Cleo

For Tabbi, my beautiful, inspiring girl,
with thanks and love from the M. B.

ORCHARD BOOKS
Carmelite House
50 Victoria Embankment
London EC4Y 0DZ

This edition published in 2015 by Orchard Books

ISBN 978 1 40833 409 6

Text © Lucy Coats 2015

A CIP catalogue record for this book is available
from the British Library.

1 3 5 7 9 8 6 4 2

Printed and bound in Great Britain by Clays Ltd, St Ives plc

The paper and board used in this book are made from wood from
responsible sources.

Orchard Books is an imprint of Hachette Children's Group,
and published by The Watts Publishing Group Limited,
an Hachette UK company.

www.hachette.co.uk

LUCY COATS

ORCHARD

1

Death Comes to Alexandria

The Royal Palace of Alexandria, Egypt
Four Years Earlier

I stood in a dark, stuffy room full of people I hated, trying my hardest not to cry one single tear. Princesses aren't supposed to, you know; at least, not in public.

My precious mother was lying on a painted bed, dying, and my heart knew there was nothing I could do now to save her.

It should have been so easy.

The most powerful goddess in Egypt was meant to be on my side, but apparently she wasn't listening to me right now. I'd had my palms raised up to the heavens, begging her constantly since my mother's accident. How hard would it have been for her to answer one tiny prayer? Just one – that was all I asked.

It's me, Isis. Cleo. You chose me at birth, remember? I'm your special favourite. Please save her, Isis. Please!

But no. Just when I really needed her, my patron deity disappeared and went silent. I was so very angry with her about that, but I couldn't show it.

It might sound as if I was a spoilt royal brat with no feelings because I refused to cry when my mother was dying. But I wasn't.

Not crying took everything I had. There was a lump in my throat the size of a camel's foot, and my eyes felt as if the whole Nile welled up inside, just waiting to pour out of them. I'd got my nails dug so far into my palms that I could feel the skin breaking, and then the slow, stinging seep of blood.

'Never show anger, fear or grief, my little pusscat. Never let them see you're weak.'

That was the last thing my father the Pharaoh – the great and wondrous Ptolemy Auletes – said to me three days ago, when he got on his grand ship – the one with a thousand or so oars – and sailed away to Rome with my little half-sister, my two baby half-brothers and the precious flute he seemed to love more than any of us.

If only he'd taken my mother and me too.

If only he'd made her his Pharaoh queen, then none of this would even be happening.

Egypt is supposed to have two Pharaohs.

One for Isis, one for Horus – protectors of the Double Throne.

Maybe that's why my goddess wasn't listening to me.

Maybe it was all my fault.

Maybe I should have tried harder to stop him going away.

I wouldn't have left my kingdom to rot just because a few thousand angry Alexandrians were rioting and threatening to throw me off my throne. And I most certainly wouldn't have sailed all the way to the other end of the Great Green Sea just because I owed a pile of money to some old Roman.

I was pretty sure my father was a big fat coward, showing fear, like he'd told me not to. Ptolemy rulers aren't supposed to run away and leave their people behind, or their daughters, or their gods.

But, hey, even if he wasn't here now, he was still the Pharaoh, which meant he was lord-of-everything and could do what he liked, mostly, including leaving me and my mother to sink or swim in this hellhole of a palace.

At least, it had been me and my mother till yesterday.

Till her so-called accident on that deserted flight of stairs.

Soon it was going to be just me, and that scared me half to death.

I thought if I concentrated on my father's last command, maybe the little hissing voices in my head wouldn't be able to come in, wouldn't be able to spit horrible words like 'alone' and 'abandoned' at me.

It wasn't working very well.

All I wanted to do was to throw myself on the bed and hug my mother tight. I longed to hold her hands – those soft little hands that had stroked my hair only yesterday morning; those slim fingers which had held mine steady as I traced kohl round my eyelids with her own jewel-ended stick for the first time last year. But I wouldn't give anybody in that room the satisfaction of seeing me break down. If I cried, Tryphena and Berenice, my Evil Sow half-sisters, would say it was because I wasn't a proper princess. They had said that a lot since my father left. But I was. I really was. It was just that, as I said, my mother wasn't exactly the official queen. My father used to call her his queen of hearts in front of everyone, though, and me his pusscat princess. When Pharaoh says you're a princess, you are, believe me. Anyway, I was recognised as Princess Cleopatra in the priests' scrolls, and that's about as official as it gets.

Nobody could imagine how much I didn't want my mother to die. But the physicians had told me at dawn that she was starting on her journey to the gods and there was nothing more they could do for her. I commanded them. I screamed that Isis would curse them to eternal death. I even threatened to have them beaten and fed to the jackals if they didn't make her well again. But they just bowed and backed out of the room, shaking their wrinkly, bald heads just like a lot of vultures anticipating a nice fat piece of carrion. The next thing I heard was the sound of the deathwatch drums.

Boom boom boom, they went. *Boom boom boom*.

That was when I started praying to Isis even harder.

Oh, Isis! Where are you? Where were you when Mama fell down those stairs? Did you see what happened? Did she really slip? Or was she pushed? Please save her! Please! I'll do anything for you. Anything at all.

But Isis still wasn't listening.

The person on the bed didn't even look like my own dear mother any more. She was barely breathing, lying there so still and small under her favourite blue linen sheet, the one embroidered with lilies. I had put that over her poor, broken body myself, just in case it made a difference. I hoped it might help her get better if she had something pretty around her. But it didn't. (Or, at least, it hadn't so far.) And having the official crowd of palace gawpers there to witness her passing wasn't helping either of us. I'd tried to stop them coming in, but what could I do? I was still an undergrown child in their eyes, and the deathwatch was in the stupid religious rules my tutor had been drilling into me since I was old enough to talk. I could hear his prissy voice in my head now.

'Everyone must witness the passing of a member of the inner court, whether they want to or not – the god Horus himself has decreed it.'

It was only two months since they'd called the deathwatch for my half-siblings' mother – my father's 'official' Pharaoh queen – just as all the whispers about him draining the royal treasury started. I remember feeling sorry for Tryphena and Berenice and the little ones then. I didn't now.

Oh, please, Isis, Queen of Heaven! Oh, please, Horus, Protector of Pharaohs! Oh, please, all you great gods! Don't take my mother away from me. Don't leave me all alone.

Hot, thick anger and a cold, clammy grief warred inside me as I glared over at Tryphena and Berenice, standing on the other side of the room, half hidden in the thick pall of lotus-flower incense which crept into my nostrils like fog. Evil Sow sisters might sound a bit overdramatic as a description. But in their case it wasn't. They really were vile sows (no offence to pigs, even if they are considered unclean things by some). I could see the two of them grimacing at each other, and their tightly folded arms and bored, beautifully painted faces under elaborate hairstyles told me just how much they wanted to be out of here, and hated having to stay. Now that our father the Pharaoh was gone, they didn't think my mother should even be counted as a member of the inner court, just because she was only half Greek. I mean why does a bit of Egyptian blood even matter these days? What difference does it make to anything? It wasn't as if our father was exactly legitimate either – though it didn't do to say so openly.

Of course, my horrible sisters had been plotting to take power since the minute he'd left. Did they have something to do with what had happened to my mother? Oh, why hadn't I been there when she fell? Why hadn't someone called me away from my lessons in the Great Library sooner? Maybe I could have saved her if I hadn't been so immersed in the brand new scroll Master Apollonius had brought me that morning.

Swish swish swish! I pitied Tryphena and Berenice's slaves, endlessly fanning those sweaty bodies with golden palm leaves, swatting the flies away with giraffe hair whisks. Can you believe that only three short years ago the two of them had seemed like glamorous idols of sophistication to me? All I had wanted back then was to grow up just like them. I had learnt enough since then to know that beauty on the outside can hide a nest of venomous asps within.

I saw Berenice lean over to Tryphena. Her lips moved, and her whiny, whispering voice drifted across the room, breaking the silence.

'Oh, really! Can't Father's whore-bitch even do dying right? How long do we have to stand here, anyway? I've got a new jewel merchant from Nubia coming in this afternoon and I wanted to watch the sacrifices after that. It's such fun when they scream for mercy.'

As if she had heard, my mother opened her pale, blueish lips slightly and sighed. Only I could see the misty golden *ka* soul form that rose upwards from her body – a perfect mirror image of her mortal self. Only I could see the door opening in the air, the tall jackal-headed figure stepping from his reed boat and slipping into the mortal world. Only I could see his immortal hand stretching out to draw my mother's soul through and sail off with her to the underworld realm. She held out her own hand to him and didn't even look back once. That was what finished me off.

'Please don't go. Oh, please, Anubis,' I whimpered to the shepherd of souls, falling to my knees, giving up the battle to hold back that torrent of stifled tears, 'P-please don't take her…' But it was too late.

My mother's mortal self drew one last gurgling breath as the door in the air snapped shut. She was no longer in the room.

There was only an empty body lying on a bed, and I was left behind, weeping.

Everything looked blurry through the veil of my tears. I could hardly breathe. And then I heard my sisters start in on me, just as I'd known they would. Tryphena gave me a menacing, sideways look with those hateful green eyes of hers as she flicked her nearest slave on the ear. He didn't dare wince, of course.

'Fetch the embalmers and get this dung out of here, you. Mind you clean the room out properly afterwards, too. It stinks. I think I'll use it to store my second best sandals in.'

Then she pointed one of her long red-ochre painted fingers at me and hissed like an angry cobra.

'As for you, snivelling little bastard, you're a disgrace to the name of Ptolemy, you swotty, scroll-loving runt. You'd better start running, and hope your precious goddess and her priestesses can protect you. Because this palace is finally mine now – and I wouldn't want anything bad to happen to you, would I? Like falling down a flight of stairs?' Suddenly she looked extremely smug, like a well-fed cat, lifting one dark eyebrow so that the minute rubies which decorated it glittered like tiny drops of shed blood.

It was at that exact moment I knew for sure my mother hadn't had an accident.

I saw Berenice shoot Tryphena a jealous glare, so quick I almost missed it, and then her face fell into its usual simpering, sycophantic expression as she sniggered behind her hand.

'Yes, Pharaoh isn't around to protect his skinny little pusscat now, is he? And nor is his half-breed concubine-bitch. Tryphena's right. I'd definitely start running if I were you. Fast.' Her voice whipped out as sharp as a hornet's sting on that last word.

I scrambled to my feet, my legs trembling under me like a newborn camel's. I felt the humiliation and rage rise up from my belly, joining the choking grief, making my neck feel as if their two pairs of hands were closing round it. But I refused to be silent, whatever it cost me. I refused to be beaten down. Words bubbled up inside me, words I'd needed to say ever since my mother's accident. They came out thick and slow and difficult through my swollen throat.

'Isis will p-protect me,' I said, my treacherous child's voice squeaking and younger than my ten summers, however defiant I tried to make it sound. 'She sees both your h-hateful hearts, a-and it's not a pretty sight. Just you w-wait! She'll put my father the Pharaoh back in his rightful place and then you'll b-both be sorry. Remember that when you scheme to sit on thrones that aren't yours. Remember!' I said again, my voice suddenly loud and strong, echoing with an overtone that I knew wasn't entirely mine. 'My goddess will be watching you!' And then I walked past the guards and out of the room, with my head held high, as a proper Ptolemy princess should, ignoring the rising screams of outrage behind me.

I have to admit, though, once I was safely on the other side of that gilded door, I abandoned my dignity and took to my heels. I fled through the dark, stuffy palace corridors as if the fiendish serpent Apep himself was after me. As I ran, the unstoppable sobs started to rise again. All I wanted was to get away, to escape, to go anywhere but back there where my mother's poor abandoned shell lay so still and silent. I no longer cared about anyone seeing my Nile flood of tears, or about the unattractive snail-trail of snot running from my nose. My sandalled feet flew over the marble floors, towards the one person who would understand how I felt, the person who'd been with me since I was three years old – my only true companion in this poisonous palace – Charm.

Charm was my best friend, body slave and all-round fixer of everything terrible, and I couldn't even imagine life without her. She had never let me down yet, but what if something had happened to her? Would she have our bags packed and ready as we'd planned so hurriedly last night? The lessons my mother had drummed into me over and over since my father left – lessons about treachery and being prepared to run – began marching round my brain again like a squad of soldier ants as the walls flashed by me. One of my sandals was working loose, but I had no time to bend and tighten the strap. If only she'd taken her own advice there wouldn't have been any so-called accident, and we might all be running away together.

But now it was too late. Tryphena hadn't been joking about something bad happening to me if I stayed. I knew she'd steal my father's place as Pharaoh as soon as she could, so there was no time to lose if I was going to avoid 'slipping' down a flight of stairs too. Or something even worse, like being thrown to her horrid pet crocodiles. I shuddered, imagining sharp, white teeth tearing into my soft flesh.

We had to get out of the palace – tonight.

I tore past the chanting column of palace embalmers and priests of Seth coming up out of a dark stairway. I didn't want to look at them. I knew who they were and where they were going, and I didn't want to think about it, or go anywhere near them, the unclean beasts. How could anyone bear to delve about in dead bodies? I shuddered, smelling the decay and salts of natron underneath the aromas of cedar oil and myrrh that hung about their stained red linen robes.

And then it happened.

My loose sandal strap finally snapped in two. I tripped over and crashed into a tall boy at the rear of the line. All I took in at first was that he was dressed in ordinary white.

'Oof!' he grunted, grabbing me round the waist to save me from the inevitable fall. A moment later I was sprawled heavily on top of him, my nose pressed into his chest. All I could think of was that he didn't smell of death and decay at all, but of the comforting odours of my favourite place in all the world – the Great Library. Breathing deeply, I made out dusty papyrus, dry reed, beeswax, ink cakes and a subtle, sweet boy musk all of his own. I raised my head and found myself looking down into a pair of deep brown eyes, dark as wet Delta mud, long eyelashes clogged with oily kohl at the roots. Somehow, all the world seemed to stop for a long minute, and then start up again in a different rhythm.

Didn't I know this boy? Surely I did! There was something about him that was familiar. I examined his features silently. Curved nose – though not as strongly curved as mine – slightly chapped lips that quirked and dimpled at one corner, skin the colour of burnt honey, and a curtain of hair so black and straight and shiny it could have been cut from rare heavy silk. I reached out to touch it, wanting to tangle my fingers in it, to stroke its softness. It looked so comforting. But then adult hands were under my arms, lifting me, setting me back gently on my feet. I came back to myself suddenly. What had I been thinking?

'Apologise to the Princess Cleopatra at once for your clumsiness, librarian Khai,' said the red-robed embalmer who had parted us.

All of us knew it had been my fault – but no one was going to say so. This boy was a commoner, and I was still a Ptolemy. My father would have had him beaten for even coming near me.

'I'm very sorry, Your Royal Highness. Please forgive me,' the boy said, bowing, but not afraid, as so many were, of my family (and with good reason – those pet crocodiles of my sisters' were very well fed). His voice was low and roughened, not yet a man's, but nearly. He spoke Greek with a slight Egyptian accent, and that was when I knew him. He was the boy from the Great Library. The one who'd got down a scroll for me several months ago from a shelf I couldn't quite reach, and spoken to me as if I was a real person, not an untouchable Ptolemy princess. He'd made me blush redder than a ripe plum as his hand touched mine. Charm had seen that, and teased me about it mercilessly, till I threw pillows at her. He was the boy I'd had pleasingly forbidden thoughts about for nights afterwards – until the trouble with my father began and drove him out of my mind.

He'd smiled at me then, and he smiled again now – just the flash of a crooked white grin, and something else in his eyes I couldn't quite work out. Was it sympathy? Then the red-robed priest dragged him back to his place at the end of the line, and he was gone, leaving a strange knot tied around my heart that I didn't understand, together with a mystery. Why was a librarian like him with the stinking embalmers and Seth priests? What did they need with a scroll stacker? Had he been sent to the unclean ones as a punishment? I shook my head, bending down to kick off both sandals. I couldn't think about him now. The fear of what my sisters might be sending after me lent wings to my bare feet as I began to run again, but the boy's face stayed in my mind. *Khai*, I thought, the memory of that kind smile somehow lending me courage.

His name is Khai.

I whispered it out loud to myself.

'Khai.'

It meant 'royal scribe', and that seemed like a good omen, somehow. Scribes and scholars had always been my friends.

And this particular Khai came from my favourite place in the world, the Great Library. Maybe my goddess was finally listening. Maybe she had sent him to me as a sign.

Suddenly, colliding with him seemed like a small luck talisman to hold onto. My sorrowful heart beat more strongly, urging me onwards, and I sent a quick thank you thought his way, though I was painfully sure I'd never see him again.

The women's quarters were eerily deserted and silent for the time of night. There were no sounds of laughter and gossip, no welcoming open doors, no familiar smell of patchouli, sweet honey cakes and damp, oily kohl pots wafting out on the evening breezes. The tall, ochre-painted corridors were empty and silent with menace.

Something was wrong. I slowed to a halt, panting. Suddenly the air around me felt thick with danger and the small hairs on the back of my neck rose. I'd learned to take notice of that warning instinct since before I could remember.

So I tiptoed forward cautiously, peering round each corner as I went. The marble felt smooth and cool under my sweaty bare feet, which made small sucking noises at every step as the floor tried to cling onto them. I was right to be wary. Outside the highly decorated door to my rooms stood two massive Nubian guards, white uniform kilts perfectly aligned at knee level, holding spears whose sharp silvery tips looked as though they meant business. The new and shiny silver amulet of foul Am-Heh round their thick necks made me bite my lip hard, but I couldn't stop a tiny gasp escaping. Were matters in the palace worse than I'd thought? Were my sisters openly worshipping the demon god of the fiery lake now? Were they truly turning their backs on Horus and Isis and Ra and favouring the Devourer of Souls? If they were, then the true gods would be very angry. The whole of Egypt might be in danger, not to mention the house of Ptolemy and the Double Throne.

Whatever the truth was, the two of them had definitely worked fast. They must have instructed their pet mercenaries even before the drums for my mother's deathwatch sounded. No wonder Tryphena had looked so smug. Slowly, trying not to make another whisper of sound or let them see me, I edged my head backwards, my heart battering against the prison bars of my ribs so hard that I felt sure they must hear. But I wasn't slow or careful enough. The guards' heads both went up like desert sighthounds at the minuscule flicker of movement, and without a word they stalked forward in unison, spears lowered, silent killers on the hunt for their prey.

Me.

I whirled and ran from them, bare feet slipping and slithering as I fled down the corridor and away. My only advantage was that I knew every twist and turn of the women's quarters, every door, every column, every alcove, and they didn't. My heart fluttered and beat frantically, trying to flap its way out of my chest as I skidded left, right, left again, trying to confuse them. Their legs were so much longer than mine – I had to keep ahead, had to. I didn't dare look behind me. The sound of heavy sandals pounded over the floors, echoing off the walls, telling me I was doomed, lost, dead.

No! I thought fiercely, my earlier anger at my goddess blooming within me again. *No! I know I wasn't born to die like this. I refuse! You'll see, Isis, if you won't save me,*

I'll save myself! But they were empty words, and I knew it. My breath was coming in desperate gasps now, air clotting and clogging my lungs as if it was an enemy. Dark spots had begun to cloud my eyes, when I saw the damp, mottled column that marked the entry to the ancient water cisterns and the underground slave passages that ran alongside them. It was a big risk, but it was the only chance I had now. I ducked behind it, hoping the running guards were still one corner behind, hoping they wouldn't see me, hoping they didn't know the passages existed in this part of the palace. This was it. I had no more left in me. I threw myself inside the hidden entrance and slid down the rough clay wall behind the column, burying my face in my own armpit, biting the cloth of my robe, trying to muffle the gasping sounds that came from me no matter how hard I tried to control them. I smelt of stale fear and panic even to myself. The sound of sandals was almost on me now, and I tensed my whole body, willing them onwards, willing them to be blind and deaf and stupid, willing myself small and invisible, praying once more to my deaf and silent goddess, asking her to grant me the one small piece of luck I needed to survive.

Whether she did or not, I'll never know, but the guards kept on going. I knew I had only minutes to get away before they realised they'd lost me and retraced their steps. I opened my eyes and forced my brain to think, forced my trembling legs to stand up and move into the dim darkness of the tunnel.

Had the guards killed Charm already? Or taken her? She'd never desert me – I knew that – so she must still be in my rooms. She must. I had nothing in me to vomit up, but I felt bitter, stinging bile burn the back of my throat at the thought of losing her as well. Oh, why hadn't we made a back up plan? Why hadn't I asked her to meet me at the docks? With only the thought of her to cling to as comfort, I had to stuff down my panic. The belief that she was alive was all that was keeping me going, and that meant I'd have to get into my rooms and rescue her. But how?

Please, Isis, help me. You've got my mother now. Don't take Charm away too. Please! I prayed again. A soft breath of air touched me, caressed my cheek like a finger. It smelt of sand and the memory of wild desert places. Suddenly I was seven again, feeling the thrill of excitement as Charm led me through the secret slave passages, squeezing at intervals past the cool rounded bellies of the massive underground stone cisterns which supplied all the water for the palace. We'd stuffed our hands in our mouths to stifle giggles as we sneaked up steps and into dusty closets to spy on Tryphena and Berenice in their chambers, and hidden behind pillars to see my father dispensing justice from his throne.

With a small shiver, I also felt the claustrophobia, the sense of stifling air and the endless fear of being caught and punished – except that this time the punishment wouldn't be a beating. It would be death. I searched through those old memories urgently. Which way had we gone? Could I even find the way back to my rooms without Charm as my guide? I didn't have any choice. I'd have to try.

I tiptoed forward carefully, slowly, looking back over my shoulder at the smallest sound, dreading the slap of sandals. Even I, young and child-short as I was then, had to stoop in the cramped, damp earth-smelling spaces, and the foul smoke-reek of the widely spaced lamps made my eyes sting, though I welcomed their faint light. Over and over again I took a wrong turn in the dimness and had to retrace my steps, feeling more lost and alone every time. Once I heard male voices in the distance, making me freeze like a startled mouse, ears straining towards the sound, fearing that my sisters' guards were finally on my trail. By a miracle I met no one, though, and some homing instinct, whether it was my childhood memories or something else, led me true. When I eventually recognised the flight of steps up to my own quarters and saw that there were no guards waiting for me, I raised my palms and thanked Isis for keeping me safe, just in case she actually had. It never hurts to be polite to a goddess.

The slaves' doorway to my rooms was nothing like the painted and ornately carved main entrance. It was far humbler, just a narrow opening of crumbling clay bricks leading into a small, dark closet whose shelves were piled high with too-small robes and worn sandals. It smelt of dust, musty linen and old leather. I could see a shimmer of light ahead of me, and I crept inside, once more holding my breath and taking care not to knock anything over. I poked just my big nose and one eye round the edge of the door into my bedroom. My legs were trembling again, and I reached out, grabbing onto the smooth, cool marble for support. I couldn't see any guards, so I slipped inside, ducking low, just in case.

'Charm!' I whispered, using only a tiny breath of sound. 'Charm! Are you there? It's me, Cleo. We have to go!' There was no answer, and my eyes flickered round the room again, frantic with fear. Was she lying in a pool of blood somewhere, unable to answer? But then I heard a tiny, muffled noise from inside the painted chest behind my dressing screen, which usually held bed linens. The lid creaked open a crack, and a small, brown hand emerged, then another, and then a head covered in tight, black curls. Charm's eyes were huge, dark pools as she slithered out, and laid the lid silently against the wall. Her skin was the ashy colour of dried mud, streaked with fear and tears and I wanted to run to her, to hug her to me tight and never let go. But I knew I mustn't. There wasn't time. I put my finger to my lips and beckoned her towards me. She shook her head, though, and knelt down again, fumbling with something inside the chest till I nearly exploded with the effort of not shouting at her to hurry. The seconds dripped by as I waited, terrified, for the guards to come back and hear something, to burst through the doors and catch us, but slowly, inch by silent inch, she dragged out two bundles wrapped in rough linen. Picking them up, she came to me, her bare feet soft and noiseless. And then, finally, we ran back into the slave passages as if Am-Heh the Devourer himself were at our heels.

The Great Harbour was loud with bustle and noise, even this late at night. It was the hot Shemu season, in the month of Payni, when men preferred to work in the cooler darkness. There were ships unloading goods from near and far, and the reflected light of the distant Pharos flared and shone over it, making shadows dance like black ghosts. Lines of slaves snaked down every gangplank, carrying reed baskets of wheat and walnuts, piles of raw fleeces and huge clay amphorae of wine towards row upon row of patient donkeys and supercilious camels. The air smelled faintly of mint, fresh coriander and other herbs brought in from the countryside, but the main odour was of unwashed bodies, animal dung and the eternal, unmistakably familiar brackish scent of the Nile Delta at harvest time. No one took a second glance at two young girls with bundles on their backs. Why should they? It was a common enough sight.

I shifted my burden and looked around, feeling the rough cloth of my tunic scrape against my skin. My unbound hair felt lank and sticky and unwashed in the heat, my face was still stiff with the dried salt of my tears, and my feet were bruised from the stone of the streets. I wasn't used to this. Princesses didn't go barefoot or in disguise – not unless they were escaping from Evil Sow sisters and certain death, anyway. I bit at my thumbnails, feeling the skin beside them rip and tear. I was trying to stop doing it, but the small pain of the familiar bad habit distracted me from my greater fears.

'Where's our barge, Charm? What if it isn't here? What if they've already left?'

'It was tied up over there,' she answered, pointing down the docks. 'I checked twice this morning, and one of the other slaves told me it was due to be emptied out just after sunset and leaving upriver for Saïs at first light.' She craned her neck and stood on tiptoe, trying to see over the crowds. 'That's it – the one with the bare decks. Apparently the captain is very greedy, and he'll take a bribe without asking too many questions. They say he's also very superstitious, which might help us.'

I craned my neck too, but I couldn't see anything. I was too small, and my bundle was too heavy. Suddenly I shrank down, as a squad of soldiers marched past. Could they be looking for us already? Charm put out a comforting hand and squeezed my shoulder.

'Don't worry, Cleo. They're just the normal harbour guards – they patrol all the time. You don't have to worry unless we see the palace lot. Your sisters, curse their names, won't let out the family secrets to ordinary soldiers, you can be sure of that.'

I knew she was right, but suddenly everything I'd been through already that day crashed in on me, and I caught my breath on a sob. Charm pulled me close.

'You can't cry, Cleo, not now,' she hissed, giving me a tiny shake. 'We have to get on that barge and away from here. You can't draw attention to us!' She pulled me along behind her, dodging and weaving through the busy throng as if she was an eel. And there it was. The barge that would take us away from here, upriver to safety, away to the priestesses of the House of Isis at Saïs, where I hoped my sisters held no sway. That was as far ahead as I could think for the moment. All we had to do now was find an opportunity to sneak aboard without being spotted.

It soon came. As a pushing and shoving fight broke out between two roaring, spitting camels in a narrow alleyway, we took our chance and scurried up the gangplank while the only two crewmen left on board turned away to laugh at the violent animal brawl. Dropping to our knees so as not to be seen, we crawled hurriedly towards the only obvious spot to hide – an untidy pile of sail at the foot of the mast – and pulled it over ourselves. The thick linen smelt of mouldy flax and muddy river water, but I was so tired that I didn't care. I fell asleep almost at once, my head pillowed on Charm's belly, holding her hand as if it was the last safe place left in the world.

2

Sanctuary at Saïs

I woke to the creak and sway of a moving boat, the shouts of men, and the splash of oars on water. Charm's palm pressed me down hard as I tried to sit up, confused and thirsty.

'Don't move!' she hissed. 'We have to stay here. The longer it is before they discover us, the better. And let me do the talking when they do find us, just like we planned – or your Greek accent will give us away for sure. Promise me you won't go all princess on me, Cleo. I know it's hard, but you have to act like you're just a humble acolyte of Isis!'

That was the story we'd come up with so hurriedly the night before last. We were going to say that Isis had told me in a dream to go to the temple at Saïs and serve her, but that my strict father had forbidden it, which is why we were stowing away. It was sort of true – and maybe it would work. In this smelly, stuffy place, with the hard deck digging into my hipbones, it sounded flimsy and far-fetched, though.

Are you pleased I'm going to your temple, Isis? I didn't know where else to turn to. You're my only hope now that my mother's gone.

As if I'd summoned that horrible deathbed just by thinking, the grief rose up in me full force again and I started to cry – soft, dry, hopeless sobs which shook my whole body. I was so tired, and I wanted my mother so badly at that moment. I tried hard not to feel angry again about what had happened the night before when Isis hadn't answered my prayer – hadn't saved her – but it was no good. Suddenly I felt like screaming, shouting, shaking my fists at all the gods and goddesses, including my own. Instead I swallowed a musty clump of dust and started to choke. Charm pulled my head into her shoulder to muffle the sound as I began to cough loudly and uncontrollably. I felt Charm stiffen, and I heard heavy footsteps hurrying towards us. Then the corner of the sail was snatched back, and I saw a man's fat, oily face glaring down at us. He reached in and dragged us out, one at a time. His hands were rough and *he* wasn't gentle either, flinging us down on the deck like sacks of onions. I was suddenly even angrier, sprawled coughing and wheezing there at his feet. If he'd laid even a fingernail on me in my father's palace, he wouldn't have lived to see the next dawn. But as I struggled to get enough breath to shout at him, I felt Charm's hand on my wrist, squeezing hard, and I remembered just in time. I wasn't a princess here, was I? I was just an ordinary girl on her way to do the goddess's bidding.

'Two little runts,' the man grunted. 'Two stowaway girl runts stinking up my nice clean barge. I've a good mind to pitch you over the side for the river-horses to eat.' He leered at us, his brown, broken teeth showing between his puffy lips and his stinking breath sprayed over us like fog. It smelt of rotten meat and stale barley beer. 'How would you like that, little runts?'

I bit back a shriek. I hated river-horses, with their fat, bristly brown bodies, and those enormous yellow-toothed jaws. I could imagine being torn apart by them only too easily. I'd seen it happen when I was very young. The young hunter had been showing off for the Pharaohs on their silver barge, and had slipped and fallen right into the middle of the angry beasts. His blood had stained the water like spilled red ink.

My mother had wiped away my tears then, and my

father had promised to protect me.

Neither of them was here now. We were at the mercy of this stupid man's whim.

'Oh, please, magnificent captain,' Charm cried out, flinging her arms round his ankles. 'Spare us, and the blessings of Isis shall be upon you. We must reach the goddess's temple at Saïs before dusk today. She has summoned my mistress to be her acolyte.' Then her voice dropped to a whisper, as she jingled a small purse. 'We can make it worth your while, great one!' His hand flashed down in a moment, grabbing the little bag, and he opened the neck, looking inside. His stubby, grubby fingers ferreted about, and he pulled out a silver coin and bit it. His eyes narrowed, and a look of sly greed came over his face as he turned away from the interested glances of his rowers, cradling the purse to his huge belly as if it were a child. He bent down towards us.

'Maybe I am going to Saïs, maybe I am not. This worthless amount of coin is not enough to get both of you there, however. I will need more to even consider it. After all, how do I know you are not runaway slaves who have stolen money from their master? I honour Isis, blessed be her name, but why should I believe this lying tale of yours?' As he spat a slimy green glob over the side of the barge, we looked at each other in panic, and I felt sick and weak as Charm scrambled to her feet, pulling me up beside her. Wasn't this man supposed to be superstitious? Why would he risk offending Isis when he had a purseful of silver in his hand? It was more than some men would earn in a whole year. Charm started to talk, gabbling fast, scrabbling in her waist pouch for the silver bracelets we had hidden there just in case, but if the jewellery didn't tempt him, or he took it and threw us overboard anyway, we were truly finished. I closed my eyes and started praying silently and desperately to my goddess again.

O dear Isis. I really do want to serve you. Please send a sign to make this idiot believe us. Please help us to get to Saïs.

Charm's voice babbled on and on, begging, pleading for him not to throw us overboard but I blocked it all out, concentrating only on trying to make my goddess listen to me.

And then, quite suddenly, I realised that the only thing I could hear was the plash and creak of oars. I opened my eyes to see Charm and the captain gawping at something over my left shoulder. All the colour had leached out of his face, leaving it an unattractive shade of grimy brownish-grey. I turned to see the Eye of Ra rising behind me. Just above its first golden-pink rays flew a flock of sacred ibis in the shape of a familiar symbol – the loop-topped Knot of Isis herself.

The captain shook himself slightly and stared at me as if I was either a freak of nature, or something holy. I couldn't tell which.

'Ship oars and set the sail, you lazy beggars,' the captain shouted, his voice only trembling a little. 'We must reach Saïs by dusk. No stops, no excuses.' He bobbed his head to me and gestured towards a coil of rope in the bow. 'Make yourself comfortable, bird-blessed of Isis,' he said.

I let out a breath I didn't even know I'd been holding.

Thank you, dear goddess, I said silently. *I won't let you down, I promise.*

That was pretty much the first and last prayer of mine Isis would answer for a long while – though I didn't realise it then.

We arrived at Saïs in good time, with a stiff breeze filling the sail all the way. In fact, we were there well before dusk, and the captain insisted on escorting us to the temple gates himself, muttering about making an offering to the goddess. I nearly told him to use the coins he'd taken for our passage – I noticed he hadn't given them back, despite his awe at seeing Isis's sign – but I didn't. He'd remember us all too well anyway, and I didn't want him to hear my voice. Charm was right, even though I spoke reasonably good Egyptian, (unlike my stupid sisters, who despised scholarship of any kind), my Greek accent marked me as a member of the royal court. It was a dead giveaway. I started to feel nervous again. Was Saïs far enough away from the palace? Would I be safe? Or would my sisters' evil influence reach out and touch me even here?

Unfortunately, once we'd persuaded one of the acolytes to take us to the high priestess, it seemed that it might. The high priestess was a tall, willowy woman called Taia, with breathtaking green eyes and a generous mouth, and despite my shabby dress, she believed me when I told her who I was and why I needed sanctuary. I really tried to behave like a princess and the chosen of Isis in front of her. Truly I did. I stiffened my spine and stood up straight. I smiled my father's most sphinx-like smile. I used all the skills of oratory I'd been taught, making my voice coo at her like a mourning dove and command her like a general in turn, till I was hoarse and sweating. None of it worked.

'You must leave at once, Princess Cleopatra,' Taia's

voice was implacable. 'It's too close to Alexandria here. There are palace spies everywhere in the temples. We couldn't protect you properly. No. I think it's best if you go down to the care of our mother house at Philäe. No one will think to look for you there, and we will spread the word that you have died of a fever. That way you can, as you say you wish to, dedicate your life to Isis in peace. I will write the letter to High Priestess Jamila now.'

I'm not proud of what happened next. My only excuse is that I was much younger then, and it had been a long and frightening couple of days.

I lost it completely, right there in front of her, drumming my heels on the floor like an enraged toddler. I didn't want to leave for some far-off mud hole temple in Upper Egypt! I just wanted to curl up somewhere and mourn my mother in peace.

'I won't go! I won't! I won't!' I shrieked. But I did. I had to. Taia practically tied me up and made me. And because she was a high priestess of Isis, and I'd come to her asking to be an acolyte, I was bound to obey her. So the next morning I found myself bundled onto another barge, a more comfortable one this time, veiled and dressed in the white of a trainee priestess, with Charm at my side and a chest of money and jewels for my upkeep.

I wept like a clay watering pot almost all the weeks of

the long, dreary way to Philäe. Well, I wept when I wasn't cursing and swearing empty vows of death and revenge against Tryphena and Berenice.

Charm says I was a total nightmare, and I nearly got us thrown off the boat with my eternal wailing, but most of that sad journey passed in a blur for me, to be honest. I do remember noticing the occasional field of blackening grain and diseased cows float past as we rowed upstream. But I was so distraught I couldn't even make myself care enough to ask which of the gods were warning of their displeasure by cursing Egypt's crops and beasts that season. None of it mattered to me right then.

All I knew was that not being able to mourn my mother properly and attend her funeral rites was driving me nearly mad. Questions ran through my head like Nile water through a sieve. Was her embalming done properly by those unclean red-robed beasts and their Seth death priests? Did she have all the right grave goods in her tomb to take with her to the Underworld? Did they put her in the Sema where she should have belonged, alongside my father's Ptolemy queen, or just throw her body in an unmarked hole somewhere? There was no way I could find out now if it had been done right, or if my vile sisters had interfered somehow, and it bothered me like an itching sore on my soul.

Strangely, my only comfort was that I thought librarian Khai might have been there with her. Whatever dreadful thing he'd done to be assigned to the embalmers, he had definitely gone with them to collect my mother's body. I liked to think that once the priests of Seth had her, he saw their oh-so-secret rites done properly with his scribe's eyes and wrote it all down.

Maybe he'd hidden a scroll away somewhere in the Great Library, and one day I'd take it down and read exactly what happened. I tried not to dream that librarian Khai himself would be the one to give it to me. I shouldn't have been thinking about someone like him at all, really – but he kept on creeping into my head like an obstinate mosquito. My old life in Alexandria was gone forever – and him with it. However much his kohl-rimmed brown eyes and white smile came into my daydreams, I'd never be able to go back to the palace – not with Tryphena and Berenice on the Pharaoh's Double Throne.

Yes, that's right. My Evil Sow sisters were joint rulers of Egypt now. At least that meant there *were* two Pharaohs on the Throne. Maybe that would be enough to placate the gods and turn their wrath aside from the crops and beasts – if Tryphena and Berenice ditched the vile Devourer and turned back to Isis and Horus, of course. I prayed they did for all our sakes.

The proclamation about our two new rulers came upriver on a fast felucca yesterday. High Priestess Jamila – the ghastly camel-toothed head of Philäe who I despised already – announced it to a temple full of white-clad acolytes and priestesses a week after Charm and I arrived at our new home. You could scarcely even call it a home, what with the heat and the flies and the smell of wet mud and assorted dust and dung. Hearing her say it out loud felt like an elephant had kicked me just under my ribs and crushed my heart. I had to gnaw my own lip nearly in half not to scream with rage.

Because, of course, why would a lowly acolyte even want to scream at such joyous news? High Priestess Jamila bundled me and Charm into isolation as soon as I arrived and made both of us repeat my story over and over till we were word perfect. The old Princess Cleopatra had died of a fever. I was just Cleo now – a normal acolyte from a rich family of merchants with my faithful slave at my side. Not royalty. Nobody special at all.

Jamila couldn't stop me thinking, though.

How dared those bitches steal my father's place? He was the true Pharaoh, not them. I would have been willing to kill them for that alone, but I still hoped my father would come back across the Great Green Sea one day soon and do it for me. A little voice inside me said he wouldn't, though. He was probably having too good a time playing his flute to Julius Caesar and all those warlike Romans, teaching my baby brothers to fight with barbarian swords and spoiling my little sister Arsinöe to death with foreign sweets. He'd probably forgotten all about the bastard daughter he left behind, even though I missed him and my mother so much it sometimes felt like someone put a hook in my guts.

No. My mother was dead, and it was no good relying on my father to come back and save Egypt from my Evil Sow sisters and their dark god. One day soon I'd ask Isis to help me go and fetch him home, but until then, I'd just have to grow up really quickly and learn to be a proper priestess in this river-horse infested hole of a temple.

And with my luck, that could take me years and years.

3

Black Kite at Dusk

Four Years Later
The Temples of Isis, Philäe

I stretched lazily, feeling the slave's strong thumbs stroking over my back in small, delicious circles. The smell of rose-and-cinnamon oil filled the warm air, and the thin coverlet lay heavy on my naked hips and legs, almost too hot for this summer day. Through my half-closed eyes I could see the black silhouettes of swallows, dipping and darting against the harsh blue of the early Akhet sky, hunting for airborne bugs over the Nile, and, as usual, the wretched river-horses were splashing and snorting in the reeds by the far shore. I shuddered. One of the big ones had attacked a village fishermen with its great yellow-toothed jaws only yesterday. His body had been torn right in half when they brought it into the temple for the goddess's last blessing, and there'd been a nasty trail of red stains dripping from underneath him that brought back bad memories. River-horses might be sacred to Tauret, but I was still terrified of going anywhere near them. I had vivid nightmares about threats of being thrown to them by that stupid barge captain, all these years later.

Closer by I could hear the faint domestic sounds of our evening meal being prepared in the temple kitchens below. The wet *slap slap* rhythm of barley dough being kneaded against stone was peaceful and comforting, and I slowly drifted in that half-dream state between sleep and waking, floating on a tide of memories.

'Aaaah,' I murmured, flinching as Hu hit a particularly tight spot by my right shoulder. 'Just there. Press harder.' I was always horribly stiff after dancing practice, and today I'd worked for Priestess Maia till the sweat poured off me like rain. Even the fat, sleepy eunuchs had sat up and taken notice of my moves in the Dance of Isis Rising, and, by Horus, those half-men are hard to impress. The only thing they usually sit up for is food.

I wouldn't have been half as good as I was now without Charm, though. Night after boring night for over two years she had counted out dance steps over and over again for me in whispers. There was a lot of giggling from us both at first as I stepped and wiggled in the privacy of my room. Charm was a great giggler, but I didn't let her put me off – at least, not much, not after I got serious about it. It was really hard at the beginning, and I took ages to get the moves right because I wasn't very used to dancing – I was more of a sit-in-the-library-and-study-stuff girl. Scrolls – and the treasure within them – had always been what I loved best. Knowing things is one of the ways a woman can be powerful – and so I'd crammed my head full of every subject I could lay eyes on. If I was going to be useful to Isis, I needed to be ready for whatever she asked of me.

I have to say, though, my new-found love of dance came as a bit of a surprise to me. I didn't know it was possible to lose myself so fully in the physical, nor that the mathematical precision of the swirling steps would make me feel so connected to my goddess. At first I ached in places I didn't know could ache – and then I got aches on top of those aches till it hurt even to twitch my little finger. Isis is a demanding goddess, and she likes her priestesses to learn all her arts to perfection. That means dances to honour her sensual side as well as all the other more educational disciplines, and I'd vowed when I arrived here that I was going to be the youngest girl ever to be raised to full priestess even if it killed me.

Unfortunately that meant I'd really earned my unwanted reputation as the swotty scholar girl who pestered all the teachers to give her more rhetoric and algebra, and learned too many new languages in her spare time.

All that hard physical work was worth it, though. None of the other girls was even close to dancing like I had that morning. Well, they wouldn't be, lazy things. All they did was flirt with the priest-acolytes when High Priestess Jamila and the other priestesses weren't looking. I had seen Jamila watching me earlier in the courtyard, and she had nodded and given me one of her rare smiles as she left. Her long camel teeth and all-seeing eyes still creeped me out a bit, but maybe her being there meant something. It had certainly seemed unusual at the time. She was normally too busy pulling the strings of temple politics to bother with watching us girls dance.

I almost didn't dare to think it, but maybe the Council of Eight might be going to raise me to full priestess the next day. That would be the day I turned from a girl to a woman – and that should be marked somehow, shouldn't it? After all, who could be more suitable than me to pass the testing of Isis? Surely she must want me, the one she'd chosen at birth, to serve her as a priestess at the very least?

I squeezed my eyes tightly shut, so that the sunlight made strange red and black patterns behind my lids and prayed silently.

Oh, please, dear Isis! Please give me a sign. I'm so fed up with being an acolyte and answering to all those dried up old crows in their boring white robes. I want to be someone…do something. Tomorrow I'll be properly grown up. I want to serve you… I want to…

I didn't finish the prayer. I didn't dare to. I couldn't even admit what I really wanted to myself, let alone to my goddess, although I was pretty sure Isis already knew. She knows everything.

Inevitably, a pair of mud-brown eyes slid into my drowsy mind just then. Ever since I'd left Alexandria four years ago, that unsuitable librarian boy's eyes had crept into my dreams. I'd kind of got used to those eyes being in my head now, though I didn't want to admit, even to myself, how much I'd miss them if they went away. Just lately they'd been appearing more and more, and for the last few weeks I'd been hearing Khai's voice too. It was all strangely real, and quite disconcerting. The things he said to me under the cover of night's dreamworld made my sleeping breath come faster, and even thinking about them in the daylight made me blush. I didn't understand it at all. Even if he had got really gorgeous eyes, he was still just a librarian, and, even worse from my goddess's point of view, he was somehow attached to those Seth-loving embalmers. I'd only ever seen him twice in my life. How could he continue to haunt me so? Maybe it was because I had such intense memories of everything that happened the day my mother died. Maybe it was because he'd been my talisman of hope ever since that terrible time, my dream that everything would turn out all right for me in the end. Whatever the reason was, I found it extremely disturbing – but not in a bad way.

Go away, Khai! I told him, as his eyes smiled at me, and I moved restlessly under Hu's gentle fingers. *You're just a figment of my imagination. Just a dream. You're not real – you can't be.* But those mud-brown eyes with their thicket of kohl-rimmed black lashes stayed in my mind, crinkling seductively at me as if they knew I didn't mean it, until my belly felt as if it was full of thick, sweet heat.

Oh, I'm real, Cleo. You just don't know it yet.

His dream voice was like slow-poured honey, but with an effort I pushed it – and him – out of my head. I couldn't afford to think of Khai like that. It was pointless and silly to mope after a boy who I'd never see again –

one who should be forbidden to me for all sorts of sensible reasons I could never think of when he was there in my head. Although he wouldn't be a boy any more, of course. He'd be a young man. Grown up, like me.

I'd certainly come a long way from the frightened, skinny child I had been back on that awful night when Charm and I escaped up the Nile on that smelly cargo barge. Those first months at Philäe had been a pretty dark time for me. I missed my mother and – yes – my father so much, and it took me a long time to adjust. If I'm honest, when I wasn't studying on my own I was just like a wounded desert lioness, fighting and scratching the other girls until none of them would even speak to me.

Some of them still didn't, and I really did regret that. It wasn't their fault that my mother was dead, but I took it out on them anyway, and they hadn't ever forgiven me for being such a surly hellcat. Cleopatra the princess was dead of a fever and I was just the ordinary merchant girl Cleo as far as they knew – why should they treat me differently from any other orphan who wanted to serve Isis?

As it turned out, it was all too easy for me to forget I was a princess. I certainly didn't behave like one those first long months. Charm was my saviour, as usual. She kept on reminding me that I was still a princess inside, and that my gutter behaviour wasn't going to get me anywhere. She was right. I behaved like a brat, not a Ptolemy, and I needed her to tell me so. After all, she was the only one who knew my two secrets now, apart from High Priestess Jamila – and I had no idea how Jamila had found out about the second one, because neither Charm nor I had told her. I hoped it was Isis, because if anyone else knew, I was in deadly danger.

There was the secret that I was still alive – and then there was the other one. That was the secret which could get me killed quicker than a cobra's strike if it got out. Everyone here knew that my dead mother dedicated me to Isis at birth – and that was true. It was the reason Jamila gave out for why I was here in her temple. It was common knowledge, though of course nobody knew who my real mother was. But there was more – and that was the really dangerous bit.

This is how my mother told it to me. On the day I was born, Isis appeared to her in a dream – and not just any old dream, either. The goddess told my mother that she was giving me a magical gift, and that I was going to be under her special protection all my life. Gifts from the gods are pretty rare and at first my mother said she didn't really believe it. The immortals are known to be capricious, and as I didn't show any signs of magic when

I was born, she thought no more of it. But as soon as I could talk I began pointing and babbling about seeing immortals in the temples, and that was when she was sure that the dream – and the gift – was real. I knew it scared her a lot – it's almost unheard of for any human to see the gods (well, apart from people in the folktales old women tell in the marketplace).

I lost count of the whippings I got if she even noticed me twitching an eyelash at a god or goddess in public. She told me over and over that I had to keep it quiet, keep it secret, that if it got out, I would be killed. She was probably right – back when I was little, all the palace schemers would have tried to use me for their own ends, or seen me as a threat to their own power and had me murdered. I don't even want to think what my Evil Sow sisters would have done with me. Any sort of magic makes people very nervous. I know that now.

I also knew that after every big sacred feast day, I was shaking for hours afterwards from pretending everything was normal. Well, anyone would be. It was disconcerting to say the least, seeing Bastet the cat goddess munching on the fish offerings, or star-strewn Nut climbing down her ladder in the sky, or falcon-headed Horus swooping down to scoop up the meat-smelling smoke from a choice sacrifice. The immortals do like it when we mortals throw a party for them. The only time I ever saw Isis, though, was when she waved at me as she watched her priestesses dance at the river feasts. That was all she ever did these days. Wave. It was why I'd been so frustrated. If I was so special to her, why wouldn't she take any notice of me?

Charm was the only one I could talk to about any of it. She was convinced Isis had something amazing in store for me. I wasn't so sure about that. I mean, what did I have that made me worthy of the attention of a goddess? I was just the supposedly dead bastard third daughter of an exiled Pharaoh, and after four years I'd pretty much given up on the childish idea of rescuing my father from the Romans, or expecting Isis to put him back on his throne – at least, that was what I always told Charm.

But it did niggle at me. Why would Isis give me the gift of seeing immortals if I was not supposed to do something with it? I just wished she'd tell me what she wanted from me, but whenever I prayed to her and asked her to explain, I just got a big fat silence. It had been like that ever since I got to Saïs. She waved at me, but that was it. It was infuriating.

That wasn't to say she hadn't been listening. I'd been a short, skinny runt all my life, and only Charm knew how fed up I'd got with being jeered at and called 'Stuck-up

Stick Girl' and 'Her Snooty Flatness'. I was used to Charm having curves. She was three years older than me, after all. But it became even worse having a boyish body when the other girls my age were becoming womanly in all the right places. So I asked Isis to do something about it, and I think maybe – just maybe – she did. It all happened suspiciously fast, anyway.

Perhaps I was just a late developer, but it did feel odd to have transformed from short, gawky skinny Cleo to still short, but just-a-bit-voluptuous, siren Cleo in two short months. I definitely wasn't comfortable with it yet. For a start, I'd had to do all the dance moves differently to cope with the, um, bouncing. If it was Isis who changed me, she definitely went a little over the top in that area. Don't get me wrong, I wasn't ungrateful at all – but I wasn't sure it was worth the sour looks and snarky remarks from the other girls since my own slim but plentiful curves came in. At least no one could say the goddess had meddled with my nose, though. That still sat in the middle of my face like Nekhbet's big hooky vulture's beak. I always felt a kind of kinship with her when I saw her around the temple sacrifices – us big-nose girls have to stick together.

I wriggled uncomfortably, all the languid pleasure of the massage draining away as I thought about my terrible relationship with the other girls in the temple. I really had tried to make friends with some of them over the years, but they were always too wary of me for it to work. Most of that was my own fault because of my bad behaviour at the beginning – but now, well, I felt as if I had the plague or something. It was all the fault of one of the handsomer priest-acolytes. Shu had suggested I might like to 'dance' with him late one night, rocking his hips suggestively, and leering at me in front of everyone. I was so embarrassed.

Unfortunately Shu was the one all the other girls were after, and it didn't seem to matter that I sent him away with a curse and a soundly slapped face. That just made them all think I was even more stuck up, and stupid as well as swotty. I wasn't, but how were they to know that? However hard I tried to make friends, they could see I would never really allow anyone to get close to me except Charm.

'Blast them all to Anubis anyway!' I snarled crossly, sitting up and snatching the sheet across my chest. Hu backed away.

'Has this unworthy slave caused the honoured acolyte pain?' he asked, voice trembling a little. Oh no! Now I'd upset him. Hu was nice, and he had gentle hands. In the early days he'd sometimes brought me illicit honey cakes to cheer me up. So I plastered a smile on my face to reassure him.

'No, no. Not you, Hu. Don't worry. I was thinking of someone else. Several someones, in fact.' I started to lie down again, but before I could do so, Charm came racing through the door without her usual polite knock. Her normally neat hair was bursting out of its restraining band, rioting in a mass of damp black curls over her sweaty forehead.

'It's come! It's come! I think the Council of Eight have summoned you!' she said, gasping out the words as if she'd been running for a week. 'Look! This was on the bed when I went in to put away your dancing robes.' She waved a scroll of papyrus in the air. The four beribboned seals on it clinked and clanked gently against each other as she did so.

I was up and off the massage bench in a second, ignoring the proper robe Hu held out to me, flinging the sheet round my naked body any old how. I snatched the message out of her hand and hugged her as we capered and jumped round the room like maniacs.

'Open it, open it!' said Charm, breathlessly. 'I want to know what it says.'

I glanced at Hu, suddenly wanting him out of the room, and dismissed him with a wave of thanks. He bowed and let himself out, closing the heavy wooden door softly behind him.

'C'mon, Cleo,' said Charm, bringing me back to myself. 'What does it say? I can't wait any longer. Imagine me – the body-slave to a proper full priestess. Maybe even the high priestess herself one day!'

I gave her a friendly swat on the arm as I scanned the outside of the scroll for clues. It had my name written on it in normal writing, but suddenly I almost didn't want to open it. Did they really think I was ready to be a full priestess? Was I good enough? Then I frowned, puzzled. I recognised the seals of the high priestess, the priestess of novices and the priestess of ceremonies, but what was this fourth one? It definitely wasn't one of the ones we'd learned about in Priestess Halima's lessons on precedence and hierarchy. I should know – I had come top in all the tests. I stared at it more closely, trying to puzzle it out. It had just a single hieroglyph on it, one I didn't recognise immediately. Did it say 'secret', or was it 'hidden'?

'C'mon,' said Charm again, impatiently. 'What are you waiting for? Isis to give you permission or something? Open it, Cleo.'

Slowly, my hands trembling slightly, I unknotted the intricate fastening and unrolled the papyrus. It crackled slightly as it opened, and there were just three hieroglyphs written inside, ones I recognised immediately.

Temple.

Dark.

Moon.

I knew exactly what they were meant to tell me. I was to go to the main Temple of Isis at the dark of the moon – tonight, just as my birthing day dawned. I stood staring at it. This wasn't the usual way a priestess was summoned to her testing. I'd seen the papyri older acolytes had received often enough. This one should simply have shown me a picture of the Knot of Isis. My belly started to roil.

'I'm scared, Charm,' I said. 'Something's not right. The council seals are all fine, but there's this extra seal, look! I've never seen it before and I don't know whose it is. And the council always has the raising ritual at noon, not at night.' I'd seen so many raising ceremonies – watching with longing eyes as everyone crowded round the new priestess, hugging and welcoming her in the bright noonday sunlight. Was mine to be different, then?

Charm gulped and look at me with big eyes. 'Maybe it's Isis,' she whispered. 'Maybe she wants something – some repayment for her gift of sight. Maybe it's the call you've been waiting for all these years. I've always said she's got big plans for you.'

My mind started to whirl. Could Charm be right? Was it Isis? Did my patron goddess finally want some service of me? Was this the sign I'd asked for? And then, despite the heat, a shiver of cold ran up my spine as I thought of what was written on that unknown seal and remembered half-heard conversations, whispered rumours and sudden silences. There were secrets in this temple other than mine.

'I hope it is Isis herself,' I said. 'I really do.'

It was just then that the black kite dived screaming through the window and landed on my bare shoulder, its sharp talons ripping into my flesh. The burning, red pain sliced through me, taking my breath away for a moment. I felt its feathers soft against my face, saw the flash of a fierce yellow eye. Then I screamed too. It was just once, but I couldn't help it. I threw my arm up, trying to bat it away. Its talons were like fierce knives wrenching themselves out of my body, and I fell to my knees, moaning, as four warm rivers of blood poured out of my tender flesh. The bird was already gone, flying out of the window again as swiftly as it had come. I heard the sound of running feet coming from the corridor outside. I clutched at the scroll instinctively, wanting to hide it.

4

The Mark of Isis

Charm looked at me, both hands across her mouth, and her eyes wider than ever, paralysed with the shock of it. There was a knock at the door, and I knew I had to do something. I forced words into my mouth, gritting them out through my teeth, trying not to faint.

'Send them away, Charm. Say I saw a big scorpion and got scared or something. Everyone knows I hate scorpions. I can't let anyone see me like this,' I set the scroll down on the bench and mopped at the blood with the sheet. There was a lot of it, and I could feel it clotting down my back in thick, sticky globs. The pain was even more intense now, a throbbing thing with a life all of its own, and I took shallow breaths to try and control it, biting my lip to stop myself screaming again. Charm was at the door now, holding it open only a crack, so that no one could see in, her voice, slightly higher than usual, reassuring whoever was outside.

'Lucky it was only one of the other slaves,' she said, closing the door and running to me. 'Oh, Cleo, let me see – it looks bad. We need to get you back to your room so I can deal with it properly.'

Somehow, my mind couldn't think straight. The effort of speaking, of thinking had cost me all I had left, so I let her take charge. She got me into the robe Hu had left folded neatly on the bench and then tore a strip off the bloody sheet and bound my shoulder tightly. I tried not to whimper, but I couldn't help it. I wasn't used to this kind of pain. Then Charm opened the door and looked out warily.

'There's no one about,' she said. 'Come quickly before the supper bell sounds.'

I don't know how we made it through the corridors to my rooms without anyone seeing us. Luckily it wasn't far. As Charm opened the door and hustled me in, I froze for a second, recoiling into her arms. I heard her gasp as she saw what I had just seen. The same bird that had wounded me was perched in the window of my bedchamber, preening its feathers, which glowed a deep chestnut in the soft light of dusk. I could see it properly now, and there was no doubt. It was a black kite, sacred bird of Isis. My goddess had definitely sent me a sign, even though I couldn't decipher it yet. I bowed, wincing as the wounds it had given me pulled, releasing a further flood of blood. A messenger of Isis deserved respect, but I eyed the bird nervously, hoping it wasn't going to attack me for a second time.

'G-Greetings, Prince of Winds,' I mumbled, the renewed pain hazing my voice and making it tremble. 'What message do you carry for me from my goddess?'

Would it speak to me? Would it turn into Isis herself, as in the old stories? But the kite just clacked its beak at me and hissed irritably, turning its back.

'I'm sure it's a great honour, having the goddess's bird here,' Charm muttered from behind me, practical as always. 'But I'd as soon it flew off back to where it came from if it's got nothing useful to say to you. I need to poultice that shoulder for you and wrap it properly. Will you be all right alone with it while I fetch some herbs and bandages from the infirmary and ask the slaves to bring me some wash water?'

I nodded, suddenly sleepy from the shock, and went to lie down on the bed, just as the supper bell clanged out from the dining hall. A crowd of chattering voices and pattering sandals erupted immediately from the rooms nearby. Someone banged on my door, laughing loudly and shouting rudely for me to come to dinner. Of course it was Kemsit, the one who'd coined my Stick Girl nickname. I groaned. I couldn't face any of them now, especially not her – and I certainly didn't want them asking any questions about my shoulder.

'I'll tell them you've got your moon-blood,' Charm said quickly. 'Say you don't want to be disturbed.'

I nodded again. I wasn't hungry anyway, and it was a common enough occurrence among over a hundred women living together for it not to occasion any remark. As she slipped out of the door, and the noise receded towards the other side of the buildings, I fell into a drowsy daze. The pain was somehow lessening now, fading like the memory of a nightmare. It seemed quite natural to me when a voice began to whisper in my ear. It sounded like the merry chime of bells, like cymbals ringing out in joy, like the stillness of a white crescent moon against a fall of shooting stars. It was a voice I'd known since I took my first breath. I felt warm arms around me, a hand stroking my hair. It was fiery hot, and yet cool as river water at dawn. I snuggled into it, knowing myself safe and loved.

The stars and I are calling you to your time of testing, my daughter. Bind your wrist with leather and take my messenger with you on your journey tonight. He will help you to find the way when the darkness falls. When you remove the bandages from your shoulder, you will find the mark of my favour. You should wear it openly, with pride tonight. The ones you meet will know what it means.

As suddenly as it had come, the voice was gone. I opened my eyes to find Charm snapping her fingers in front of my face and fanning me with a bunch of something green and strong-smelling.

'Cleo! Cleo! Wake up!' she was saying in a voice gone high with strain. 'Oh, gods help me, wake up! Please come back. Don't leave me!' The bitter scent of crushed green herbs filled my nostrils as I sat up, and I saw steam rising from a small earthenware basin.

'I'm awake,' I said hurriedly, anxious that Charm would run off and summon one of the healers in her panic. 'Don't worry, I'll never leave you.' Then I hesitated, not quite knowing what to say next. Should I tell her the truth about what had just happened? I'd never kept a secret from Charm in my life, but this was so big, so scary, that I couldn't even grasp the fact of it myself. Would she believe me? How long had I been unconscious? I looked down at the bed beside me. One long, dark hair lay there among the sheets. It wasn't mine, and it glowed slightly blue. I picked it up and twisted it round my finger tightly, comforted by this tangible evidence of my goddess's presence.

'I-I think…well, Isis spoke to me. Properly, I mean, not just in a dream. She was right here beside me. Look! She left one of her hairs behind!'

Charm gasped, dropping the herbs onto the bed, her black eyes going wide with awe, reaching out towards the glowing hair with one fingertip, wiping my doubts away with her faith that my goddess had really been with me. The hair gave a last burst of light, faded and disappeared. My finger felt the cool heat of it, lingering.

'She did? She was? Really? What did she say?'

'She told me…' I stopped, taking in a deep breath. It was terrifying to say the words out loud, and my heart was skipping and stuttering as if it didn't quite know where to settle in my chest. I let it all out in a rush.

'S-She told me that she was calling me to my time of testing, and that I had to take her bird with me tonight. And that she'd marked me somehow, here.' I pointed at my right shoulder, then started pulling at the clumsy bandages, peeling them off, flakes of dried blood raining down on the sheets. Charm tried to help, but I brushed her hands away gently but firmly. This was something I knew I had to do for myself. It should have hurt, but there was no pain at all now. Then, craning my head round to look, I saw why.

Four small perfectly healed white scars lay across my shoulder in a familiar pattern, shining bright among the bloodstains. Charm reached out to touch it with one shaking fingertip, tracing it softly. The skin felt sensitive and tight.

'It's the mark of Isis. It's the throne glyph,' she whispered. 'Oh, Cleo! I was right. The goddess does have big plans for you. Pharaoh-sized plans!'

My heart gave another great stutter of panic, and I shuddered, getting up all in a rush and walking over to the window where the kite still sat, motionless as a statue now. I breathed in great gulps of the damp night air, smelling the fetid murk of the river mixed with a whiff of barley bread and baked tilapia left over from dinner. What if Charm was right? Surely the mark couldn't mean that I was going to be Pharaoh? But what if it did? Did I really have the strength to rule Egypt? Despite all my lessons, I had no idea if I could even do it properly – and anyway, there was the small problem of my ghastly sisters occupying the throne right now.

'Please, Charm,' I choked out, my throat tight with terror. 'Don't ever say that again. You mustn't. I can't think about being Pharaoh...about going back to that cesspit of a palace. Just...don't.' My voice fell to a whisper as the fear turned cold and sour in my stomach – somehow she'd brought all those old insecurities from my childhood crashing in on me as if it had only been yesterday. I reached for my polished mirror with a shaking hand, holding it up at a distance so that I could see my shoulder, wanting to check again how my goddess had marked me. There was no doubt about it. The throne shone bright on my skin among the bloodstains. What did it mean? How could I ever show this sign in public? Someone would carry the rumour of it and me downriver to the palace in Alexandria, and then Tryphena and Berenice would be sure to find out I was still alive. I would be as good as thrown to Am-Heh's crocodiles after that – unless Isis protected me.

'Listen, Cleo,' Charm said, coming up behind me and putting her arms round me. 'If it's the goddess's will, how can you fight it? If Isis wants you to be Pharaoh, you will be – and you'd better start getting used to the idea. Anyway, I quite fancy being the Pharaoh's simple body slave!' She took hold of my shoulders and whirled me round, dropping to her knees in an exaggerated parody of the obeisance given to the reigning Pharaoh while sticking her tongue out and making stupid goggle eyes like a frog. It made me giggle in spite of my fear. She could always cheer me up – she always had been able to.

'Don't be an idiot, Charm!' I said. 'And don't try to pretend you're just a simple body slave, either.' She had been my best friend since I was three and my father had sent her to me as a present after she was captured. She had been six. 'The first thing you ever told me was that you were a princess too, remember?'

'I'm still a princess,' she said, and only I would have heard the trace of sadness hidden deep in her words. 'It's just that the tribe I'm a princess of doesn't exist any more.'

I felt guilty then. It was my own father who'd destroyed her people, hunted them down to the last man and woman. Charm and four other children had been the only survivors. They'd died of a fever as soon as they'd arrived in Alexandria. She was now the only one of them left. I leaned down and pulled her up, squeezing her hands tight. It was my turn to do the cheering up.

'Well, you're just as much a princess as I am in my eyes. And don't you forget it again!'

Charm smiled. She was never down for long.

'You can buy me a nice heavy crown for my next birthday to remind me, then,' she said. 'With jewels on it.'

Just then the kite shook itself, its feathers ruffling up and then falling back into place, smooth as burnished bronze silk, and I remembered that Isis had told me to take it with me to the temple. I sighed, eyeing its fierce beak, and those sharp talons digging into the sill. However was I going to persuade that thing to get on my arm?

Charm had her back to me now, gathering up the squashed herbs from among the bedsheets. Tears suddenly stung my eyes as I turned and took a step towards her.

'Oh, Charm,' I said, the reality of my goddess's words sinking in properly for the first time. 'How on earth am I going to do this?' The herbs pattered to the floor as she turned and saw my face.

'I don't know,' she answered, her black eyes serious. 'But we'll manage together somehow, like we always do. Now come here and let me wash all that blood off. You look like a warrior who lost a fight, not a prospective Pharaoh at all.'

I laughed again. It hurt my throat, somehow, but I took comfort in her belief and her practicality.

'I do, don't I?' I said, as she bathed it all away with the warm water, wiping my body with gentle hands and then patting it dry. 'Now, O my Worker of Miracles, all we have to do is find some leather to wrap round my wrist!'

* * *

It was eerily dark with no moon, though I could see Sihor, my birth star, already brilliant on the horizon. I would have to hurry. I had to be at the temple soon. I scrabbled among the clothes in the closet, pulling out the light loincloth, the breastband and the one-shouldered pleated dress. Whatever the testing was going to be, I must look my best for it. The fine cream linen was embroidered with carnelian beads, and I flung it on, knotting the golden cord around my waist before winding the attached shawl round and round, over and over again, back and front, till it tucked into the cord again. I fumbled for my lightest dancing sandals, bending down to fix the beaded thong fastenings around my slim ankles, and then picked up my mirror again, setting it at an angle so that I could do my make-up. I shook up the oily kohl in its tiny enamelled bottle, dipped in the slim wooden stick, and started to outline my upper eyelids with a steady hand, staring at my reflection. I saw a golden-skinned, oval face, framed by a mass of heavy, dark honey-coloured hair and ruler-straight fringe. My left eyebrow quirked slightly under a high forehead, making me look a little lopsided, and my sea-blue eyes and curved nose marked me out as a true Ptolemy, as did my slightly pointy chin. No one could deny my lineage, even if I was the Pharaoh's bastard.

I wiped the excess kohl off the stick, and, taking it by its decorated end, ran the sticky black paste round my lower lids, elongating them so they almost met my already darkened eyebrows. Then I smeared a touch of red ochre on my lips and cheeks, rubbing it in till they glowed.

By the time Charm returned, panting and sweaty with the heat of running, I was almost ready to go.

'Here,' she said, holding out a bundle. 'It's kidskin. I got it from one of the camel boys. He was going to make it into a pair of slippers for his girl, but I said I'd give him a jar of beer for it tomorrow. I didn't say what I wanted it for,' she finished hurriedly, seeing the question in my eyes.

'Will you bind it round me, please? Then I'll see if the bird will hop on.' I held out my left wrist, and Charm wrapped the soft layers around it, over and over. Surely the bird's talons wouldn't hurt me through that? I got up to go to the window, but as soon as I rose, the kite launched itself off the sill, gliding over on silent wings and landed on my hurriedly outstretched arm. It uttered a quiet cry and settled, folding its wings neatly. I could just feel the prick of its talons pressing into me. It was much lighter than I had expected, but I still had to tense my muscles to hold it steady. I drew in a deep breath.

'I'm ready,' I said, though my stomach felt as if it had a swarm of locusts crawling inside it. Charm's lip started to tremble.

'What if you don't come back, Cleo?' she asked. 'What will I do then?'

'I will come back,' I replied. 'I told you before. I'll never leave you.' But Charm's lip only trembled more, and two fat tears spilled down her cheeks. It was very unlike her to be this emotional.

'But if you don't?' she insisted. I used my free hand to reach out and hug her close, making the kite wobble on its perch and snap at me angrily.

'I'll be back before you know it, silly. Isis would never make us be parted. I won't let her. She knows how much you mean to me. Now come on and help me find the best way to sneak through the corridors. The others are sure to be asleep by now, but I don't want to take the risk of meeting anyone on the way – specially not Kemsit. That would be a disaster. Then you can come back here and keep the bed warm till I'm finished in the temple. I'm sure it won't take long.' My voice sounded surprisingly strong and confident, given my turbulent locust belly, and Charm seemed reassured. At least, I thought she was. She took a lamp from an alcove and covered it with a dark piece of cloth, and then peered out of the door, her head turning left and right.

'Come on, Cleo,' she hissed. 'All clear.'

We flitted through an endless-seeming maze of sandstone passageways, shadows swaying like ragged wraiths behind us. What seemed familiar in the daylight was mysterious and menacing in the dead of night. I followed the light of Charm's shrouded lamp, and at each cautious step I became more and more frightened. Who – or what – would be waiting for me in the temple tonight? It was territory so unknown that I couldn't even imagine where it might lead me. I focussed on keeping calm, not showing my fear to Charm, keeping my wrist upright so that the bird didn't fall off. It helped me – a little – but all too soon we were at the steps to the main temple, and it was time.

'Go on back to our room,' I said, making a huge effort not to let my voice shake, standing straight and tall with the bird beside me. I gave Charm a gentle push with my other hand. 'I have to do it alone from here. Please, Charm. Don't make it harder than it is already. Just go. Now.'

She gave another soft sob, but she obeyed me, saying nothing and looking at me over her shoulder only once. I had to bite hard on my lip not to call her back. It seemed horribly cold and frightening without her as the sound of her footsteps receded, and I stood in the absolute velvet stillness, looking up at the sky, waiting. The kite was almost a comforting companion on my wrist now. Its presence meant that I wasn't totally alone. Even the howling desert jackals on the other side of the Nile were silent now, the river-horses asleep in the reeds, the sacred ibis in their nests. The moon was dark, and the stars themselves seemed to be looking down on me. I felt very small and insignificant under their gaze. Then I saw Sihor, the star of Isis, and the light under which I had been born rise over the temple roof and I walked up the eight shallow stone steps and halted in front of the great bronze-bound carved pillars which marked the entrance. Two tall painted statues of Isis flanked them, and, straightening my shoulders, I reached out my hand, touching the right one for luck, then I stepped between them and in. My sandals scuffed slightly on the sill as I entered, and I smelt old incense and the dusty scent of holiness. The temple was totally empty and dark. Even the stars above me seemed dim.

There was no one there.

No one at all.

The kite flapped its wings once, startling me. It sounded as bold as a thunderclap in that noiseless place.

'Hello,' I called, soft and cautious. 'Hello! Is anybody in here?'

But the sound of my voice fell into a deep well of silence, and my quiet words drowned, quite unnoticed.

Or that was what I thought in the hushed minutes that followed, minutes that dragged out like hours, marked only by the rolling drumbeats of my heart. My arm began to hurt from the weight of the kite. I tensed my muscles harder in the effort to hold it steady, shifting from foot to foot. I was beginning to doubt myself.

Had I misunderstood what Isis had said? Was I in the wrong place? Where were the ones my goddess had told me I would meet?

Then, as if in answer to my questions, a line of pale light appeared at my feet. I startled and jumped backwards. As the kite let out an irritated hiss, and snapped at me again, the stone floor in front of me opened with a harsh scraping sound, revealing a set of rough steps lit by dim, flickering lamplight. A stench of stale air and rancid oil rushed up at me.

'Enter now into the realm of Isis for your testing, and be judged if you dare,' said a disembodied voice from far below, remote, cold and unseeable in the gloom. I couldn't tell whether it was male or female. 'But know this. Isis sees all, hears all, demands all. Those who are judged unworthy along the way will be made blind. Those who cannot find the path will fall into darkness. Those who are lost will wander forever, tombless and damned. Are you ready to enter Her realm, acolyte?'

Wonderful. Sounds like a real festival of fun, I thought, trying to ignore the tremble in my knees. I willed my voice not to shake, trying not to be afraid, remembering that I bore my goddess's own mark on my shoulder and her bird on my wrist. Squeezing my eyes shut for a moment, I gathered my courage and Isis's blessing around me like a cloak even as the sour taste of fear welled up in my throat. Then I opened my eyes wide and gazed down into the shadows. There was only one answer I could give.

'I'm ready!' I said.

'Then come to us,' said the voice below.' And let your lips now be sealed and silent till the end. If you can.'

Us? How many of them were there? And just one of me. Those last three words still hung in the air, but they only made me more determined, not less. I stepped forward boldly, my head held high.

Never show anger, fear or grief. Never let them see you're weak.

My father's words unearthed themselves from my childhood memory, offering themselves to my present need.

All right, then, whoever you are down there, I thought. *I'll show you my Ptolemy princess face. I'll do whatever it takes to get through this. I'll make my goddess proud.*

But as I set foot on the tenth step down, all the lamps blazed up with a clear white light, leaving me blinking and blinded. Then they went out entirely as the stone ground closed over my head, shutting me in. I stumbled, threw out my right hand towards the wall, about to clutch at it for support, then snatched my fingers away, biting back a scream. A horde of pale, glowing scorpions, led by a monstrously huge white one, covered the dark grey stone, stingers curved up in menace, claws poised to pinch. It was right then that I knew this was going to be even less fun than I'd imagined.

Scorpions were my number one least favourite insect of all time, even if they had once been Isis's guards when she was on the run from Seth. Ever since I'd seen Hesi, one of my childhood nurses, swell up and die from being stung, I'd hated their primitive shape, their scuttling, sly gait, their air of menace and death. But I couldn't let that fear stop me. I wouldn't. So I kept on walking downwards into the darkness, lit only by the faint greenish glow of the clattering, rattling insects which kept pace with me on the wall as I went, on and on, deep into the earth beneath the temple, till my legs ached and I lost count of the steps I'd taken.

The bottom took me by surprise. Expecting another step down, I lurched forward, biting into my tongue as my jaw clacked shut with the impact. The hot, salty-iron taste of blood filled my mouth, and I swallowed it down silently. My left arm was nearly numb now, and I was having to support it with my other hand, but I was still glad of the kite's company. It meant I wasn't totally alone in this place where I could see almost nothing except pale, glowing scorpions.

I felt the brush of tiny legs on my bare toes and then a sharp stabbing pain. The horde of scorpions had left the walls now, and were streaming across the floor, across my feet. A tiny one hung from my ankle, stinger jammed in to the hilt. It hurt like a needle under a nail – small, sharp pulses of pain that grew and grew. Would I too swell up like Hesi had? Would I die here in the underground dimness?

I shook my foot frantically to get the beastie off, leaping back from the rest in disgust, but I couldn't escape them. I both heard and felt the wet crunch of insect bodies dying underneath my sandals, nearly biting through my lip, holding in the screams of disgust and pain that wanted so badly to come out. I could smell the ichor leaking out of the foul creatures, a thin, bitter scent that mixed with the damp mustiness of stone and lingered in the back of my nostrils. But I wouldn't give in, however much I hated the revolting things. The kite beat its wings angrily at my sudden movements and dug in its talons hard, breaking through the numbness and making my muscles jerk with a further agony. I couldn't soothe it with words, so I reached out with one shaking finger and stroked its soft feathers, hoping it wouldn't bite me again.

The light was even fainter now. I could just make out the tail end of the scorpion horde disappearing round a corner into what looked like a narrow passage. I didn't want to follow them, but I had no choice unless I wanted to be left in total darkness. They were my only source of light. So I walked on behind them, shuffling my feet back and forth to try and get rid of the scorpion slime and sticky bits of carapace from the bottom of my sandals. My ankle was throbbing even worse now, and I could feel it swelling as I walked. *I* won't *die like Hesi. I* won't! I thought fiercely, over and over again, willing the throbbing to go away.

The passage got narrower and narrower, closing about me so that I had to hold my arms straight out in front of me to fit and hunch my shoulders inwards. The kite's silhouette bobbed up and down in front of me like a black beacon. I knew I wasn't going to be able to hold onto it much longer, but I clenched my teeth together, trying to put all the pain out of my mind, concentrating so hard that I almost didn't register as the passage widened out into a larger space. Suddenly the scorpion horde disappeared down a small hole in the ground, far too small for me to follow. Although I hated those scorpions, I wanted to put my foot over it, wanted to stop them going, wanted to beg them not to leave me in the dark. As the last insect vanished, taking the dregs of the light with it, the kite launched itself off my arm with a wild *Screeee!* and flew off.

There was no time to think. I fled after it, straining my ears for the soft beat of its wings, but it was no good. I could hear nothing but the sound of my own running feet on bare rock. Isis's messenger had deserted me, and I was all alone in a darkness so deep that I felt as if my body had dissolved into it and become nothing. I had never been so alone. The words I'd heard earlier hit me like a slap.

Those who are judged unworthy along the way will be made blind. Had I been judged unworthy somehow? Was this my punishment? Was I to be left here, blind forever, searching for a way out until I died? Was my last memory of sight and light really to be those horrible scorpions? It was unthinkable, and yet I was beginning to believe it was true. I pressed my fingers hard into my eyeballs, hoping to see a comforting flash of white when I released them, but the darkness still reigned inviolate.

5

The Sisters of the Living Knot

I don't think I'd ever realised how stubborn I could be till then. Even the time when I was five and had refused food for four days until Charm was allowed to eat with me didn't compare to this. I tried not to think about being blind forever, or about swelling scorpion stings. It made me too afraid. Instead I focused on the hot, confused ball of anger and determination inside me. What did Isis really want of me? I'd worked so hard to learn all the arts a priestess needed in the years since Charm and I had come to Philäe, trying to find a way to please my goddess and make her proud of me. I could talk politics and religion with people in ten different languages, I knew by heart all the paths the stars trod through the heavens, I could brew a love philtre or a healing draught, play a seven-stringed lyre, dance to make even a eunuch feel desire. But how to find my way out of a lightless hole underground without even so much as a spark to guide me was something that had never come up in my lessons. Oh why had Isis left me in this horrible place? Why had she honoured me with her mark and her bird messenger earlier tonight if it was all for nothing? Did she actually want me to fail? No! I wouldn't believe it. I couldn't.

This must be a test of a different kind – a test of my character or my endurance. If Isis didn't want me to show off the skills I'd been taught, I'd learn different ones. Right here and now, I would make it up as I went along. I would find a way to get out of this pit if it killed me. I'd show my goddess and that doubting voice what I was made of. I rolled my stiff shoulders, stretched my aching arms out in front of me once more and took one careful pace forward, then another, then another, fighting the fear, stamping it into the stone with each step. If I was really blind, I'd have to learn to walk again without light, and I might as well start right now.

With my sight gone, all my other senses were heightened. It was very hot and stuffy, and I could still smell the damp, musty scent of the stone all about me, but now there was something more earthy about it, more green, something that conjured up reeds and mud. Was I near the river? Underneath it? I thought about the weight of all that Nile water above me, filled with hateful river-horse jaws and shivered.

Back and forth, back and forth, I waved my arms as I walked; left and right, left and right until suddenly my fingertips grazed over something cold. I whipped them back at once, clutching them to my chest, and then, turning cautiously, sent them questing out again to explore. Whatever this was, it was man-made – it felt slippery and smooth, like polished marble or onyx. As I rubbed my fingertips over it, I could feel raised lines and curves. Concentrating hard, I put both palms flat against the wall and swept them outwards, then up and down. Yes. There were hieroglyphs written there. What were they? I traced the lines and curves of the picture signs over and over, willing my fingertips to see what my eyes couldn't. Was that an adze or an axe I could feel? Was that the sign of Hathor or the girdle of Isis? And what was the line that wound back and forth like a snake?

I closed my eyes, though I had no need to, finally seeing the shape and meaning of the glyphs inside my head.

Turn around and change direction, Isis-chosen. Chosen of Isis, change direction and turn around.

Whichever way round I read it, it seemed to say the same thing, seemed to say that my goddess was still on my side. So, setting my back against the wall, I did what I'd been told and walked forward, trusting that Isis knew what she was doing. The green, earthy smell was stronger now. A breath of different air wrapped itself around my calves, and with no more warning than that I lost my footing, sat down hard on my royal behind and slid downwards, plunging feet first into something wet and warm.

I sank like a stone for about a second, hit bottom and pushed upwards, spitting and spluttering. I struggled to my feet, feeling soft mud sucking and squelching round my toes. Then, blinking and screwing up my eyes, I looked around me in the dim, steamy air and found I wasn't blind after all.

Being able to see again felt so good that I almost forgot to be afraid – almost, but not quite. Because as I stood up to my knees in the brackish, muddy water of an underground lake, I felt eyes watching me from the shore. Where were they? I turned my head this way and that, searching. There! Half-sunk in the mud at the edge of the lake. Blind, white piggy eyes with black pupils. Dead eyes that didn't blink. I stared back at them, legs twitching and itching to run, and teeth chattering like bulbuls in a thornbush. I edged myself around slowly, not wanting to turn my back on them, but needing to know what was there. Behind me rose a high red cliff, with a waterfall streaming down its centre, straight into the lake. The din of water hitting water almost drowned out the small, clicking sounds of my fear – almost, but not quite. I looked up at the grey sky, which shone with an unnatural, flat light, trying to work out where I should go next, trying not to think about those blind white eyes boring into my back.

A *screeee!* pierced the air above me, and the kite swooped over my head.

Screeee! Screeee! Screeee! it went, urgent and loud, warning me. I looked over my shoulder. The dead eyes on the shore were moving. I could see broad, pallid, sharp-toothed heads heaving themselves out of the mud, launching bloated ghost-white river-horse bodies into the water – towards the place where I stood. I froze, unable to move even a fingernail.

Screeee! Screeee! Screeee! The kite shrieked again, chivvying me to move, flying back and forth across the face of the water, across the wet, mossy steps that I now noticed leading up the cliff beside the waterfall. Forcing myself into action, I turned and dived towards them, arms and legs flailing in terror, cursing inwardly as the wet pleated skirt clung round my legs, hampering my efforts to swim.

The thick mud of the lake had sucked my best dancing sandals off already, and the red beads on my shawl hung heavily from the soaked linen, like solid drops of blood. I tore it off and flung it behind me. It landed with a *splosh!* and I heard the wet clack and crunch of jaws tearing at it. A rush of water hit my back as one of the dead-eyed river-horses charged me, jaws gaping wide. Its fetid breath filled my nostrils, making me gag. I kicked out with my legs, hit dense, solid flesh, pushed it away with all my strength. My robe ripped as one sharp tooth snagged on the hem, just by my calf, and I worked frantically to undo the golden cord round my waist. As it came loose, I tore the shoulder fastening apart, gave a desperate wriggle, and was free. I made one last wild push forwards, grabbed onto the steps and heaved myself upwards, feet slipping on the slimy moss as the whole herd of ghostly-looking beasts surged and crashed against the stone, roaring out their frustration.

I was dressed only in my loincloth and breastband now, but I didn't care. All that mattered was that I was away from the dead-eyed nightmares, trying not to fall, scrambling up the steep cliff any way I could, and the kite was above me always, calling me, guiding me onward. By the time I reached the top of the steps, my bare feet were cut and bleeding from the rocks, my knees were a red ruin, my nails were ripped ragged and my hair was a dense, sodden mat dripping cold trails of muddy water down my back. The kite met me there – perched on a rocky pillar beside a small copper door, which shone brightly in that grey, dim place despite the green streaks of verdigris on its surface. I nodded my thanks to him as he took off again, one small chestnut feather falling from his wing, spiralling through the still air and landing at my feet. As I bent to pick it up, the kite let out a last *screee* of farewell and disappeared from sight.

Fine mist from the waterfall fell on my nearly-naked body, soothing it. I staggered towards the copper door, pushed it open and fell inside on my hands and knees, eyes closed, panting. If Isis had anything more to throw at me, she would have to wait. I needed a moment to get my breath. I jerked with shock when I felt someone behind me, felt soft, warm hands under my armpits, helping me to my feet. A finger reached over my shoulder and touched my lips, cautioning me to silence. I didn't need to be told, though. I'd held my tongue this long. I wasn't going to fail by screaming now.

As I opened my eyes and looked around me, I saw a small, low room, painted with glowing pictures of

Isis in all her glory. They seemed to shimmer and shift as if they were alive. A heavily-veiled woman, wearing white robes, now moved round in front of me. Beside her stood a silver tub, filled with steaming water. A strong smell of roses perfumed the air and I saw that the bathwater was covered in floating red petals. The woman beckoned me forward, helping me out of my loincloth and breastband, giving me a hand to step in. I was so tired – too tired to worry about being naked in front of a stranger, too tired to wonder who she was and what she was doing here. Thankfully, I sank down past the petals and into the water, trying to ignore the stinging in my hands, knees and feet. A moment later she lifted a long-necked pitcher and poured a cool stream of asses' milk over my body. The familiar, slightly sweet smell made my eyes prick with tears as the liquid flowed over my breasts and down my belly like gentle, smoothing hands. I hadn't had an asses' milk bath since I left Alexandria – since my mother was alive. It was bliss after what I'd been through, even though I didn't understand why. Had I somehow passed the testing? Was this the end? What was going to happen to me now? Questions were bubbling up in me like water from a deep spring, but I closed my lips on them. I would not speak or make a sound till I was told to.

The woman washed my hair with a lotion that smelled of sunshine and rosemary. She combed out the tangles in silence, then she helped me out of the bath, dried me, and anointed my many wounds with a green, pungently-scented ointment which soothed and healed them at once. Before I had any time to wonder at that, she pointed to some robes like hers, but of a lighter material, hanging on a hook, together with a clean pair of white kidskin dancing sandals and new undergarments. I put them on, then looked at her questioningly. She pointed again, and as she did so, another door appeared in the wall – out of nowhere. I stared at it dumbly, unable to feel the awe I knew I should. It was a grander door than the last, precious ebony wood inlaid with jade and pearl and chrysolite, with a handle of gold.

This will be the last part of your test, my Chosen. It would please me greatly if you perform it well.

I whirled round at the familiar voice, which filled the room with quiet thunder, seeking a glimpse of my goddess made flesh, but there was no one there. The room was now empty. I pinched myself, hard. Was I really awake? How could I not have noticed that my goddess was in the room with me? Had Isis really just acted as my body servant? Why hadn't I tried to see her face? The small pinch pain told me I was and she had.

Pride filled me, and a shivery sense of awe, though I couldn't yet believe it had been real. Her hands had felt so human in my hair, and on my wounds. I wanted to reverse time, to go back and throw myself at her feet in worship. She had done me such great honour, it was nearly impossible to take it in.

I won't let you down, dear Isis, I thought fiercely, gazing at her picture on the wall. *Whatever task lies ahead, I'll do it better than anyone ever has or ever will.* Then I seized the golden handle in my right hand, turned it, and pushed open the door.

I stepped into in a dark, red-walled room, lit by cedar torches in silver and ebony brackets. Their spicy fragrance permeated the air, and a shimmering haze drifted upwards from their clear, still flames. Eight priestesses in full ceremonial robes sat across from me on thrones whose high golden backs culminated in a Knot of Isis. I recognised none of them except for High Priestess Jamila. Between them and me lay a huge open pit, covered with a widely-spaced mesh of thin, curved boards of polished wood arranged in a strange looping pattern. I stepped forward, looking over the edge, and recoiled. At the bottom of the pit was a roiling, boiling mass of hissing serpents, black and brown, green and gold, biting at each other's tails and spitting drops of venom.

'Cleopatra, daughter of Ptolemy the Flute Player, acolyte of our goddess,' said a veiled priestess. I recognised her cold, remote voice at once. 'There is only one dance across the pit, only one true way of Isis. If you make a wrong step or take a wrong turn, you will fall, and the serpents will be your escort to the land of the tombless dead. That is all. You may begin when you are ready.'

I sucked in a breath. Only one dance? Only one true way of Isis? I looked at the narrow, looping boards with a closer eye. There were several places I could step onto them and begin, but which was right? I saw a small symbol painted on the end of each board: cow horns, a feather, an eye, a moon. Definitely not the horns or the eye, then – those were for Hathor and Ra – but what about the feather and the moon? Both of those could represent Isis.

A picture of a small, spiralling feather flashed into my head. Had the kite given me a sign? A clue? Did the feather mark the path I must dance? And if so, which dance should I choose? I ran through them all in my head, counting steps out with mathematical precision, seeing the movements. Not the Night dance nor the Noon – those both had straight lines in them, and there was not a straight line to be seen here. None of the dances of Desire – those involved a lot of swaying and suggestive hand strokes, but not much foot movement. I went over them all, one by one until there was only one left which fitted, the most difficult of all – the dance of Isis Rising. There was a small flat bowl of chalk to my right. I stooped to it, scooped up some of the white dust and rubbed the soft kidskin soles of my sandals with it. I needed all the help I could get. Then I stepped onto the feather-painted board and began, putting my fate and my faith in the kite's wings.

I didn't look down, I didn't think. I just trusted my body to find the pattern of the dance, let it flow from movement to movement, in a kind of trance of graceful arcs and arabesques. I could feel the steely power of Isis within me as I kept my eyes soft and unfocussed, resolutely ignored the hissing, writhing mass beneath me. I refused even to consider the idea of falling, forcing all thought of what lay below from my mind. Instead I imagined I was floating lightly from board to board, my feet remembering the twisting, turning steps as if I'd been in the sunny courtyard of the temple, with the fat, lazy eunuchs looking on. All those years of practice came together in one fluid, beautiful series of steps, in which my whole body moved in a perfectly executed prayer to my goddess.

I knew I'd done it the moment I fell into the last

whirling spin and knelt at the priestesses' feet, arms outstretched, head tipped back in ecstasy, shoulders bare, opening myself entirely to the judgement of Isis. I was aware of eight quickly muffled gasps as the mark of Isis on my bare right shoulder began to glow with a brilliant golden light.

'Welcome!' said eight voices in unison. They sounded slightly choked. 'Welcome, beloved of Isis.' There was a distinct pause. 'Welcome, O marked and chosen one. You were summoned and have come to us through darkness, pain and fear. You have passed the time of testing and are reborn in Her sight. The Sisterhood of the Living Knot receives you, its newest sister, in the name of Isis. Come forth, join us. You have been long awaited.'

I straightened myself and scrambled to my feet, light-headed with relief. I'd passed my testing, I could speak. I wanted answers, and I was going to get them. Whether it was hunger or the fact of having passed my ordeal, I was feeling a bit light-headed, ready to challenge anything or anyone.

I fixed my gaze on the one familiar person here. High Priestess Jamila's homely, camel-toothed face looked a little strange in the company of her seven peers, all younger than her, some much more beautiful, but I found it a strangely comforting sight.

'So, am I a proper priestess now, or what?' I asked her, my voice sounding a little hoarse from disuse. 'What's all this about being marked and chosen? And who are the Sisterhood of the Living Knot?' If this was to be my priestessing ceremony, there was nothing here I recognised – no feast, no crowds of congratulatory acolytes, nothing familiar to hold onto. I needed to know where I stood, and why this was so different from what I'd been expecting.

She glanced at the veiled priestess before she replied, almost as if asking permission to speak. That was definitely odd. Wily old High Priestess Jamila wasn't given to asking permission from anyone – she was the queen of political game-playing in the temple – but maybe she was outranked. The veiled priestess nodded at her sharply, just once, confirming my thought. High Priestess Jamila was definitely not the head sister here.

'Well,' said High Priestess Jamila. 'I suppose you would have questions, Cleopatra, it being you. Come! We will show you all you need to know, priestess of Isis.'

Well. That was one question answered, anyway. I was now a real, bona fide priestess of the goddess. I couldn't wait to see Charm's face when I told her. Youngest priestess ever, just as I'd dreamed. She'd be so happy for me! Immediately I thought of her, I began to get anxious.

How long had I been away? I couldn't tell if only minutes had passed, or hours. I hated to think of her all alone in my room, waiting for me.

'Can I send a message to Charm first?' I blurted out. 'Only she'll be…' My voice tailed off into nothing as all eight of them turned and looked at me incredulously. 'What?' I said, suddenly defiant. 'She's my best… I mean, my body slave. She worries. I want her to know I'm safe and well.'

Jamila raised her eyebrows and shrugged her shoulders, looking at the others as if to say, *See what I have to put up with?*

'Very well,' she said. 'A message will be sent to her. Now come, Cleopatra, there are things you must know.'

Several hours later, my head was reeling with all those hidden temple secrets and more, and my stomach was making noises like a starving warthog. I'd been lectured on all the rules of the sisterhood, made to read a massive pile of scrolls and then lectured again by each sister in turn about why I mustn't tell anyone anything about any of it. When they'd been founded (ages ago), what they did (pulling the strings of power for Isis, and spying, among other, darker, things), who they were (the brightest and best from every temple in Egypt). It was a lot to take in, and any kind of studying always made me hungry. If I'd been in the library, I would have eaten at least a plate of sticky honey pastries by now, and possibly two. All I'd been given so far was a glass of disgustingly warm barley beer and a couple of dry rolls with curd cheese. My stomach was not happy.

I rubbed my eyes, which felt as if they had an entire desert full of grit in them by now. All I really wanted was to go and find Charm, get some proper food and then to lie down and sleep somewhere, preferably for several days. But the veiled priestess, whose name was High Sister Merit, had just given me a prophecy by some old sister called Holy Salama to read. It made my head want to burst. Because it was apparently about me.

I read the cramped script again and again, trying to understand it.

In the days of the floodtime of Sihor, star of Isis Rising, the marked one shall also rise, with the throne shown clear on her shoulder. The marked and chosen one shall wipe out the betrayer's sin. She shall seek the bloodied magic key to the hidden tomb and bring it forth. Thus will my ancient oath to She Who is Hidden be met once more, and our powers restored.

It still made no sense whatsoever.

'So,' I said to High Sister Merit and High Priestess

Jamila, who were by now the only two sisters left in the room. 'The whole sisterhood has been hanging around since forever, waiting for someone to be marked with the throne sign by Isis? And now I'm her?' I ran my fingers over the small still-glowing white scars on my shoulder. There was no doubt, they were definitely there. I was the one marked with the throne. 'But why me? Why now? And why didn't Isis explain it to me herself?'

That made both of them go all purse-lipped and tight-faced. Maybe Isis didn't speak to them, and they were jealous of me or something. That made a kind of sense – and I was desperately trying to find some sort of sense in all of this.

High Sister Merit frowned at me. She'd taken her veil off now, and I noticed that her otherwise perfect egg brown cheeks had a net of shiny dark scar lines criss-crossing them, as if long ago someone had taken a very thin blade and cut spiderwebs into her face. It gave her an eerie, otherworldly look.

'The ways of Isis are mysterious. You insult the choice of our goddess by speaking of her so lightly, Chosen. Will you refuse your destiny?' she asked. 'For it is written…'

'Yes, yes I know,' I interrupted, too tired to be polite. 'It's written. I'm not stupid! I've just read it about ten times. Holy Salama's wretched prophecy. But what does all that about betrayers and bloody keys and hidden tombs and oaths and powers all mean? And who is She Who is Hidden? I don't understand what it all has to do with me.'

'We have studied the prophecy scroll for many long seasons,' said High Sister Merit, icy and formal. 'Some of our sisters have devoted all their waking hours to meditating on it, asking for guidance as to the will of our goddess, some have gone to seek answers out in the world at great personal cost to themselves. Some of our number have even died. You are the only one in that time who has come to us from her testing marked with the throne by the goddess herself. You are honoured beyond all other women. You are both marked and chosen, there is no doubt.'

'I know,' I said (and I did, really, I did). 'I know how lucky I am to be the chosen of Isis. It's just that I still don't know what any of it actually means.'

There was an awkward silence.

'High Priestess Jamila and I have had many, many debates about you over the last few months,' High Sister Merit said at last. 'We have always known you were destined for the sisterhood. One or other of us has been watching you in secret since you were born. You are not the only one our goddess visits, you know. Some of us said you were not ready for your testing yet, others of us said that Isis would be served best by testing you early, while you were still young enough to be advised.' Jamila sniffed loudly at this, her disapproval evident. 'But when Isis made it plain that we were to call you yesterday, none of us knew that you would emerge from your testing as the marked and chosen one. That was a surprise to everybody, and it changes everything. You now hold the destiny of Egypt – maybe of Isis herself – in your hands.' High Sister Merit paused, tapping one long fingernail on the table. There was an angry fire and a hunger in her eyes as she looked at me that made me very uncomfortable. What did she want from me? The destiny of Egypt? The destiny of Isis? What was she talking about?

'Oh, for Isis's sake!' Jamila burst out. 'Show the girl. Nothing is served by hiding it from her. She is the marked and chosen one, whether we like it or not, and she must face her fate and do Isis's will, or everything will be lost.'

'You overreach yourself, High Priestess,' said High Sister Merit coldly, glaring at her. 'Stick to your petty temple scheming, and let me handle the affairs of the sisterhood. I know my duty. I know what is at stake.' She turned back to me, reaching out with her long fingers, grasping my head with palms that felt unpleasantly hot and damp. 'Look! Look at me! I will show you the vision that Isis, in her wisdom, gave me at my own testing. It will explain everything.' I had no choice but to look at her. She held my skull in a viselike grip. My blue eyes met her black ones, and I fell into them as if they were a deep well with no bottom.

I was in a room with a young woman a few years older than me, dressed in the robes of a priestess of Isis. Great, heaving sobs shook her shoulders. I tried to go to her, but I had no body, no voice. All I could do was watch.

'Why, Isis? Why?' she said, sobs thickening her voice.

I knew how she felt. I'd often asked our goddess that very question. Suddenly, the vision slid a bit, and a man was with her in the room. He was very handsome, but I felt a lash of contempt and hatred spike through me as I saw he wore the amulet of a priest of Seth, and the red garb of an embalmer. What was a priestess of Isis doing with garbage like him – a worshipper of death, disorder and deception? The woman was on her knees, clinging to his thighs.

'I've been summoned, Tebu. I-I have to leave Alexandria.' Her face turned bitter and angry under the tears. 'This is the last time I'll ever see you. I'll never sing again either, never speak to a living soul. I'm going to be stuck out in the desert with…' Her hand flew to her mouth as the words burst out.

'Stuck with who? Doing what, my dove?' said the man. His voice was too smooth and caressing, and I didn't trust it or him. 'Tell me what your goddess has done to make you cry, my poor Sera.'

'I m-mustn't,' said the woman, scrambling to her feet. She looked frightened. 'Truly. I've said too much already. You must go, my love. I shouldn't have summoned you. It's too dangerous. If we're caught…'

'But I want to know where you're going, my pearl.' I heard a bullying hardness creep in behind the caressing tones. 'And I can see you want to tell me. Think of it as a parting gift between lovers. It would mean so much to me if I could picture what you are doing in your new home.'

'I-I mustn't. I can't. But…oh, Tebu!' The woman flung herself into his arms. 'Oh, Tebu, I shall miss you so. I'm going to be so lonely in that wretched place. I wish you could come with me. I think Isis must be punishing me for being with you. Just because she hates your god – it's so unfair.'

As she began to weep again, the filthy priest cajoled her, flattering her beauty, her exquisite voice, dripping his wheedling words into her ear, trying to get her to betray my goddess. Anger welled up within me. How dare he? And how could she? Because now the sisters' secrets were spilling from her mouth like honey from a jar.

'There's a cave...in the desert. It belongs to the Old One – the grandmother of all the gods...the Hidden One. Isis swore an oath that we would guard what's in the cave, just four of us s-sisters, with nothing but sand and howling jackals for company. Whoever is summoned has to stay there till she dies, and...and, oh! Isis takes our voices from us, s-so we can't tell what's in there or where it is...and we have to live on dates and camel milk. I hate camel milk!' The woman began to sob again and rock herself to and fro. 'Oh, why, Isis? Why must you take my voice? Didn't my songs make you happy? Was my music not pleasing to your ears?'

The man shook her roughly.

'Tell me, my dove. Tell me what's in the cave.'

'I can't,' she wailed, pushing him away, stumbling backwards. 'Something magic, some ancient treasure is all I've been told. I don't know! I won't know till I get there – and then I won't be able to tell anyone because my voice will be gone.' Her voice now rose to a shriek and she began to flail about as if possessed. 'Go! Go! My goddess calls me to her!'

The room wavered around me, dissolving and reforming into the lush green of an oasis at dawn. A trickle of smoke from a dying fire rose into the still, sultry air. Four white camels and two calves lay resting on the rocky ground under the palm trees, beside a red sandstone cliff. The quiet splashing of a small flock of waterfowl was all that disturbed the glassy surface of the deep green pool. Then there was a flicker of movement as four women, dressed and veiled in white, appeared from the mouth of a cave in the cliff face. In total silence three of them scattered, one to tend the fire, one to milk the camels, one to fetch water. The last stayed just outside the cave, watchful and alert.

The scene quivered and went misty before clearing again. I would have gasped if I'd had breath. Now it was dark, lit only by an immense fire in the midst of the oasis and four bodies lay scattered about on the ground, legs and arms splayed like discarded white-clad dolls, throats gaping wide like screaming mouths. The sand was stained with pools of darkening scarlet around them, flickering in the flame-light. Suddenly, a hoarse, agonised shriek sounded from inside the cave, followed by a great roaring and a man was flung out of the entrance. There was a flash of blinding light and sound which burst upwards in a great white column, scattering across the deep blue sky, spilling across the stars like milk. I heard a cracked old voice cry out, in a language I did not understand, twinned with a younger one – the voice of Isis herself. The voices sounded both angry and afraid, and the rage and mourning of them burned my ears like fire.

The man stumbled away, bleeding heavily from wounds both on his body and his face. It was the Seth priest, the filthy embalmer, Tebu. His red robe was ripped, and five deep scores slashed across his shoulder and belly. They looked as if they had been made by the claws of some beast too huge to even imagine. I tried to move, but I was held fast. I would have helped whatever beast it was to kill him if I could.

Then a fierce storm wind blew about me. Swirling sheets of sand rose up from the ground, filling my vision, blotting out the stars, so that they might never have existed. Even though I had no physical body here, I felt the gale's unnatural power, unleashed and uncontrollable, like the beast whose voice I heard over and above it all, howling out a song of death and oblivion. In less time than it took me to draw a silent breath, the desert had covered the entire oasis, hiding all traces of it, burying the murdered bodies – and whatever else lay in the cave – in a rippling ocean of sand.

I was whirled through the stinging air, and moments

later I was riding with the murdering dogslime, Tebu, as he galloped through the night, groaning and trying not to topple down onto the neck of his camel.

I crouched at his shoulder when he stopped at dawn, saw him draw a crude map on a ragged piece of papyrus with his finger, heard his vile Seth-chant as he dipped it into ash from his fire and his own foul blood to make a sludgy red-tinged ink, which glowed with some strange kind of magic.

I hovered on the wind with my enraged goddess as she struck and struck at him and the map with lightning, saw the lightning flash rebound off Seth's amulet, leaving him unharmed as the god's power surrounded him with a glimmering green protection.

The scene lurched forward in time, and I felt my unbodied belly roil with sickness. Impotent with fury, I watched him creep along an alley, his handsome face now blackened and ugly, saw him stumble through a painted arch I felt I should recognise.

The picture blurred again, and now he was crawling through a narrow scroll-lined passageway, past a malachite green statue with a donkey's head, past a pile of skulls whose red eyes watched with silent menace. I saw him fumble the map out of his clothing and into a plain ebony box, reaching up with an effort to place it on a shelf, before he fell to his knees, sobbing for his god to take the pain away.

And then, with a jerk, I found myself back in my own body, staring into High Sister Merit's eyes. My own eyes were blurred with tears and rage.

'How could she?' I burst out. 'How could Sera have taken that vile Seth-creature as her lover? What was she thinking to betray our goddess like that? Why did Isis not strike her down? Why was she chosen as a sister in the first place?' I still didn't understand what any of it had to do with me.

High Sister Merit looked at me almost approvingly. 'Hold onto your anger, Chosen. It will serve you well. You are right. Traitor Sera brought shame on every sister, living and dead. Her betrayal caused Isis to fail in keeping her oath to protect the Old One, her grandmother. Because of that betrayal, Isis is gradually losing much of the power she once had. Egypt is slowly dying because our goddess cannot protect us as she once did – crops fail, there are plagues among the beasts and the people...' She lowered her eyes for an instant, as if ashamed of something, and then her expression flashed back to its normal coldness.

I frowned, not understanding.

'Losing her power? B-but Isis is the most powerful of all the gods, isn't she? She's the mother of Egypt. All the other gods bow to her…don't they?' My words trailed off apprehensively. Was my goddess not what I thought she was? A long ago memory drifted through my head. Blackened grain, bloated cows. Was this what Merit meant? Had I been wrong back then to think the gods were showing a brief displeasure? Was it worse than that? Was my goddess's protective power really failing?

'Not any more,' Merit said, and her voice was bleak. 'Though none know this but the highest of us. When the Old One retired from the world and lay down in her tomb to rest, in the days before our ancestors' ancestors came to this land, Blessed Isis became the vessel for much of her power. But that power was always linked to the fate of Egypt, and to the Old One herself. That is why Isis made a solemn oath to her grandmother to protect her cave tomb and the magical treasures that lie within for the rest of time. We sisters of the Living Knot were originally formed as a band of warrior maidens by our goddess to provide a guard for the Old One and carry out that sacred duty.' She stopped, clearing her throat, which suddenly sounded choked and thick.

'We have not been able to honour our sacred trust for

hundreds of seasons, because of the wretched traitor Sera's flapping tongue, and now nobody can find the Old One's cave, including Isis. Her grandmother has shut her out.

'Our goddess would not speak to any sister for many seasons after traitor Sera's betrayal. It was a long, dark time of silence and weeping till She favoured Holy Salama with knowledge – but it is only now that She has revealed the vessel chosen and marked to carry out Her purpose. You saw that enormous burst of light – that was a great part of Isis and the Old One's combined power being strewn across the heavens. With every season that passes, a little more of it is drained away and lost and Isis becomes a little weaker. If she does not regain that power soon, Egypt and her people will die – and our goddess will dwindle to a mere shadow.'

A long, icy finger stroked my spine from top to bottom, and I shivered with a kind of sick dread as the words of Holy Salama's prophecy finally sank in.

'Is that what it's about, then?' I whispered. 'I'm the marked and chosen one, so I have to wipe out the betrayer's sin and save our goddess and Egypt? But I don't understand. How can I do that?'

High Sister Merit scrubbed her hands over her eyes. It made her look almost human for about a second.

'We think that the "bloody magic key" in Holy Salama's prophecy means the map which the accursed Seth priest drew,' she said.

'But how is the map magical? And how will getting it back restore Isis's powers?' I interrupted.

'We think that the priest used Seth's own power, and his own death spells, to bind some kind of strong magic into the ebony box. Both box and map are now hidden from Isis's eyes. Her grandmother has decreed that Isis may not return to her tomb without that map, and our goddess thinks you are the one to bring it to her. Until that is done, her power will weaken further, and Egypt will slide further and further into famine and chaos.'

Beside her, High Priestess Jamila stirred, tapping her foot on the floor, and her thin lips pursed before she spoke.

'The point is, Cleopatra, that little by little, Blessed Isis is growing weaker. She is still powerful, of course, but the loss is having an effect on the whole of Egypt, as Merit has told you. It is not just crops and beasts and plagues. Her temples are failing too – and now the lesser gods have started to steal away her power. Gods like foul Am-Heh.' Her mouth closed like a trap, as if she'd said too much, and suddenly I had a bad feeling about this. Am-Heh was the vile god my sisters worshipped. There were definitely things High Priestess Jamila and High Sister Merit still weren't telling me, I was sure of it.

'So, where exactly do you think this magical map is?' I asked slowly, dreading the answer I knew was coming.

High Sister Merit, met my eyes with her hard, clear gaze. 'We know from our most recent investigations that the priest Tebu died from his wounds, and that his shrivelled body was found in the secret archives of the Brotherhood of Embalmers, underneath the Great Library in Alexandria. We are now quite certain that the map is hidden somewhere in there.'

Immediately, I knew where I'd seen that painted arch before. How could I have forgotten it? It led to the Great Library in Alexandria. Now I understood. At least, I thought I did.

'Let me get this straight, then,' I said slowly, ticking the words off on my fingers, feeling as if I was in some kind of twisted dream. 'You want me to go back to the city I fled from four years ago, in fear of my life. You want me to break into the secret archives of the Brotherhood of Embalmers and find some long-lost magical map! And you want me, ME, to get back Isis's powers and save the whole of Egypt?'

My voice rose to a near-shriek as I lost what little calm I had.

'Are you mad? I've never been taught anything about sneaking and spying, and I wouldn't go near the filthy Seth-loving embalmers if you paid me in stardust and diamonds! Oh, and by the way – do you know what my Evil Sow sisters will do to me if they find out I'm alive? They'll probably throw me to Am-Heh's fat, overfed crocodiles the minute I walk through the door. If I'm lucky! There's no way I can do this! No way! You might as well kill me now!'

I was on my feet before I knew it, panting for breath. I couldn't go back to Alexandria! I couldn't! What was Isis thinking?

'Sit down, Cleopatra!' said High Sister Merit. 'It is not we who command you to do this, but Isis. Will you defy your goddess? Do you dare to tell me that she has marked and chosen the wrong girl? Where is your courage? Where is your sense of duty to your goddess and to Egypt?'

High Priestess Jamila broke in, not giving me a chance to answer, using her most imperious tone – the one she used to command obedience from errant acolytes.

'See, Merit! I told you she wasn't strong enough for this. I knew we should have waited!'

High Sister Merit just looked at her. For a second the air between the two priestesses popped and crackled with hostility. Then High Priestess Jamila's eyes dropped under High Sister Merit's disdainful stare.

'Oh, have it your own way,' she muttered. 'I bow before the will of Isis. May Her will be done.' Then she turned and marched out of the room, leaving me alone with the scary high sister.

Was this really my destiny? Maybe Isis really did want me to go to Alexandria and find this magical map. But High Priestess Jamila had got one thing right. Why did it have to happen right now? My brain almost refused to work any more, overwhelmed by everything that had happened to me in the last few hours. I just didn't have the energy to stop the overflow of hot tears which started to drip down my cheeks, and I slumped forward onto the table, half-sobbing, nearly defeated. I wanted Charm so badly at that moment that I would have done almost anything to hear her voice, to ask her what I should do, what I should say.

My first day as a priestess wasn't meant to have been like this. It should have been full of sunshine and rejoicing with a big feast, and dancing, and hugs and congratulations – that's what every other new priestess of Isis always got. All I had was a stomach full of fear and the head of a secret sisterhood determined to send me to the one place I dreaded more than anywhere else in the whole world, on a quest that was so big it was incomprehensible. I felt somehow cheated, despite the great honour Isis had given me.

'I won't go,' I said miserably, summoning up one last bit of fight. 'You can't make me.' But I somehow knew High Sister Merit and Isis between them would wear me down in the end. How could they not? The fate of my country, my people, and the power of my goddess herself were at stake.

6

The Road to Alexandria

It seemed I was right. The head of the sisterhood was
even more stubborn than I was. She was like a great wall
of granite, implacable, unyielding. Despite my tears of
exhaustion I still battered myself nearly senseless on her
before I gave in to her demand that I return to Alexandria
to find that gods-cursed map for Isis. I'd tried crying,
pleading – everything – but none of it had worked. I
might have got past scorpions, ghostly river-horses and a
pit of snakes, but none of them were a patch on High
Sister Merit.

My goddess hadn't had to say a word. She already
knew how relentless the head of the Sisterhood of the
Living Knot was. She'd given her the job, after all.

Once she'd got her way, High Sister Merit was all

action. She hustled me, stumbling and disoriented, along underground passages I'd never known existed, then up into the dark, silent corridors of the Philäe temple I knew so well. Whatever day it was now, I could tell it was near dawn. The lightening sky was a clear, pale pink, promising another blazing Akhet morning. I was so tired that I almost fell through the door of my rooms. Charm was asleep at the end of my bed, sprawled out anyhow on top of the covers. I lurched towards her, but High Sister Merit grabbed my arm, her hard fingers pinching my flesh painfully.

'Remember, say nothing to your slave of the sisterhood or your mission,' she hissed. 'I will see you later today to give you more instructions. Sleep now. You will need it.'

I nodded, not meeting her eyes. I would have said yes to anything at that moment if it got rid of her and allowed me to sleep, but of course, I lied. Did she really think that I wouldn't tell Charm, the person I trusted most in the world? Did she really think I would go back to the snake pit of the royal palace without my best friend to watch my back? I crawled into the bed beside her, the minute High Sister Merit was out of the room, meaning to shake her awake, meaning to tell her everything. But I was too exhausted to do more than lay my hand on her shoulder before darkness took me.

I woke to the sound of a door slamming, drowsy and still dazed from the events of the night. The flood time had arrived with my birthday, as it always did, and I could hear the change in the sound of the swelling waters of the river. The air was hot and muggy, and I could feel the sweat starting under the heavy hair at my nape. I stretched out a hand, groping beside me sleepily. But nobody was there. I sat up all in a tumble, forcing my eyes open, my heart beating fast. Where was Charm? Why was she not beside me? I blinked, looking around, trying to focus. There was no Charm to be seen, only wretched High Sister Merit, sitting on a stool by the window, upright and cool as a stone column, watching me.

'Where is my body slave?' I said, clamping down my panic and putting on my most imperious princess voice. I might as well start practising it.

'I have sent her away,' said High Sister Merit, clearly unimpressed. 'To pack for you. It will be a long journey. There are things you must know about the arrangements which have been made for you. It would not be appropriate for her to be here. She will return to you later, when it is time for you to leave.'

'All right,' I said, trying to sound reasonable and grown up as well as imperious. A few hours sleep had given me a little more energy to argue with her, but all I could really do was try and bargain with her for some small concessions.

'She's definitely coming with me, though. I want that understood right now. She knows the palace better than I do. She'll be a help if I need to send a message or something. No one ever looks at slaves.' I kept my voice hard, as if I didn't care, as if it didn't really matter. High Sister Merit wasn't fooled for an instant, of course. I'd given myself away last night when I asked to send Charm a message.

'You will go to Alexandria openly, as the special emissary of Isis,' she said, as if I hadn't spoken. 'I have already sent messages by bird to the sister in the temple on the isle of the Pharos, and she will help you if she can.' She frowned, and her lips sucked in as if she'd just eaten a bitter fruit. 'You yourself must not trust anyone but that one sister in Alexandria. The temples of all the gods are riddled with spies and corruption, and in the palace itself, Am-Heh gets stronger by the day, may his name be cursed. His dark power threatens the Double Throne itself.'

My mouth dried, so that I could hardly swallow. The hound-headed Devourer was the most terrifying of the Underworld gods, eater of a million souls, render and ravager of human flesh. If he had plans to oust Isis and Horus, and take over as the sole god behind the throne, we were all in big trouble. My sisters' growing worship of him was one of the reasons why I had chosen to flee to the temple at Saïs four years ago. I did wonder why High Sister Merit looked so sour about the Pharos temple, though.

'How will I know who she is?' I said. 'I mean, how will I know for sure that she's a sister? And what guarantee do I have that the so-called Pharaohs won't arrest me as soon as they realise who I am? They think I'm dead. It's not much good if I'm thrown to Am-Heh's crocodiles the moment I get there, is it?'

High Sister Merit sighed impatiently.

'You will know, because we are all marked by our goddess – here, like this.' She pulled open her robe to reveal a glowing white scar in the shape of the Knot of Isis on the outer slope of her left breast. 'We have the living Knot of Isis set in our flesh. You are the only one of us who is marked with the throne on her shoulder. As for the rest, when you arrive, I have ordered my own most reliable contacts at the royal court and in Alexandria itself to spread the story that you have been chosen by the goddess Herself to give counsel and comfort to their royal majesties the joint Pharaohs of Egypt. In that way, you will be seen as a part of the official court, and will be able to move around as you wish. I am sending two of our best eunuchs with you to take care of everyday details in your personal chambers and you will have an honour guard of warriors of Isis around you in public places to keep you safe, as well as a food taster to prevent poisoning. They have all been informed of your identity, though not of the details of your true purpose. Your sisters will surely not dare to harm an emissary of the goddess.'

I looked at her incredulously as she handed me an official scroll with at least seven seals stuck to it. If she thought that, then she didn't know my sisters one bit. They'd always done exactly what they wanted. A piece of paper on its own wouldn't stop them killing me if they felt like it.

'You will present this when you arrive at the palace. It is your formal accreditation in the name of Isis Herself. Suitable royal dress has been provided for you. You leave today,' she said in a voice that brooked no arguments.

'B-b-but what about finding the map?' I cursed the slight shake in my voice. 'You haven't given me much to go on. Where will I start? How do I find the archives of the brotherhood? How do I even get into them? What if I'm caught?'

High Sister Merit frowned at me for about the fiftieth

time. She had the uncanny ability to make me feel less like the newly chosen and marked of Isis and more like a stupid child. It was humiliating, but I'd learnt my lesson. I wouldn't challenge her again – or at least not yet.

'You will have to tread carefully. Members of the brotherhood are dangerous – and their Seth priests guard their secrets carefully, as some of our sisters have found out in the past, at the price of their own lives. But we have had a secret contact planted within the brotherhood for some time,' she said. 'He will make himself known to you and aid you if he can. That is the only help I can give you for now.' Her voice sharpened. 'You have been given the chance to save our goddess and Egypt – so do whatever it takes, Cleopatra, or by Her name I will see to it that the rest of your miserable life will be short and extremely painful.' I heard the pent up fury in her voice as she turned to the window, her hands gripping the sill as if she would strangle it.

'Why?' I asked, my voice sounding strangely quiet after the crash of her rage. 'Why does it matter to you so much?' I needed to know – needed to make sense of her odd intensity.

She turned to me, and I saw the track of one lone tear down that cobweb-scarred cheek. She wiped it away impatiently, clearing her throat.

'I was born in the Pharos temple,' she said. 'I grew up there, among the vileness, hearing the name of my goddess taken in vain but helpless to stop it, learning things no child should have to, seeing sights...' She paused for a long second, lost in the past, running her fingers over the thin scars criss-crossing her face, as if remembering old pain. 'When I was summoned to the sisterhood, when Isis gifted me with vision, she...she showed me that Sera, the betrayer, had come from that vile place too. You cannot imagine my deep shame that my temple had spawned such a monster – I felt tainted by her, and I vowed to Isis that I would set things right if only She would give me the chance. But now She has chosen and marked you. A mere girl, favoured by my goddess above all others.'

I met her eyes, flinching slightly at the raw anger I saw there. What could I say? I *was* a mere girl. But Isis *had* chosen me, marked me for a reason. Surely she couldn't let me fail in this unimaginable task she'd set me? High Sister Merit's hand shot out, gripping my shoulder, her face swooping so close to mine that I could both feel and smell her slightly acid breath on my cheek.

'I will keep my vow, Cleopatra Chosen. Even though you have been marked by our goddess, I promise you this. You will succeed in finding that map, and bringing it back here, or one of us will die, and it won't be me.' She strode to the door, flinging it open. 'So you see, you really don't have a choice. Now, come – it is nearly time for you to leave.'

I followed at her heels, brain working furiously. Clearly failure was not an option, so I needed a plan. The trouble was, right now I couldn't think of one.

A giant wave of relief crashed over me at the sight of Charm standing safe on the dock under the hot, pitiless gaze of Ra's shining Eye, piles of bundles stacked around her, waiting while two large high-sterned feluccas tied up. Beside her stood several porters, the two eunuchs and the honour guard of six warriors of Isis, their shields bearing the silver Knot of Isis. This was my entourage, and the sight of them was making me very nervous. It wasn't only me that was nervous, either. I could see Charm fidgeting, twisting the end of her belt round and round her finger, tapping one small, sandalled foot. Then she turned and saw me. I could tell that she wanted to run to me, hug me, but I shook my head slightly, warning her. All the questions I knew she was bursting to ask me hung over her like a cloud of buzzing sandflies. But there was no chance for us to talk, with High Sister Merit hovering over me. She reminded me of a hungry vulture eyeing up a drowned carcass as she muttered last minute instructions into my ear. Eventually, though, the porters packed everything on board, and it was time to leave. I stalked up the gangplank with High Sister Merit's last words hissing in my ears.

'Tell nobody about the sisters on pain of your own death, remain silent about your mission, remember what I have told you, and above all honour Isis.'

I wanted to roll my eyes, but I didn't quite dare. I swear Isis had given that woman the power to sniff out any kind of disrespect, I didn't want to ignite her temper again. I understood now why Jamila bowed to her – High Sister Merit was a raging force of nature all by herself and I couldn't wait to be away from her and alone with Charm, if we could ever manage to be properly alone on a boat.

I sat between two bundles under a small canopy, keeping out of the way as the two crewmen scurried about the sharp-nosed prow of the lead felucca, with its painted blue eyes, pulling ropes and following the shouted orders of the steersman. As the white, triangular sails crept up the mast, the desert-dry breeze filled them, and the boat started to move away over the water. I watched as my island home of the last four years fell away behind me, the grey buildings slipping past like washed-out ghosts in the shimmering wet heat. Would I miss it? I thought I would. I'd been safe at Philäe as anonymous Cleo, ordinary girl, subject to the same rules and regulations as everyone else. Now I had to find my Princess Cleopatra persona again, draw my royalty around me like a cloak, deal with my Evil Sow sisters again. The felucca heeled sharply to one side, white foam fizzing and singing past its sides as it wove in and out of the islands. My fingers clamped onto the mud-smelling wood in front of me, gripping it till my nails turned white. There was only one person I needed now High Sister Merit was out of sight. I turned to look for her. Charm was sitting on the other side of the boat, staring over at me, her face full of worry. She was flanked by a matching pair of the warriors of Isis and the two eunuchs.

'Attend me,' I said carelessly, beckoning her to me, knowing she would understand my cold tone even before I told her why. I must try to start as I meant to go on. No one in the palace must know what she meant to me, and I didn't yet know if I could trust my own household. It was best to be wary of everyone for now. If I had to play haughty princess-priestess in public, she would have to play humble slave. Neither of us would like it, but it was the only way I could think of to keep my best friend out of danger.

'Yes, Highness,' she said, lowering her gaze and scooting over to kneel before me. 'I hear and obey.'

But I could see the almost invisible smile hovering at the corner of her mouth as she fussed with things around me, playing the role of slave perfectly, as I'd known she would. Just having her there made me feel more comfortable, and I gave her hand a quick squeeze when nobody was looking. She squeezed right back.

We passed the First Cataract just before dusk, hauled through a narrow passage between the rocks by a gang of waiting slaves, chanting their traditional song of 'Ha! Yalesah!' over and over again as they pulled on the ropes. The Nile was beginning to flood properly now, rising and spilling over its banks, blotting out the reeds, swirling round the rocks with a hungry sound. Did Isis still have the power to control it, or would the waters keep on rising till the whole of Egypt was drowned, I wondered. It was not a comforting thought.

It was nightfall before Charm and I could speak properly without anyone overhearing, and then only in whispers when everyone else was sleeping. The stars above were scattered thickly, like jewels across the night sky. I wondered if I would miss their brightness in the city. We huddled together on a pallet spread over the hard boards, listening to the ever-increasing rush and flow of the Nile beneath us, which almost drowned out the whine of the mosquitoes. I had several big red bites already. I could feel them itching and swelling.

'What's going on, Cleo? What happened to you? Why are we suddenly going back to Alexandria?' The whispered questions poured out of Charm like water from a goatskin bottle. I explained as best I could, hurriedly skating over my ordeal in the realm of Isis, concentrating on telling her what I had to do and why.

'I was so worried,' she said, when I drew breath. 'I didn't know what was going on, and I didn't dare ask anyone. I just sat there, waiting and waiting until your message came, and after that I was so tired I fell asleep. I'm sorry, Cleo, I should have stayed awake. I should have been there for you when you came back. And then that priestess, High Sister Merit, she sent me away and…and…all I wanted was to talk to you – to see you were all right!'

I couldn't bear it. She sounded so miserable and guilty, and none of it was her fault. I hugged her tightly, rocking her, comforting her, as she had so often comforted me in the past.

'I keep telling you,' I whispered. 'I'll never leave you. You've got me for life – at least you have if those Evil Sows don't sacrifice me to wretched Am-Heh's crocodiles as soon as we get to Alexandria.'

I felt her hiccup on a tiny Charm giggle.

'Poor me,' she whispered, hugging me back. 'Stuck with my crocodile food best friend. What a terrible fate.'

Later that night I dreamed of Khai again, but this time it was different. This time I really saw him properly – not just his eyes. It was only a flash, but I knew it was him, even though he'd definitely grown up in a *very* good way since our last encounter. Those deep, dark eyes were unmistakeable, of course – except this time they seemed older, and there was the pain of a hunted animal in them. He was leaning against a Pharaoh's empty throne, looking directly at me, and he said just five words.

Trust me, however it looks.

At least, that's all I remember. Of course, I couldn't stop thinking about it when I woke up, or for the weeks afterwards – because I had exactly the same dream every single night. There wasn't much else to do on that wretched boat other than think, unless I wanted to list dead trees, gaunt faces and every other sign of Isis's receding power I saw along the banks – and there were enough of those to fill a whole shelf of scrolls. Grown-up Khai had seemed so serious, so unlike the previous dream Khai whose eyes and voice had caressed me with words like 'beautiful' and...well, lots of other stuff that still made me blush to remember.

Why had things changed? I'd always half thought he was a figment of my imagination before this – but now I wasn't so sure. Were the dreams I'd been having for so long real? Was Isis sending me a message here? Could it be that the boy I'd secretly fantasised over for so long was somehow connected to my goddess? I hugged the small hope to myself all the way down the river. It was better than worrying about sisters and crocodiles.

With sails, the journey took less time than it had going upriver all those years ago, but both Charm and I still thought we'd be on those wretched boats forever. The Nile was in full flood now, bringing the rich, black silt which should make the crops grow tall and plentiful when and if the waters receded. We sped downstream on the back of its rushing torrents, a fair wind from the south in our sails, past groves of gnarled mulberry trees, past the tall tufts of endless papyrus-filled swamps, past armies of rustling date palms with their heavy burdens of unripe green and orange fruits. I counted off places as we passed them – Thebes the Great, Abydos of the Tombs, Memphis of the White Walls, Heliopolis, city of Atum – just for something to do, but in between times Charm and I mostly stared out at the ever-spreading waters and flooded fields. Amongst the healthy living things were myriad stark reminders of looming death and disaster – and the smell of rot hung heavy in the air as whole bloated and stinking herds of plague-dead cows and goats floated past us. I turned away from them in the end, my eyes filled with frustrated, angry tears, trying to come up with a workable plan for when we arrived – and for finding that cursed map as soon as possible afterwards. I kept an eye out for river-horses, but the ones I saw kept well away. Somehow I couldn't seem to summon up my old fear of them any more. Perhaps it had died with the ghostly white ones I'd escaped from in the realm of Isis.

When I wasn't staring or thinking, I took the trouble to get to know each member of my new household during those long weeks we spent on the journey – moving from boat to boat whenever we stopped, trying to gauge whether they were trustworthy, finding out their names, where they came from, whether they had families, small nuggets of information about what food they liked, what their hopes and dreams were. I'd learnt from my bruising first experiences with the other girls at Philäe – this time I wanted to make sure I started out my new life with allies, not enemies, so I smiled charmingly and listened carefully to what they told me, keeping a polite princess distance, but forging the first chains of loyalty between us. At least, I hoped so. They were my household now, and I'd need them to be on my side.

The eunuchs, Dennu and Dhouti, were both middle-aged men with shaved heads and deep crinkles round their eyes which spoke of humour. They were less plump and a lot fitter than most – at least they looked as if they could move quickly enough if they needed to. I liked them at once. The six warriors of Isis were all younger, except for their tall captain, a black-haired, dark-faced suspicious-eyed man called Nail. His name meant 'winner', so I hoped that was a good omen. They all seemed devoted to my goddess, and their obvious familiarity with the weapons they carried definitely made me feel safer. The warrior I liked best from the start was Sergeant Basa, who was as large as a plough ox, with bulging muscles to match. Unlike Captain Nail, he laughed a lot. It was a hearty, comforting sound, with a jovial wheeze at the end, and the other men were relaxed and comfortable around him.

My taster, Am, on the other hand, was a vacant-looking, lanky boy who slept a lot and ate first from every pot – when he wasn't pestering everyone in sight to throw Senet sticks with him. I didn't blame him a bit for the sleeping. It wasn't a job which encouraged much intelligent thinking time. Am was the only one I wasn't entirely sure about – so I made sure he never travelled on the same boat as Charm and me until I realised that he was exactly what he seemed: gormless.

I knew the moment we left the Nile and entered the still waters of Lake Mareotis. I could see the faint dawn flicker of the Pharos far off, warning me that we were near our destination. As we crept our way slowly into the canals and along to the Harbour of the River, I saw the tip of its familiar rounded light tower start to loom above the city and my heart began to beat faster. The beautiful marble buildings along the south wall of the city, the enormous painted statues, the endless temples – each one revealed itself to me in the pale mauve-pink light of the rising Eye of Ra as we passed. The almost-forgotten scents of Alexandria wafted into my nostrils – the musky smoke from ten thousand cooking fires, the smell of charred meat, baking bread and spices, rotten vegetables, malodorous dung and night soil, overripe fruits, and overlaying it all, the pungent reek of black delta mud and salt from the Great Green Sea. I shut my eyes for a moment, breathing in the smell of my childhood. But I was not that scared child now. I was both princess and priestess of Isis, with a sacred duty to perform for my goddess. I straightened my back.

'I won't let you down, dear Isis,' I whispered into the soft breeze. 'I promise.' A breath of air touched my cheek. It smelt of the desert and wild places. Overhead I heard a kite's high, screaming call. My goddess was listening and that made me both glad and hopeful. I turned to Charm.

'It feels good to be home,' I said quietly. 'I didn't think it would.'

'Ha! You're just looking forward to being able to order everyone around, O Mighty Princess!' she said, bowing extravagantly. She'd started doing that to make me laugh, but we'd decided it was good practice for her public role as humble and unimportant servant. 'That's if you don't get served up to the crocs first.'

'Thanks for reminding me,' I said. 'Now, O Magnificent Body Slave, I need to speak to my brave warrior captain and his cohorts. Summon them for me, will you?' I waved a hand in the direction of Captain Nail, Dennu, Dhouti and warriors Haka and Sah, who were all on duty. Charm's mouth fell open for a moment. Then she grinned behind her hand, not letting anyone see.

'They're only on the other side of the deck, O Excellent Wondrousness. You could summon them yourself,' she whispered.

I looked at her down my large nose, putting on my best princess face.

'But why would I, when I have you to do it for me, O Tremendous Folder of Robes?'

Sticking just the tip of her tongue out at me, she went to fetch them.

I sat enthroned on a rug-covered sack as the five men shuffled over to me on their knees. The steersman bit off a curse as the felucca rocked wildly with the movement in the narrow channel. Charm settled herself at my feet, and five pairs of eyes looked up at me, waiting. I looked back, steadily. I'd already decided what I was going to say.

'This won't be easy. You already know there are many enemies ahead who will wish us all harm, but me in particular.' I took a deep breath, hoping that I really could rely on their discretion. 'That includes both the Pharaohs, who currently think I am dead. Trust nobody in Alexandria unless Charm or I tell you to. I haven't been here for many years, so I don't know how things stand in the palace, but you should be aware that our goddess may not be everybody's first choice right now. That's what I'm here to try and change. Eat nothing unless Am has tasted it first. Inspect all gifts for poison, take no bribes, and look out for each other and me. Report anything even a little suspicious to Charm or Captain Nail.'

I looked them each in the eye before continuing my orders. None dropped their gaze from mine.

'Dennu, you will summon a proper litter for me and Charm as soon as we land, and hire porters for the luggage. Dhouti, you will find out when the next Pharaohs' audience is taking place. We will go straight up to the palace and announce ourselves. Remember, I am merely the emissary of Isis for now. Nobody is to know my real name yet – and none my purpose. Captain Nail, you and all your men will flank me as soon as I descend from the litter, Charm, you will be immediately behind me. Whatever happens today, remember we are under the protection of Isis herself, blessed be Her name.'

'Blessed be Her name,' they all chorused after me, hands thumping against silver-Knotted shields. As our two boats navigated their way through the crowded waterway, I truly hoped my goddess was still listening. We'd need all the help we could get.

The Harbour of the River was busy even at this early hour. Dennu leapt off the felucca to do my bidding, as soon as the crewmen had tied up in the first free berth, and before long both parts of our little group were reunited and gathered at the edge of the dock, bags and bundles all around us. Captain Nail and burly Sergeant

Basa gave swift orders to the warriors, and Charm and I were quickly hemmed in by large male bodies, protecting us from being bumped and battered by the crush of stevedores loading and unloading cargo. Baskets of silvery fish and small waterfowl were abundant, along with the usual endless supply of young papyrus stems and roots in tottering piles. There seemed to be no shortage of food here, anyway, though I noticed that some of the vegetables were blackened at the edges and somewhat musty-smelling. Only the best was shipped to Alexandria, though. I stood there, breathing it all in, until Charm elbowed me discreetly in the ribs.

'Oh, dear Ra,' she whispered, pointing. 'Look at that!'

Dennu was back, with several strong-looking porters, who lifted our bags and bundles onto their heads as if they weighed no more than a feather. He'd also brought the litter, carried by four bearers of ill-assorted heights, so that it dipped down and up like a drunken sailor as it moved along.

'I'm sorry, Chosen,' he said. 'It was the only one available. Would you prefer I found you another?'

I shook my head.

'No, I'd rather get there. Just tell them not to go too fast, please.'

The bearers laid the thing down on the ground, and

Charm and I ducked in under the low roof, arranging ourselves on the thin blue cushions. It smelt rather of its last occupant, clearly someone who thought that an overabundant scattering of ambergris and patchouli would mask the pungent scent of body odour. I grimaced.

'This is going to be fun,' I said, clinging onto to one of the wooden corner pillars as the bearers settled the carrying struts onto their unevenly matched shoulders.

The litter rocked sickeningly from side to side as we passed through the south wall of the city, so that Charm and I had to clutch at its painted edges to keep from falling. There were many people in the wide, paved streets at this hour of day, rushing about among the huge statues of sphinxes, falcons and gods, chattering and shouting to each other in a mixture of languages. I'd forgotten how many different races lived here – pale Gauls with blue tattoos, hurrying Jews with long beards and prayer shawls, traders from Tyre and Carthage, dark-skinned Ethiopians from the south, women with dangling copper earrings and jars on their heads, others with heads wrapped in brightly-coloured cloth. All the world was here, and I felt momentarily proud that I could talk to many of them in their own tongues – if I'd wanted to, that was. At that moment, I didn't. I was concentrating too hard on not being sick.

I wished I'd never asked Dennu to summon the wretched litter now. I nudged Charm.

'How bad will it look for my priestess dignity if I get out and walk?'

'Very bad,' she said. 'Even worse if you throw up all over yourself, though.' She looked a little green herself, but she had her thinking face on.

'What?' I asked. She shook her head.

'Nothing, really. But . . . well . . . what will we do if the palace guards won't let us in, Cleo?'

'Of course they'll let us in,' I said, more confidently than I felt. 'I'm the emissary of Isis herself. They can't stop us.'

She rolled her eyes.

'I knew having that title would make you too big for your sandals,' she said. 'Now shut up, O Queen of Confidence, or I might be the one throwing up all over you.'

I was wrong. The guards tried quite hard to prevent our entry, crossing their silver-tipped spears with an aggressive thump when we first appeared. The sound of raised voices shortly afterwards made the litter bearers turn tail, tipping and rocking us even worse as they frantically shuffled around in their desire to get away from any trouble.

'Quick, Charm, stop them,' I hissed at her behind my hand. 'It'll look bad if I do it.'

She looked at me, raising one dark eyebrow. I could see she was shaking slightly, but she jumped out anyway.

'Yes, O Most Excellent Emissary,' she said as she went. The litter lurched to one side, then the other, and I was nearly thrown out. Charm set her hands on her hips and stalked forward, glowering.

'Sons of dogs. Cowardly curs. How dare you treat the emissary of Holy Isis like this? Are you not ashamed? Do you actually want the goddess to curse you with a plague of suppurating boils on your sorry behinds?'

Slowly, painfully the litter turned around again, as she continued to abuse them mercilessly.

Captain Nail was doing some shouting of his own. His deep, gravelly voice floated back to me, demanding our entry to the palace. I stared straight ahead, trying to look aloof, as my position demanded, slowly clenching and unclenching my hidden fists. It was not my place to lower myself in outsiders' eyes by interfering. I had to let the captain and Charm do their jobs, but it was very hard.

My captain eventually forced the guards to back down, and permission to pass was given. Nail and his burly warriors had won this first verbal battle of the day. I was sure there would be more before it ended. As we made our way through the gates, I gave the guards one disdainful glance. Each was wearing the amulet of Am-Heh round his neck, but the silver was tarnished and their white uniform was grubby and unkempt. It was a dispiriting outward sign of the demon god's filthy power.

One of the lower chamberlains was summoned, and we soon found ourselves housed in a small pavilion in the grounds of the palace, complete with a sunken bath. It was an unimaginable luxury after so long making do with a quick wash in the river. As Charm was giving orders for hot water and food to be brought, Dhouti approached, bowing low.

'The next Pharaohs' audience is at the third hour before sunset, Your Highness. You are expected.'

I interrupted before he could go on.

'Did you tell anyone my name?'

He bowed again.

'No, Highness. I followed your instructions to the letter.'

'Thank you, Dhouti. You may go. Rest. Have something to eat, after Am has tasted it. It's been a long journey.' I smiled and dismissed him.

The bath was bliss. I made Charm share it with me. We both stank of weeks of boat damp overlaid with added odour of litter. Then, when we'd dried off, she unpacked our bundles as I napped a little. The boy Am arrived with the food, and tasted a morsel of each dish. Thankfully, he didn't keel over, so Charm and I ate hungrily, stuffing ourselves with the familiar Alexandrian dishes we hadn't eaten for so long. We cooed over spicy fried liver and curled, crunchy pieces of squid sprinkled with sea-salt and fine ground pepper from the Indies. We licked every morsel of honey syrup from our fingers after we guzzled the flaky almond pastries, and fell on the hot raisin cakes as if we were starving beggars. All of it was delicious after weeks of garlicky beans, sour beer and stale barley bread.

We had to wash again before she dressed me in the ceremonial court robe of a priestess of Isis, draping its white linen folds around me, and helping me to tie the traditional Knot of Isis at the front. Last of all she put up my hair and secured it with amber-headed pins underneath a sheer veil.

'Do you want to wear these, Cleo?' she said, holding out my mother's heavy gold necklace and armband. They were all I'd been able to save of her jewellery when we fled, and they were very distinctive, set with a royal cobra's head, decorated with lapis lazuli. I remembered the day my father had given them to her in front of the whole court, playing her a beautiful tune on his old flute.

The thought of them both together, as they never would be again, gave me a small, hard lump in my throat.

'Yes,' I said. 'Why not?' If this wasn't the perfect occasion to show them off, then what was? It had been too dangerous to wear them at Philäe – a simple acolyte like me would never have possessed jewellery bearing royal insignia. The gold felt cold against my skin at first, but as they warmed, I imagined my mother's touch from beyond the tomb, giving me strength and courage.

I needed it as I walked slowly through the hot, bright light of afternoon, past the pale marble colonnades and statues of gods, past groves of trees and beds of scented flowers in the palace grounds, flanked by my six warriors. In my right hand I carried the sealed scroll, my left was folded tight around a clammy palm. I made myself loosen my stiff fingers.

You've survived glowing scorpions and ghostly river-horses and a whole pit of snakes, I thought fiercely. *Your goddess is on your side. You can deal with two Pharaohs and a court full of sandal-licking flatterers.* I moved through the painted passages and into the first ivory-panelled hall with a strong but strange sense of familiarity. Was I really back here again? The magnificently carved ebony doors of the throne room were thrown wide open, and I stepped through into the opulent stink of the crowded room, my guards pushing past chattering purple-cloaked officials and advisers, ambassadors and their retinues, solemn scholars, leopard-skin decked priests and others of the court just there to show off their hair or clothes. Then I stopped dead. My two sisters sat raised above me on ornate golden thrones, the jewelled white diadems of royalty bound round their brows, but I only had eyes for one person. The young man in the red robes of an embalmer who was lounging at Tryphena's feet, her ringed hand casually stroking and stroking his long black hair as if he were one of Bastet's holy cats.

Long, black hair so straight and shiny it could have been cut from rare heavy silk.

Deep brown eyes dark as Delta mud.

They were eyes I knew as well as my own.

They were eyes which had been haunting my dreams for the last four years.

I felt as if an invisible hand had punched me in the guts.

7

The Boy from the Brotherhood

All the air whooshed out of my lungs. I couldn't breathe. It was him.

Khai.

All my happy dreams shattered into sad little fragments around me.

It was Khai, and Tryphena had him in her Evil Sow clutches.

Not only that, but the red robes told me he belonged to my goddess's worst enemy, Seth.

I opened my mouth to scream my impotent rage, but nothing came out. All at once I felt powerless and small and betrayed – feelings that were all too familiar to me in this place, this palace, this pit where everything

I loved was always destroyed.

I heard my sisters cry out in shock, saw them point long, gold-painted nails at me, nails like Harpies' talons.

'Who is this impostor?' yelled Tryphena, her voice as spoilt and pouty as ever.

'Why is she wearing the sign of our own royal cobra? Arrest her!'

As two Nubian guards moved towards me at a run, I came back to myself, jerking out of my stupor. Hard warrior bodies shoved themselves forward to hem me in, making a tight protective ring around me, spear tips bristling outwards, silver-embossed shields making a wall in front and behind. I thrust my feelings of hurt, and, yes, jealousy, away, stuffed them into a locked box. Instead I put on my princess mask, turning my face to still, cool marble.

'Halt!' I said, my voice high and clear and commanding, just like High Sister Merit's. 'Touch me at your peril.'

The guards stopped for an instant, looking confused.

'Listen to your Pharaoh, not her,' Berenice screamed at them. 'Arrest that girl immediately. She's lying. Rip that jewellery off her and bring it to me. I recognise it. It belonged to our late sister's mother – she must have stolen it.'

The Nubians started forward again.

A Nile cataract of anger rushed through my whole body, and I felt the mark on my shoulder burn under my robes as if my rage had lit it. How dare they? Could they not see that I was surrounded by the warriors of Isis? Did they really dare to disrespect my goddess so publicly? Merit and Jamila were right – Am-Heh's forbidden power had indeed grown strong here if they did. I closed my eyes for a second, calling on my goddess silently.

Please dear Isis, show them. Give them a sign. Make them believe in you. Make them believe in me.

A breath of air caressed my cheek. Once again, it smelt of desert herbs and sunlight. It gave me the courage I needed.

'I am the Princess Cleopatra, chosen emissary of Isis,' I shouted above the clash of spears around me. 'Sent by the goddess herself to advise and bring comfort to their Magnificent Radiances the Pharaohs!'

And then, quite suddenly, there was an awed silence, broken only by the sound of a hundred indrawn breaths. All eyes were fixed to something above my head, and every face showed a kind of glazed awe. I glanced quickly upwards, to where a red glow suffused the air. Clearly Isis had done something extraordinary and unusual – but I couldn't see what it was, and there was no time to look. Seizing the moment, I pushed the crossed spears in front of me aside, and stalked forward, towards the double thrones, forcing my face to be blank and emotionless.

'But you can't be Cleopatra,' Tryphena whispered, paling underneath her bejewelled makeup. 'You're dead. They told us you were dead of a fever.'

'I think you will find that I'm quite as alive as you are,' I said to her, my voice a vicious whisper. Much as it pained me, I dropped to my knees before them both, and held out my scroll of office, the dangling seals clinking delicately. 'My credentials, Your Magnificences, signed by every high priestess of Isis in the land,' I said, loud enough for everyone to hear.

As I spoke, Khai stiffened and sat up straight, frowning as if he was puzzled by something. My sister's hand fell from his hair, shaking slightly as she accepted the scroll from me, and he tossed his head as if to rid himself of the feel of her. Kneeling, I was right at eye level with him, and once again I could see the oil sheen of the thick kohl lines around his lashes. I stared at him furiously, trying not to think of all the nights I'd spent lost in dreams of him, trying not to remember the way his dream hands had felt, his dream mouth on mine.

His lips were still slightly chapped, and they still quirked and dimpled at one corner. His smooth skin was still the colour of burnt honey. I still wanted to reach out and touch him. He caught my eyes for a moment, and mouthed six silent words. Only I could see them.

Remember, trust me, however it looks.

Then he turned away deliberately, and snuggled into Tryphena's throne again, gazing up at her adoringly. Berenice was leaning over. She pushed him impatiently out of her way, as if he was just an annoying piece of furniture.

'What does it say?' she asked.

'See for yourself,' said Tryphena, handing it to her. The shock and fear on her face smoothed away, leaving a mask as expressionless as my own. Then she cleared her throat and waved a hand at me, plastering a smile onto her over-painted face. I didn't trust it any higher than the first block in a pyramid.

'Arise, emissary of Isis. We welcome you to our court, both as the chosen of the blessed goddess, who has honoured us with her presence today, and as our long-lost sister.' She clapped her hands together in front of my face, making me twitch back. 'Let there be feasting tonight! Let the best rooms be prepared. Let the court rejoice that Princess Cleopatra is returned to us! Now leave us – this audience is over.'

There was a brief scatter of applause as I rose gracefully to my feet. I had done it! I was in! But I had no time to wonder. Tryphena had risen too, and all the court dropped to the floor and bowed their heads down before her. She leaned forward, pulling me up towards her, and tucked her arm in mine.

'Come, Cleopatra. We have much to catch up on.'

'Yes,' said Berenice, tucking her hand into my other arm. 'We certainly do.' She poked Khai with one gold-sandalled toe, and dropped my scroll in front of him. 'Here, library boy – file this somewhere.'

'Yes, Magnificent Majesty,' he mumbled into the floor.

All of a sudden I felt like biting them both, but I didn't let it show for an instant. Instead I turned to Tryphena as we strolled towards her royal apartments, followed by our silent guards, who eyed each other with belligerent wariness, and by a meeker gaggle of slaves and attendants.

'Who's he?' I asked casually.

It was Berenice who answered.

'Oh, him – that's Tryphena's latest boy toy. Pretty, isn't he? He's supposed to work for the Brotherhood of Embalmers in that old library you used to spend so much time in, but Tryphena can't seem to do without his hair under her fingers. Can you, dear?'

'He entertains me, that's all,' said Tryphena. 'Shame you sacrificed your own pretty boy to Blessed Am-Heh's crocodiles last week, sweetie – you'd have one to stroke too if the god hadn't found him so tasty.'

So it was true, then. They were sacrificing to Am-Heh openly. It was the worst sign yet that the true throne gods had been ousted.

I could hear the undercurrent of spite in both their voices. Nothing had changed there. They might both play by the blank-faced court rules of political skill now, but they were exactly the same Evil Sows underneath. In a way it was comfortingly familiar. I'd learned a lot about political skill while I'd been at Philäe. I could probably deal with my sisters on their own. What bothered me more than their sniping was the aura of darkness which hung about them both – especially Berenice – trailing behind like a smoky plume of dusk. I thought I could see something within it – the evil glint of a hound's eye, the curve of a crocodile's claw, the grey rounded rear of a river-horse. I shivered suddenly. Was this Am-Heh in person? Was I seeing the Devourer himself? The hairs on my spine rose and prickled, I would have to tread extra carefully until I could work out how things stood.

The sitting room of Tryphena's royal apartments was entirely changed from my father's day. Gone were all the joyful scenes of musicians and dancers, gone were the finely embroidered hangings depicting stories of Isis and

Horus, Zeus and Hera. Instead, the walls were decorated with a red so dark it looked like old blood. Painted on them in gold were things I didn't want to look at too closely – rent limbs, screaming faces, and among them always, in his lake of fire, the horror of Am-Heh's hound-headed, crocodile-legged, river-horse-bodied form, jaws agape and dripping with ripped apart entrails. Amongst a scatter of large cushions, two heavily jewelled couches stood in a corner of the room, their scaly golden legs and reptilian feet continuing a theme that was becoming distressingly familiar.

As Tryphena and Berenice let go of my arms and arranged themselves on the couches, slaves and eunuchs running to bring cool drinks and fans, I stood there, not entirely sure what to do next. I knew the outwardly friendly behaviour was put on. But what did it mean? What did they want of me?

'Sit, dear sister,' said Tryphena. 'And why don't you dismiss your handsome warriors? I'm sure they must be hungry and thirsty after their efforts to defend you. Let's be cosy, just like old times.'

I nearly laughed. Old times? Cosy? Who was she trying to fool? I wasn't the scared little sister any more, and it was best they learned that now, Pharaohs or not.

I turned to see Captain Nail twitch an eyebrow

downwards. I didn't need the tiny signal.

'I'm sure they'll survive,' I said drily. 'My warriors of Isis will be just fine staying right where they are.'

Tryphena and I stared into each other's eyes for a brief second, then she looked away. First round to me, then.

'As you wish,' she said, pretending that she didn't care. 'Now, do tell us, dear Cleopatra. How did you survive that dreadful fever which killed so many?'

'Oh, yes, do tell,' said Berenice. 'Because, you know, Tryph and I would have searched until we found you if we'd had even a hint. We so longed for you to be in the palace with us.' Both their smiles and their words were as false as a cobra in a kite's nest, and they knew I knew precisely what they truly meant.

Inwardly, I sent a small curse High Sister Merit's way for making me into a spy. I was going to have to pretend now as if my life depended on it – which in a way it did. This was the bit I'd dreaded having to explain. Charm and I had worked and worked on my cover story on the boat, though, and now I prayed to Isis that my sisters would believe me.

Of course, I told them nothing of my unhappiness, nothing of my loneliness, nothing of the Sisters of the Living Knot. Instead I painted a picture of a feverish child who had been saved by her goddess, then an ambitious girl clawing her way up the ranks of priestesses, stopping at nothing to get what she wanted, supported by Isis all the way until she became her chosen emissary, with the full power of the goddess behind her. I emphasised that last bit quite a lot.

'I told Isis there was nothing I wanted more than to come back here,' I said, my own smile as sickly as theirs. 'To be in my rightful place, with my family again.' I let a small tear trickle down one cheek.

'How sweet,' said Tryphena. 'I'd quite forgotten how sentimental you can be about your relations. We must make sure to spend lots of time together.' A slave bent to whisper in her ear. 'Now, I do believe your apartments are ready. Someone will be sent to summon you to the feast.'

I got up as gracefully as I could, and bowed, before walking to the door. My warriors fell in around me, and we followed the slave to where Charm and the eunuchs were waiting for us.

There was no doubt about it. My new apartments at the royal end of the women's quarters were magnificent. Captain Nail directed his men to stand guard, and began to inspect the highly-decorated outer rooms, presumably for hidden openings between the blue enamel and sapphire panels. I was glad he was being thorough. It made me feel a little safer.

As I entered the bedchamber, Dennu and Dhouti were directing palace servants to loop fine linen curtains around the bed, which was set on a dais reached by three low steps. It was gaudy and gilded, with clawed lion's feet, and a tall headboard made in the shape of carved ivory wings with the feathers picked out in mother of pearl and moonstones. Beside it stood two tables inlaid with lapis lazuli and more sapphires. It was a far cry from my simple room at Philäe. Charm had her back to me, sorting the clothes from what looked like hastily packed bundles. She turned as soon as she heard my footsteps.

'Bow before Her Highness the Princess Cleopatra, chosen of Isis,' she commanded everyone, dropping to her knees. The palace servants and the two eunuchs did likewise. It felt strange hearing my proper title on Charm's lips, and even stranger having people make obeisance to me – especially her. I wasn't used to either of those things any more. Suddenly I wanted them out of there – all except Charm, of course. I beckoned her to my side.

'Go!' I said to the others. 'I wish to rest before the feast. Dennu, make sure my taster is behind my chair.' I wasn't taking any chances. I knew my sisters would poison me at the least opportunity. It was in our shared blood. There were legions of ruthless murderers and despots on the Ptolemy side of our ancestry.

As soon as they left, I flung myself down on the soft coverlet, and patted the space beside me. Charm darted to the doorway, where Captain Nail stood planted as firmly as a palm tree in rock, closing the heavy door firmly on his muscled back.

'Tell me,' she whispered, coming back to the bed. 'What happened? We got a message to come here, so I know you weren't arrested.'

'I nearly was. It was Mama's jewellery. They recognised it, but they didn't recognise me. Well…they thought I was dead. So they set their Nubians on me again, but the warriors defended me, and then Isis did something – I don't know what – which made everyone go all silent.' I paused, the shock of Khai's appearance hitting me again. Charm knew all about my dreams of Khai – well, maybe not *all*. There are some things a girl has to keep private. But she was the only one who would understand what seeing him there meant to me. I couldn't hold it in any longer.

'Oh, Charm! Tryphena has her talons in Khai. He was just like he is in my dreams – all gorgeous – but he was sitting right there at her feet with her skinny fingers pawing at him. And he's dressed like one of the filthy embalmers. I don't understand. He kept telling me to trust him in that dream, and he did again tonight – but how can I believe in him now? How can I trust him not to betray me when he's with her? How can I trust him when he belongs to Seth the Deceiver? Maybe I've got it all wrong. Maybe…' I leapt off the bed and began to pace.

'Think about it, Cleo,' said Charm. 'Why would Isis send you dreams of him if he wasn't Hers? Why let you spend all those years doing…' She gave me a sly grin 'Doing whatever it is you do together in the dream world that makes you go all starry-eyed and pink in the mornings?'

I blushed.

'I have thought about it,' I said, trying to ignore the rising tide of heat in my face. 'You know I have. Over and over and over. Oh, if only I could talk to him. Then I'd know if it was real or not. But it looks like he spends all his spare time with my bitch sister stroking his hair and treating him like some fluffy pet dog.' I ground my teeth, hating Tryphena all over again. How dare she?

'I'll do some investigating, Cleo. I can find out where he goes when he's not with her, where he sleeps, where he eats. Maybe if I can get a message to him, he can sneak in to see you. I could bring him in through the slave passages or something, so no one would know.'

The thought of actually being alone with Khai made my heart thump a little faster. But then so did my worries about Charm's safety. It was the best plan, though, and I knew it.

'Do it,' I said. 'But be careful, O Sovereign of Sneakers. Don't get caught. I couldn't bear it if you got caught.'

She laughed.

'I'm a slave, O Mighty Princess. You said it yourself. No one notices slaves.'

'I do,' I said fiercely. 'You know I do. So you take care, you hear? There's something strange going on in this palace, something creepy – and I don't want either of us on the wrong side of it.'

Just then, there was a knock at the door. Charm opened it a crack, taking something from whoever was on the other side with a few murmured words. When she turned, her arms were full of sparkle and glitter, and shimmering material, and her eyes full of mischief.

'Apparently these have been sent to you by their Royal Magnificences, the Pharaohs of all Egypt,' she said, keeping her face carefully blank. 'To wear at the feast tonight.'

I was bedecked in gold and sapphires from neck to wrist,

made up with kohl and ochre, with my eyes picked out in lapis. My hair was braided and primped into a high coronet, and I was wearing the magnificent shimmering gown my sisters had sent me, belted with a twisted golden rope. Captain Nail had checked everything for hidden poisons, for scorpions, for pins, for any kind of danger, but there was nothing. Charm knelt and tied my sandals.

'Make sure you eat nothing that Am hasn't tasted first,' she said. 'I trust those scheming sisters of yours about as far as I could fling a camel. They're being far too nice.'

I knew she was right, but a tiny part of me, the innocent part which had once admired my sisters and wished to be like them, wanted their niceness to be real.

'I promise I won't,' I said as she opened the door to the outer rooms. 'I'll nibble like a mouse in a granary and eat properly when I come back here.' As I stepped forward Captain Nail gave a small cough. I turned towards him, raising one eyebrow. The small blue jewels above them itched slightly where the glue was beginning to irritate my skin, and I squeezed my fingers together, keeping them at my sides. He bowed low.

'Permission to leave Corporal Geta on guard inside your bedchamber, Chosen?' he asked.

I nodded. If Charm had to leave, she could make an

excuse about needing to do laundry or something, and it was best to be sure no assassin slipped inside while I was away. I sighed, making a swift decision. The warriors would have to know about the passages if they were going to guard us properly. I couldn't take the chance of someone else using them like I had.

'Charm, you'd better show Captain Nail and the rest how the, er, back entrances work,' I said.

Her eyes widened slightly, just as the captain took a step forward, his thin black eyebrows lowering for an instant.

'Back entrance? What back entrance?' He advanced on Charm menacingly, hand out as if to slap. 'Why didn't you tell me about this immediately, girl?'

I reached forward and took his arm in a hard grip. The muscles felt like they were made of sun-warm marble. They didn't give even a tiny bit under my small fingers.

'No one speaks like that to Charm,' I said, knowing I was taking a risk in showing I cared, but unable to let it go. I put on my haughtiest princess voice. 'She is mine. You will treat her with respect.'

Captain Nail snapped to attention.

'Yes, Chosen,' he said, more mildly. 'But, please, I must know about all entrances to these rooms, in order to guard you properly.'

I nodded. It was only what I'd been thinking myself after all.

'Very well,' I said. 'Do what you must. But hurry. I can't be late for the feast.'

We were summoned by a royal slave a few minutes later, and soon we were walking down the airless corridors towards the banqueting hall. Captain Nail and four of the warriors surrounded me again, with Dennu and Dhouti at my back, carrying tall ostrich feather fans. Female eyes peeped through door cracks, and whispers followed me like the hissing of wind over desert sand, but I kept my head high, looking neither to left nor to right. Charm would find out what they were saying about me soon enough. My mask was back on. I was Princess Cleopatra now, the emissary of Isis, the chosen and marked. The question was, could I keep it up?

By the third course of the feast, I wasn't at all sure I could keep the mask in place. Am was looking faintly green around the lips, not from poison (at least, I didn't think so) but because he'd had to taste so much food. I was seated between my sisters at the top table, looking down at the royal court, bathed in the light of ten thousand candles. There were dancing girls, and acrobats and a strange dark-skinned man painted with flames, who swallowed fire and spat it out again. I had been offered golden dish after golden dish. There was creamy camel's yoghurt with cumin seeds and little strips of hot, savoury bread to dip into it; there were pomegranate seeds mixed with oranges and nuts, all manner of roasted and stuffed birds, wet, silvery oysters and red-orange lobsters, colourful vegetable concoctions, towers of sweet puddings, wines and juices in jewel-encrusted tumblers and pitchers. It was excess such as I hadn't seen since I was a child. The high-ceilinged room was bright with swathes of heavy cloth in scarlet and the twice-dipped deep blues of Tyre, feathered with delicate golden embroidery. A myriad woven flowers carpeted the floors, hiding the beautiful mosaics, clashing with the cloying scents of sweet balsam and cinnamon which came from pretty golden sprinklers which the servants waved constantly around the diners, tainting the taste of the food.

I waved away a dish of Nile perch, studded with silver-dipped almonds. It probably smelt delicious, but my nose was so assaulted by perfumes that I couldn't tell any more. Despite my promise to Charm, I'd eaten more than I'd intended. It was hard not to when my sisters were pressing delicate morsels from their own plates on me, taking great care to let me see their own tasters trying them first. In between looking down their noses at the court, they chattered like jackdaws at me, trying to find out just how much influence I had with Isis, and why she had sent me. I glanced at Tryphena, toying nervously with a gilded nutshell, crushing the pieces between her fingers. How could she and Berenice have deserted the traditional gods of the Pharaohs? How could they have raised foul Am-Heh above my own beautiful goddess, above Father Ra, above Horus the Falcon-Headed? How had the gods let it happen? Why? Had they all deserted the throne they'd supported for so long? Even if Isis was weakened, the other gods were not. Or were they? There were so many things I didn't understand here, so many things that felt wrong. I suppressed a shudder. What had Isis sent me into?

There was a discreet flurry of movement behind me, and I felt a small brush of human warmth as someone knelt between me and Tryphena. Out of the corner of my eye I saw her hand drop the nutshell, reach backwards, stroke the dark-haired head by her side.

'Ah, there you are, my Khai,' she said in a low, sultry purr. 'Where have you been?'

'I was attending to my duties in the library, most Magnificent Majesty,' he said. 'The chief librarian sends his apologies for detaining me. Nothing else could have kept me from your side.'

His deep voice, so close to me, made my bones vibrate like the plucked strings of a quanun. I clenched my fists, pressed my arms close to my body, my spine stiff and upright, trying not to let even a fold of my dress touch his red robes, trying my hardest to ignore the fact that he was there, trying to pretend to myself I didn't mind. Damn him, anyway. Did he need to talk to her like that, as if he truly adored her? If I were really to trust him, he'd have to have a very good reason for acting as if he was actually pleased to be my sister's pet lapdog. Otherwise he could go and jump off the Pharos for all I cared. Then he shifted slightly, and I bit my lip on a small gasp as what felt like a thin sliver of papyrus was pushed down into the small, soft hollow in the centre of my clenched palm. The brief touch of his fingers was smooth and warm. My heart jerked with a sudden fear. What if someone had seen? I reached up to my neckline, as if adjusting my dress, and slid the small slip into the top of my breastband. The words 'my Khai' still seethed in my brain like hot wax. Was he really Tryphena's? Or had he just done something which marked him as mine – or at least as a traitor to the throne and to his deceitful god? I couldn't wait to find out.

8

Secrets of
the Library

I had to, though. The feast stretched out interminably, and my princess mask was in serious danger of slipping by the end, as my mind whirled and raced and speculated about what Khai had just given me. But it ended at last, and as quickly as I could bow to my sisters, I was on my way back to my rooms, the note practically burning a hole in my breast. I fairly shooed Captain Nail out of my rooms after he'd relieved Corporal Geta at the entry to the slave passages and replaced him with Warrior Rubi, who had feet like boats and a nose twice as big as mine. I beckoned Charm onto the bed as soon as he was out of sight, and delved into my dress. Her eyes went round as I put a warning finger to my lips, fished the small slip out and smoothed it flat.

'What is it?' she whispered.

I peered at the tiny writing, squinting in the lamplight. *Meet me in the library at dawn*, it said. *Where we first met. Come alone.* There was no signature. There didn't need to be. I knew who it was from.

'Is it him?' Charm mouthed at me, as I handed her the note. I nodded as I filled her in, speaking into her ear in a low murmur. I couldn't risk Warrior Rubi overhearing, even though I was pretty sure he was loyal to me. The fewer people who knew about Khai, the better.

'I nearly died when he gave me the note,' I said, shivering all over again as I realised the risk he'd taken.

'What if it's a trap, though, Cleo?' she asked, being Captain Cautious as always. 'Are you sure you can trust him? What if he wants to get you alone so he can kill you or something? And what does he mean by "where we first met"?'

My mind was rattling through all the options like beads on a market-trader's abacus, adding, subtracting, discarding.

'I have to know one way or the other, Charm,' I said when she'd gone silent. 'There's a chance he's the spy Merit told me about. The one who can get me into the embalmers' secret archives. I'll take the knife with me.'

Charm had given it to me after the incident with Shu, the priest-acolyte back in Philäe.

'You'd better remember to use it like I taught you,' she said. 'Up under the breastbone and thrust. Like this.' She smacked her fist hard into her abdomen to illustrate, looking fierce. 'Make sure you don't hit a rib by mistake.'

A lump formed in my throat at the thought of stabbing Khai. I so wanted to trust him, to believe he was on my side, but it was hard. Charm was right – I must be prepared to do it if I had to. I did know where he wanted me to meet him, though. I'd known as soon as I'd read the words. An image of a child standing on tiptoe, reaching for a scroll in the quieter, more deserted part of the Great Library had flashed into my head at once. An arm had appeared over the child's left shoulder, a well-muscled arm with honey-brown skin, which had snagged the scroll out of its shelf box and handed it to her with a bow and a kind word. It was the kind of thing the lonely little princess I was then had never forgotten. It appeared that Khai hadn't either, and that gave me hope.

'I'll have to go through the slave passages, and in disguise,' I said. 'How am I going to get past Warrior Rubi, though? He won't let me go alone.'

'You could tell him you're on the goddess's business

and swear him to secrecy,' Charm said, but I shook my head.

'That won't do. He's bound to run off and tell Captain Nail anyway. Soldier's honour and all that.'

She had her thinking face on again.

'Well, what about when the guard changes? I heard them talking earlier. The replacement warrior will come through this room at the middle hour of the night, about an hour before dawn to check that all is well, and then swap. Maybe we could make the bed look like you're in it, sneak you into the closet to hide, and then when the other warrior comes, I could make a big production of telling them not to wake you, and while they're distracted, you could slip out?'

I pulled her close and hugged her. 'It might just work. Did I ever mention that you are the Queen of Schemes?' She giggled, even though she still looked worried.

'You'll have to be the Sovereign of Sneaking to pull it off, Cleo. Now come and help me stuff the bed with pillows, and find something that could pass as your hair. It has to look like it's really you in there.'

It was already late, but there were a couple of hours to kill before I had to leave. Charm and I made up the bed together so it seemed as if I was snuggled tight under the coverlet, and then she coached me over and over about which turnings I should take in the slave passages. I changed into a shapeless brown slave robe which covered my curves, and scrubbed off all my make-up till my face felt shiny and tight. My hair was horribly frizzy from being confined in its tight braids and I probably looked like the back end of a camel, but there was no help for it. No one would recognise the emissary of Isis dressed like this. I wasn't even sure Khai would. A vain little voice in my head jeered at me, whispering words like 'ugly' and 'unattractive', but I squashed it down.

'He'll just have to put up with me as I am,' I said aloud, making Charm jump.

'Are you talking to yourself again?' she asked, looking at me warily. 'Or is Isis here?'

I shook my head.

'I wish she was. It might make me less nervous.' But I knew my goddess couldn't always be with me. She had other more important business to tend to, and I knew she trusted me to look after myself. I tucked the slim knife down the back of my breastband, so I could easily reach behind and draw it if I needed to. Then I slipped into the closet while Charm took Warrior Rubi a beaker of water. It was hot and close behind the clothes, and I dozed a little, to be woken by the faint sound of Charm's voice, scolding in a whisper. I shook my head to clear it of sleep. Was it time? I heard the rasp of sandals on the rough, glazed tiles. Was that the retreating Rubi? I had to risk that it was.

I stole out from my hiding place and tiptoed towards the entry to the slave passages. It was deserted, and I slid down the uneven steps into the earthy darkness just as a shadow blocked out the dim lamplight from inside my rooms. Holding my breath, expecting a warrior's shout at any moment, I tiptoed forward, setting each foot down as stealthily as a thief in a silent souk. Ten steps, twenty steps, thirty steps, fifty…it was only when I reached 500 that I relaxed a little and started to walk normally. Charm's instructions were good, and eventually I found myself just outside one of the lesser entrances to the Great Library. My heart began to hammer on my ribs, and my breath came short and fast in my throat as a scatter of confused thoughts raced through my head.

Would he be there alone? Or was he waiting with a squad of assassins, ready to strike me down? What would it be like to really talk to him? What would he expect of me? What did I expect of him? I gave myself a mental shake. If I didn't go in, I'd never find out. So I pushed the door open.

The smell of the Great Library surrounded me like a

familiar blanket – the reedy scent of papyrus and pens, dust, the sharp, acrid smell of ground ink. The palace didn't feel like home – it never had. This place did. It was where I'd escaped to when my mother was busy with my father. It was where I'd filled and fed my ever-hungry brain. It was where my only friends other than Charm lived – the scholars, the scrolls, the knowledge I craved like a tribesman in the desert thirsts after water. I stroked the wooden edges of each scroll rack with my fingertips as I passed down the narrow passageways, all deserted at this early hour. It helped to calm me, though it didn't stop the dryness in my mouth and throat.

I remembered each turn I needed to take as if I'd been here only yesterday. Left at the pigeon-holes leather-tagged with E for Epidauros, right at H for Hephaestus, on and on with the stacked scrolls towering above me to the ceiling, which was painted a rich blue and covered in constellations. Ahead of me I could see a pillar with a picture of Seshat the Scribe, patron goddess of this place, and I bowed my head to her busily scribbling image as I passed. Nearly there, then. I slowed down as I got closer, imagining my ears big as a fennec fox's, alert to every sound and movement ahead of me, then stopped. The silence was so thick I could almost touch it. And then I heard it; the tiniest noise, as if a sandal had scuffed the floor. My whole body flooded with prickles of ice, mixed with a hot excitement I couldn't suppress. There was someone ahead of me. Was it him? My hand went over my shoulder for long seconds, fingering the hilt of the knife. I knew Charm would want me to have it in my hand in case of treachery, but I just couldn't bring myself to draw it. I let my hand fall, squared my shoulders, and walked around the last corner.

Khai was standing there, staring straight at me, his hands loose at his sides. They fisted slightly as I approached him, but that was the only sign of nervousness he betrayed. Did he feel confused inside like me? Was his heart thumping as hard as mine? I couldn't tell. He dropped to one knee.

'Your Royal Highness,' he said.

Suddenly I was exasperated. Was it really going to be like this – all formal, as if we were in that throne room again, watched by a hundred pairs of eyes? He wasn't acting like he had in my dreams at all. There he treated me like a real person, not some distant royal princess. I glared at him, this young man I knew and yet didn't know at all. I wanted answers and I wanted them right now. I'd waited long enough. If my goddess wouldn't answer my questions, then by Her blood, he would, whether he belonged to Seth or not.

'Don't call me that,' I said, too cross to be careful. 'Get up and tell me what's going on, Khai. Tell me why you've been in my dreams all this time. Tell me why I should trust you. Tell me why I'm here.'

He got to his feet in one graceful movement, then scrubbed his hands through his hair, his fingers momentarily cupping his head as if to hold his thoughts together.

'What should I call you, then?' he asked, avoiding my questions. I hesitated for a second, then shrugged.

'Call me Cleopatra for now. It is my name, after all.' I wasn't going to ask him to call me Cleo like he had in my dreams – not until he proved himself my friend in the real world. He glanced away for a second, and I saw a tide of dusky red creep up from the neck of his robe to cover his cheeks.

'So, then, Cleopatra,' he said, turning back to me. My name sounded stiff and difficult in his mouth. 'You want to talk about the dreams?'

I couldn't help it. I felt the same rush of red cover my own face. Oh no, why had I even mentioned them?

He raised an eyebrow.

'That's really the most important thing to you right now?'

'No…well…yes – I mean, I want to know…' I stopped,

flustered. Why was he doing this to me? Was he just here to laugh at me? Would he go back to Tryphena and snigger with her at my stupidity? Was Seth the Deceiver behind his every word? He half-reached out towards me, then drew his hand back as I stepped away.

'I'm sorry,' he said. 'This is all very hard for me. I don't really know where to start.' He rumpled his hair again. 'I'm not used to all this. First the Pharaoh…and now you – a Ptolemy princess. I was born on the streets of Alexandria, not in a palace. I don't even know who my father was, and my mother was a temple whore who died giving birth to me. I was a street rat until I was six.' He stared at me, meeting my eyes properly for the first time, staring into them as if they were a mystery he had yet to unlock.

'Here's the truth, then: I've been having dreams about you all my life – though I didn't know who you were at first, not until I met you here in the library all those years ago. After your mother died – after you crashed into me that day…' He hesitated, drawing a breath. 'After that, the dreams came more often. I only remember fragments of most of them. Sometimes quite big fragments, but never the whole dream.' He was blushing so hard now that I could almost feel the heat rising from him. 'I really liked the bits I do remember, though.'

I nodded once, willing my face to cool down, though I felt strangely affronted and just a tiny bit disappointed. He didn't remember all of it? And which 'fragments' had he liked? The sweaty, stomach-melting ones, or just the ones where we'd stared into each other's eyes dopily? Was my dream-lover self not hot enough for his brain to retain or something? I wasn't going to ask, though I desperately wanted to know.

'That still doesn't tell me why I should trust you now, though,' I said instead, in what I hoped was a dignified voice.

'She told me you'd ask me that,' he said. 'And that I was to show you this.'

'Who told you…' I started, but he had pulled aside the shoulder of his robe, and was busy scrubbing hard at something on the right side of his chest with an ink-spattered rag he'd pulled from his belt. I stared as a familiar-shaped scar appeared in front of my eyes, lighter against the slide of his smooth brown skin over hard muscle. I had last seen that sign on High Sister Merit, just before I left Philäe. It was unmistakably a living Knot of Isis. That was not something a follower of Seth would ever have on his body voluntarily.

I tried not to let my mouth gape open like a hooked Nile perch. How could he be a sister of the Living Knot?

He was the wrong sex, for a start, and it was on the right side, not the left. Had my goddess really marked him? Or was it a fake?

'How did you get that?' I asked.

'I…' He bit his lip. 'You have to understand, Cleopatra,' he burst out, plucking at the red cloth as if it burned him. 'This isn't the real me. I've belonged to Isis since the priestesses took me into Her temple and off the streets. I owe everything to Her – and I'll do anything for Her, even pretend that I belong to Seth and the filthy embalmers. You do know I'm Her spy, right?'

I nodded slowly, my suspicions confirmed, as he went on.

'I sat up in the middle of the night about two moons ago, thinking I'd heard Isis calling me. But she wasn't – there was just this thing on my chest, glowing like a beacon in the dark,' he said. 'It…it was just after the Pharaoh started pestering me. I thought it was a sign that Isis was protecting me from her attentions at first, but then the sister came for me. She's been my contact for years, the one I give information to about stuff that happens with the brotherhood. She got me into the library when I was little, saw to it that I had scribing lessons, taught me to be a spy. Anyway, she told me I had to do it – be your sister's…' He broke off, with a disgusted

174

grimace. 'It makes me feel sick, being with the Pharaoh, having her fingers on me, listening to all that filthy Am-Heh talk and…and having to remain silent when she has her vile priests take people to be sacrificed. I try to save those I can, but it's worse than faking Seth-love for the foul embalmers. They may worship our goddess's worst enemy – but she worships the Devourer.'

He took a step towards me, his eyes intense. 'When I saw you in that throne room, Cleopatra, with our goddess's sign glowing like red fire above your head, I felt as if I was in the presence of Isis herself. I wanted to kneel down before your beauty, so clean and fine and pure. Do you know how hard it was to have to sit there with the Pharaoh's fingers in my hair, having to pretend that she was my everything?'

'I-I…' My voice wouldn't work properly. He thought I was beautiful? Really? Well, I thought the same about him, but I didn't know how to say so. I felt suddenly shy, not at all the brave Cleo who'd faced scorpions and river-horses in the realm of my goddess – our goddess, as it turned out. Surely Isis wouldn't have marked him if he were not to be trusted?

'Why do you cover your mark with dye?' I asked instead, my voice shaky but under control. He shrugged.

'It's safer,' he said. 'I can't risk anyone in the

brotherhood seeing it. Or your sisters – though that's…'
He hesitated. 'Er…getting more difficult where Tryphena's
concerned.' He gave a tiny shudder, and I tried hard
not to imagine what he might mean by that remark.

'I'm a spy twice over, you see,' Khai went on. 'I have
been for most of my life, and I've learned to be careful
the hard way. It's a path I didn't choose for myself, but
it's what Isis needs me to do so I do it willingly.'

'Me too,' I said. 'Me too.' We stared at each other in
silence, and I thought perhaps he wanted to hear my
story as much as I wanted to hear more of his.

Just then I heard a door bang, and footsteps in the
distance. Khai's head went up like a hunted gazelle's, and
then his eyes narrowed and hardened. He looked
suddenly dangerous – like the spy he was.

'We can't be found together,' he whispered. 'Can you
get back to your rooms without being seen?'

I nodded.

'But when will I see you again? There's so much more
I need to know.' I cursed myself inwardly. I hadn't even
mentioned the map yet – Isis would be so angry with me!

The footsteps were coming closer.

'No time now – go!' he ordered me. 'I'll find a way to
get word to you somehow!'

My heart gave an unexpected little wrench at

the thought of parting from him. I put a hand out, preventing him from leaving. The muscles on his forearm were tense and quivering under my fingers, impatient to be gone.

'Find Charm. She's supposed to be my body slave, but she's actually my best friend. You can trust her with anything,' I said quickly. Then I let him go and fled towards the door I'd come in by. I didn't look back once, though I wanted to very badly. He was right – we mustn't be found together, or it would mean disaster for both of us.

Charm and I had worked out how I would get out, but not how I would get back in. I pulled a fold of the rough brown robe up over my head. There would be others in the slave passages by now, early though it was, and I couldn't risk being recognised. I walked briskly through the dimness, turning my head to the side whenever I passed someone. Luckily they were very few, and they all seemed sleepy and preoccupied with their own business. I didn't stop to spy anywhere – I wasn't a child any more, and I risked more than just a beating if I was caught. As I approached my own rooms, I threw off the covering, and drew myself up as tall as possible, putting on my princess persona again. I nearly made it, but as I swept through the crumbling doorway, a body stepped in front of me, his spear haft slamming down an inch from my toes.

'Halt!' said Warrior Sah, the youngest of my guards in his squeaky-gruff voice.

I looked up at him silently in the feeble lamplight, and saw his eyes go a little frantic when he realised who I was.

'Let me pass,' I said quietly, fixing him with my best princess glare. 'And say nothing of this to Captain Nail, as you value your life, and at the peril of Isis's wrath. I have been about the goddess's business, blessed be Her name.' Well, it was worth a try.

'Blessed be Her name!' he managed to choke out, before standing aside. I hadn't much hope of him not confessing – Nail's men were almost as loyal to him as they were to our goddess, and I wasn't sure exactly where I stood in relation to either. Probably a poor third. I yawned hugely as I went into the bedchamber, suddenly exhausted. Charm was snoozing on a large cushion beside the bed, but she opened her eyes as soon as she heard my footsteps, and jumped up.

'How was it?' she asked quietly. 'Was he there? Are you all right?' I nodded, almost too tired to speak. 'Don't worry, Cleo – you can tell me all about it when you wake up,' she said, helping me out of the fusty brown robe. I kicked the sandals off and climbed the steps into the ridiculously ornate bed, sliding between the cool sheets just as I was. They smelled of lavender and attar of roses and I was asleep almost immediately. If Isis sent me disturbing dreams of Khai's slow kisses, I didn't remember them.

9

Night of Fears

I awoke to a missive from Tryphena. She addressed me as 'dear sister' and commanded me to attend her that afternoon for a session with the royal dressmaker.

'Oh, joyfulness,' I said to Charm, reading it out to her. 'Remember her? Old Nena? Breath like a stagnant pond, and the needle skills of a goddess. She makes you look great, but by the time she's pinned and pinched you into shape, you wish she'd worn a mask – or you had!'

Charm laughed.

'I'll brush your hair through with a drop of cinnamon oil. That should help drown her out. And you do need new dresses – that scary High Sister Merit woman sent some with us, but you'll need more if you're going to palace parties, and you'll be going to a lot after what happened in the throne room last night, because they'll all want you on their side now, Isis-chosen.' She looked at me seriously. 'I've done some sneaking about this morning. You've caused quite a stir among the palace busybodies, you know.'

'Tell me what they're saying, O Gifted Gossiper,' I said. Khai had mentioned something about a fiery red sign last night, but I had been a bit distracted then. Now I really wanted to know what Isis had done in detail.

'Well,' she said, peeling back my sheets and offering me a robe, 'I've heard it was anything from a huge hissing cobra to a vulture as big as a pyramid. But Captain Nail and the warriors say that a red Knot of Isis came out of nowhere and glowed above your head for a moment. They're all prouder than a gang of peacocks about it, you know. They say you showed a lot of courage.'

I felt a tiny warm spark. My goddess had been there for me when it really mattered, and my guards thought I was courageous. I hadn't felt brave at the time, though. I'd just been angry about Khai, and about the disrespect shown to Isis. Khai! I remembered him all in a rush. When was I going to see him again? We'd left so much unsaid, and I still had so many questions to ask him. I needed to find out how to get to that map – and soon.

'Were there any other messages?' I asked, putting my

arms in the sleeves she held out and keeping my voice casual. I could never fool Charm, though. Especially not when I was blushing.

'What kind of messages?' she asked, smirking slightly. I reached for the bolster from my head-rest and threw it at her as she ducked and giggled, dodging away from me. 'No, nothing yet. And you still haven't told me what happened with your dream lover, O Princess of Passion – did he kiss you for real this time?' She fluttered her eyelashes and made lip-smacking sounds. I blushed some more. I seemed to be doing that a lot lately.

'No, he did not!' I said. 'We…we talked, that's all.' I told her everything – each word Khai and I had spoken to each other was indelibly carved into my brain. 'And then someone came, and we had to leave. I told him to seek you out, to find a way for us to meet again.' I sighed. 'I think I can trust him, Charm, but why did that wretched sister tell him to become Tryphena's boy toy spy? That's what I can't work out.' A worm of jealousy wriggled in my belly as I remembered his awkwardness. 'Is he actually her lover? Why did he agree? What's the point of it, when he's supposed to be helping me find that Seth-damned map?'

Charm shook her head.

'I don't know, Cleo. I'll try to find out about him.

There's always someone in the palace who loves to gossip about the Pharaohs.'

'Well...' I started. 'Be...'

'I know,' she said. 'Be careful. I always am, Cleo. More careful than you, I expect.' She eyed the knife that lay poking out from under my sheet. I wasn't the one who'd put it there.

'You should have that with you at all times,' she said.

Just then, there was a slight commotion in the outer chamber, and then a knock on the door.

'Enter,' I said, drawing the robe tightly about me, and pulling the sheet forward a little to hide the weapon.

Captain Nail came in, towing a small, thin boy child from the lands beyond the Upper Nile whose frightened eyes half-filled his face. He carried a fan made of ostrich feathers, and as soon as he saw me, he darted out of the captain's grip, slipped behind me and started to wave it assiduously, moving the stale, warm air around the room.

Captain Nail started towards him, but I held up a hand, looking at him warily. Had Warrior Sah sneaked on me yet?

'Where did he come from?' I asked instead, though I thought I knew already.

'He is a gift from Her Magnificence the Pharaoh,

Berenice,' he said stiffly. 'To add to your consequence, Chosen.'

I held down a groan. Berenice had sent me a present. Even more joyfulness. The boy was sure to be one of her spies, even at his young age. I wondered whether she had threatened to sacrifice him to Am-Heh's crocodiles if he didn't do his job. It seemed likely. I would have to get rid of him now in a way that didn't seem suspicious, and then feed him enough information to keep him alive. He was too young to be anything but an innocent tool. I tried not to grind my teeth. It seemed I was going to have to think like a spy myself, whether I wanted to or not.

'What is your name, boy?' I asked, turning round and making my voice kind. He immediately prostrated himself at my feet, the fan making a clatter on the marble. I heard the small snap of two feathers breaking and winced. Berenice would have had him beaten for it. I would not.

'M-Mamo, Your High Graciousness,' he said, his voice as small and thin as himself, with a strong Amharic accent.

'Well, Mamo, I don't need you right now. Go with Dennu to the kitchens and tell them I said to feed you. You can't do your job properly if you're hungry, can you?'

He stared at me uncomprehendingly, and I realised that he didn't speak much of the Greek I had fallen into so naturally once I had returned to the palace. I switched to Amharic, gesturing towards the eunuch, who was standing in the doorway.

'Go thou with this man of much fat, boy child. He will feed thee.'

The head went up, and the huge eyes went round as pomegranates.

'Thou speakest my language, Great Lady?'

I nodded.

'Thy language, and many more. Now go, and then return to attend me. Later we must walk with the Great High One to find the servant of needles and cloth.'

Mamo scrambled up, then prostrated himself again, then grabbed his now limp and broken fan and fled toward Dennu.

Captain Nail bowed and left behind them. No scolding – maybe I was safe, then.

'What next?' I said to Charm when the door was safely closed again. 'A dozen maidens to scrub my back in the bath? A slave to clip my toenails? My own pet crocodile? What do those Evil Sows want of me? You were right – they're being suspiciously nice.'

'Don't you get it yet, Cleo?' Charm asked. 'You have

the open favour of the goddess they've rejected – the one who truly represents the throne. That means you could have power. Even though they have Am-Heh on their side, they must be scared silly about why you're here – and what you plan to do. Of course they're going to be nice to you – till they can find a safe way of getting rid of you.'

She was right again, of course. I should have worked it out myself. I still hadn't accepted that power and me could ever be thought of together. I had become far too used to being just Cleo the acolyte – a nobody who influenced nothing.

'Did I ever tell you how wise you are, O Most Champion of Counsellors?' I asked her.

'Not often enough,' she said, opening the door to the small but luxurious bath chamber. 'Now climb into the tub and let me do the work of twelve scrubbing maidens. You still smell a bit of those musty old slave passages.' She pulled a disgusted sniffing face, holding her nose, and I laughed. Charm could always make me laugh. That was one of the many reasons I loved her.

A few hours later, Captain Nail and the warriors escorted me to the large, light room where the royal dressmaker worked. Little Mamo crept behind me, jerking his fan back and forth as if he was possessed. It didn't do much good – the day was very hot – but I appreciated his trying. Dennu had obviously found him some new feathers for it. He had been waiting in my outer chamber, belly round and tight with food underneath his skimpy robe, and as I entered, he looked at me with adoring eyes. Perhaps no one had ever been kind to him before. I thought it was likely if he'd been around Berenice for very long. Charm had dressed me in the robes of a priestess again, with a golden Knot of Isis at my shoulder.

'Best to remind the Pharaoh Tryphena of who you are, Chosen,' she said, and Captain Nail had nodded his agreement. I certainly thought it couldn't do any harm.

As I walked through the double doors, I stared. Bolts of slithery silks from the Indies were flung everywhere, and Tryphena was poking and prodding at them, rubbing them between her fingers to feel the quality of the material. It looked as if someone had thrown a hundred dye pots around the room, a spatter of blues and oranges and golds and pinks and greens lay all mixed together on the floor, with the plain white walls reflecting their brightness. A long table stood against one side of the room, with a row of girls behind it, eyes down, each sewing frantically at a different costume. Old Nena was bustling around behind Tryphena, jewelled trims over one wizened arm, and a long, knotted string measure in the other.

A person I presumed was a cloth merchant from his dress lay in the traditional position of obeisance in one corner, guarded by two of the Nubians. He was trembling harder than a palm leaf in a simoom. The other person in the room was Khai. Our eyes met for the barest flicker of a moment, and then I forced myself to look away. I bit the inside of my cheek, but the small pain didn't drown out the sudden frustration that filled me. How were we ever going to have time to even talk about the Seth-cursed map if he was always having to play the attentive boy toy? And why did he have to? I wished I understood. I wished there was someone to ask. Where was this wretched sister of the Living Knot he'd talked about? I'd give her a piece of my mind when I finally met her.

'Ah, there you are, dear sister,' said Tryphena, turning towards me, as Khai dodged nimbly out of her way. 'This wretched merchant has failed to bring me the purple silk I asked for, and there's nothing else good enough. I was going to give him over to Am-Heh's mercy, but perhaps, if you find something you like amongst these worthless rags, I may spare him.'

I forced myself to bow low to her – hating her casual

cruelty. Every ream of cloth looked beautiful, as far as I could see. She was playing games with me, as usual, flaunting her power. That was clearly what this summons was all about – not a sisterly session of girly chat and dresses, but another way to show me who was really in charge here.

'You're too kind, Magnificence,' I said. 'I'm sure I shall find quite a few things here. Perhaps the cloth isn't fine enough to adorn your shining beauty, but I think it'll do very well for me.'

She looked at me suspiciously, sensing the sarcasm underneath my humble tone, then shrugged.

'Maybe the pink, then, or the orange?' she suggested.

Both of those would make me look like a fat flamingo with indigestion, and she knew it. Did I dare contradict her? I didn't have to. Before I could open my mouth, old Nena was scuttling forward, picking up a bolt of sea green and one of a vivid deep blue.

'Perhaps these instead, Your Radiance? Blues and greens have always suited the Ptolemy colouring.'

I saw Tryphena's face freeze for a second, and I tensed. Would she deny that I was a true Ptolemy again? I stood straighter, my fingers playing with the symbol at my shoulder, daring her to forget who I was now, what I represented. I almost saw her brain jolt as she looked at my robes and made the connection.

'Oh, very well,' she said. 'Do as you wish. I have better things to do than discuss colours. Take whatever cloth you want as a gift, chosen of Isis. And get this idiot out of here before I change my mind.' She gestured to the merchant, who let out a small submissive moan, and then she swept out followed by Khai and her swarm of Nubian guards and retainers. I looked quickly for the cloud of blackness I had seen last night, but there was nothing.

I felt a touch on my arm.

'Welcome back, princess,' said old Nena. 'Now come, let me make you look beautiful.' Her breath was as foul as ever, but not as foul as my sister's heart.

I smiled at her. Although I hated the rather sweaty pinning and standing still, I hadn't had new dresses for a long time, and a part of me was happy just to stand there and think of nothing but trims and embroidery and listen to Nena chatter on and on about what was in fashion at the court that month.

The happy mood lasted just as long as it took to get back to my rooms and find a strange woman there, dressed, like I was, as a priestess of Isis. She bowed to me.

'Chosen of Isis,' she said. 'A word in private.'

I tried not to show my confusion, swiftly putting on

my impassive princess mask. What should I do here? High Sister Merit had told me not to trust anyone except the sister who came from the Temple of the Pharos. Was this woman she? Was she the sister Khai had talked about? Isis curse Merit for not telling me her name. I couldn't very well ask her to remove her robe in public and show me her mark.

'Who are you?' I asked, stalling for time.

She cleared her throat and stared at me meaningfully.

'I am Cabar. I believe you will find my message of some merit,' she added, with considerable emphasis on the last word. I caught myself before my face moved. That couldn't be a coincidence, could it?

'Very well,' I said. 'Follow me.' Captain Nail stepped forward, but I held up my hand. 'I believe you heard the priestess. We will speak in private.' I saw his hand grip his spear till his knuckles went white.

'I will be outside the door, should you need me, Chosen,' he said, tightening his lips.

I knew he meant well, but those tight lips were beginning to annoy me. Did he think I couldn't look after myself?

Charm was nowhere to be seen, and I had the first momentary flicker of worry about her as I sat down on a couch. Where was she? But then Cabar was pulling at her robe, unveiling the glowing white scar on the slope of her left breast.

'See, you can trust me, sister,' she said, then her eyes went hungrily to my shoulder. 'Will you show me the blessing of our goddess?'

I sighed. Was I going to have to undress every time I met a sister of the Living Knot? That could get old quite quickly. Nevertheless, she had a right to see that I was who I claimed to be, so I pulled my own robe aside to show her my mark. She knelt abruptly.

'It's true, then. You really are the marked and chosen we've been waiting for.'

'I am,' I said, trying not to hate her for what she'd made Khai do. She was supposed to be my ally, after all. 'And now you need to tell me what's going on. Do you know why I'm here?' I patted the couch beside me. 'Sit down, and keep your voice low – there are always ears in this palace.'

'Yes,' she said. 'I do. Trust no one but me. Rumours are already flying around all the temples about you, and there's talk in the marketplaces too.'

'About what happened last night?'

'Yes. Our goddess, blessed be Her name, has never shown her sign openly like that in the palace before. It puts you in great danger, and not just from those here. There has been an urgent message from our sisters at Saïs. Isis has honoured their seer with a vision. It concerns you.'

'Tell me,' I commanded her, even though I wasn't sure I wanted to know. Visions didn't usually contain sweet cakes and ribbons as far as I was concerned – more like snake pits and stabbings.

'The seer saw you twice. Once was before the Dark Feast of Serapis. You held a glowing scroll in your hands, and the Knot of Isis shone above your head. The second vision was after the Dark Feast of Serapis had ended. You stood in darkness with your hands empty, looking at a scroll dripping with blood. There were two bodies at your feet, one a young man with long, dark hair, and the other a girl with short, black curls.' She stopped abruptly, as a small gasp escaped me.

My heart gave a great thump, and then seemed to stop as a creeping finger of cold slid into my belly.

'You know who they are, then.' Cabar asked softly. It wasn't a question.

I nodded.

'I know,' I said. 'And I won't let it happen. I will die myself before I let them be harmed.' I looked at her directly. 'How much time have I got before the Dark Feast of Serapis?'

'A little while. A few days, anyway. And the festival itself goes on for two days, till sunrise of the third day.'

I raised my hands to scrub them through my hair, but instead encountered heavy coils and braids. I felt a small relief as I ripped the pins out of my thick, tawny mass and let it flop onto my shoulders. The cold finger in my belly sharpened to a dagger as I realised Charm still hadn't returned from wherever she'd been. She was never away from me this long. I got up and went to the door, opening it a crack and peering through. The warrior outside came to attention immediately, and Dhouti scuttled over.

'How may I serve you, Chosen?'

'Is Charm back yet?'

'Not yet, Your Highness.'

'Then you and Dennu go and find her. Don't come back till you have, you understand?' My voice must have been sharper than I'd intended, because he prostrated himself on the floor.

'Yes, Chosen,' he mumbled. I shut the door with a sharp click.

'Your body slave?' Cabar asked. 'You care about her then? Is she the one in the vision?'

I met her gaze again. There was no point in lying. If I couldn't trust a sister, then I couldn't trust anyone. Isis had tested us all and not found us wanting.

'Yes,' I said shortly. 'And the other one is Khai, Tryphena's…well…you know.' I looked at her meaningfully. What I really meant was lover – but I couldn't bring myself to say the word out loud. If I didn't say it, it might not be true. I so desperately didn't want it to be.

'I want to know why he has to be there, with her. It's very inconvenient. I need him to help me,' I said bluntly. I thought 'inconvenient' covered it nicely. It was better than saying, 'I hate you for giving the boy I want to be my Evil Sow Sister's boy toy,' which was what I really felt.

Cabar had the grace to drop her eyes when I glared at her.

'He wasn't meant to be with her, originally,' she said. 'Originally, I placed him as our spy in the brotherhood. He was a temple orphan, you see, with no ties and nobody to ask questions about him. It was easy to get him trained up and then steer him in the right direction.' She paused, tapping one finger against the silk of the couch.

'You see, Chosen, we always knew we'd need someone to get into their secret archives and retrieve the map. We just didn't know when. Now that you are finally here, you know how urgent that is – you see how Am-Heh's power has grown. You know what's at stake for our goddess and for all Egypt. The situation with the Pharaoh may be inconvenient for you, but I have learned a great deal about the Pharaoh's dark dealings since Khai was with her. I hadn't planned it, but when Tryphena saw him with one of the brothers two moons or so ago...well... he took her fancy, and I took advantage of that. It wasn't meant to go quite so far as it has, but I have spirited many poor souls out of Alexandria and away to safety from the information he has given me. The rest – well, some of them – have been given the choice of an easier death than they might have had otherwise.' She looked at me directly. 'My speciality is in making undetectable poisons, you see.'

I filed that fact away for future reference. It might be useful.

Quite so far as it has... Cabar's words pricked my brain like thorns. It was pretty clear to me now that Khai had been in Tryphena's bed. 'Lover' had been the right term, then.

'Couldn't he just have said no to her?' I asked, even though I'd heard Khai's explanation already. I wanted to be really sure that being my sister's bed companion was one of the paths he hadn't chosen for himself.

'One in his position couldn't disobey any Pharaoh's command, and especially not this pair. And I encouraged him to think Isis wanted him to say yes after I saw her Living Knot on him.' She looked stern – nearly as stern as Merit. 'Foul Am-Heh, cursed be his shadow, has devoured more blood since your sisters seized power than he has in a thousand seasons. I will stop him and them in any small way I can, using any tool I have. Our goddess must and will be restored to her place behind the twin thrones.'

'How have Isis and Horus allowed Am-Heh to get so strong?' I whispered. 'How? Why?' I couldn't answer for Horus, but I knew about Isis, of course. Her power was draining away daily. And only I could fix that.

'The sky god is a mystery to me, and I do not presume to question our goddess,' Cabar said softly. 'But perhaps you may, Chosen.'

I would – when I had a chance. But for now, my focus had to be on finding a way to get Khai away from Tryphena. I had to talk to him about sneaking into the brotherhood's lair and stealing that Seth-blasted map, and I needed Charm to help me think of a way. Where *was* she? My distress at her continuing absence now stung me like tiny ant bites, making me restless and itchy. Why wasn't she back? Had Dennu and Dhouti found her yet? As I asked Cabar question after question – about what exactly Khai had been doing in the brotherhood for all those years, among other things – my mind was racing.

What if Tryphena and Berenice had taken my best friend? What could they hope to gain? My obedience? Certainly not my favour. Terrible scenarios played out in my mind as the hours ticked by, and I began to pace my rooms like a caged jackal. Cabar left, promising to send me messenger doves so that I could contact her easily if I had to, giving me one of the simpler secret priestess ciphers to use. She'd told me so many things, but I couldn't concentrate properly on any of them. All I could feel was Charm's absence, like a big, black hole.

A slave arrived from Nena, bearing three beautiful new court dresses in the silks I had chosen, and then another, with a command from my sisters to attend a full moon picnic on Cat Isle that night to celebrate the time of the Lotus. I paced and paced and paced, back and forth, back and forth, ordering Captain Nail to send out all but two of the warriors to search for Charm but there was no word, no sign, and neither Dennu nor Dhouti had come back with news either.

I knew it was risky to show my feelings so openly in front of Mamo the fan boy – but I couldn't help it. I felt naked without Charm at my back. I desperately wanted to go and look for her myself, but Captain Nail wouldn't let me. I knew he was right, but I didn't have to like it.

As I dressed myself in my new sea-green robes for the stupid moon picnic I couldn't avoid, I had to hold my eyes wide open and tip my head back to stop the hot tears dripping down my face and leaving black smeary kohl on my cheeks. Somehow I rebraided my hair and fumbled it back into its amber pins, settled my mother's precious jewellery round my neck and arm, and pinned the gold Knot of Isis at my shoulder. Then it was time to leave. Captain Nail was not happy. Only Sergeant Basa and Warrior Rubi had returned – and they reported no sign of Charm at all. The sergeant's normally cheery face was worn and worried with tiredness. I knew exactly how he felt.

As my depleted retinue and I processed through the gardens and down to the Royal Harbour, exhaustion and worry made my footsteps slow and heavy, and it took all my energy to force myself to keep my back straight and my head held high. It was a while before I noticed the bowing and the whispers and the flowers, and that was only because Captain Nail nudged me.

'Look, Chosen,' he said softly. 'They are offering our beloved goddess worship.'

It was true. Small knots of people had gathered along the path, servants or citizens, I couldn't tell. All prostrated themselves as I passed, throwing flowers before my feet, fragrant white and blue lotus buds, the prickly green heads of papyrus, bright red poppy petals, which smelled both sharp and bitter as I crushed them under my feet, and the blue sky rosettes of cornflower. The words 'chosen' and 'Isis' fluttered towards me on the air like delicate soul moths. I held myself straighter, nodded to those who would meet my eyes. My goddess still had their respect and love, then. That was good to know. I wondered if they would get into trouble for it, whether even now a spy was hiding somewhere around us, noting names and faces. I thought it very likely.

Please, dear Isis, protect them. Don't let them suffer for loving you, I prayed. *Don't let that foul Am-Heh devour their souls.*

I saw a twitch of movement behind a palm tree, heard a muffled yelp of pain, and then agonised choking sounds. There was the thump of a body hitting the ground, and then a huge white scorpion ran round the trunk and raised its sting in salute to me as the wisp of a man's *ka* form appeared briefly, then was seized by Anubis's hand and drawn into the darkness. It was the same monstrous beastie I'd met in Isis's realm. I knew now that it must be Tefen, captain of her seven scorpion guards. I tipped my head to it, repressing a shudder, but knowing my goddess had heard me and sent her own protector to kill the spy I'd suspected was there. No report would get back to the Evil Sows now, and my faith in Isis welled up in me and overflowed, giving me strength and courage. If she still had that kind of power, surely she wouldn't let Charm be harmed.

Would she?

10

Dark Encounters

As we reached the Royal Harbour, I saw a small barge waiting for me at the jetty. A man stepped forward, bowing low. I recognised him as one of the royal advisers who'd been in Tryphena's retinue. His large stomach wobbled as he walked, and his fat face was wreathed in a smile as false as a pickpocket's purse. He rubbed his greasy hands together and reached for my arm. Just as I was about to flinch away, a hard, warrior body interposed itself between us, a spear butt thumping between his toes. The man backed away hurriedly, his smile falling away, leaving his face momentarily blank with shock, and his mouth open. He closed it swiftly, but not before I had seen him shoot me a glance of intense dislike. I would have to watch out for him – he could prove to be dangerous.

'Nobody touches the chosen of Isis without her permission,' said Captain Nail, offering me his own arm as support to step up onto the small deck. Red embroidered cushions lined a kind of silken throne in the middle of the barge, and I sat down in it thankfully, closing my eyes for a moment. The barge rocked for an instant, as the remaining warriors, skinny Am and little Mamo climbed aboard, and then I felt the cool breeze of Mamo's feathered fan and heard the quiet *shush-shush* of oars as the slaves below began to row us round the curve of the Antirhodos breakwater and out across the Great Harbour. I listened to the soft, rhythmic chant of the rowers and let the gentle motion of the waves soothe me, their swells glittering in the warning flare of light that was the Pharos, its high beacon of flame shining out over the Great Green for all to see.

The barge rounded the tip of Drakon Island, and I stared with dark-blinded eyes towards our destination, seeing the flicker of tiny lanterns, and hearing the faint sound of music. Every splash of the oars seemed to say, *Charm, Charm, Charm* – and I wanted to leap overboard, swim back to shore, find her.

Oh, Isis! Please keep her safe till I return! I prayed. But this time there was no sign, no answer from my goddess.

As we approached Cat Isle, the music got louder, and

203

far away a single voice rose in song. With a small thud, the barge hit a gilded dock, decked with a mass of lotus blossoms. A small girl, a young acolyte dressed all in blue-embroidered white, knelt as I stepped onto land, holding up a small silver pot, shaped like a lotus flower, with an unlit candle in its centre.

'May the sacred lotus of Nefertem make the dream of your heart come true, High One,' she said.

As I took the pot from her, I wondered what the dream of my heart was. To find Charm safe when I returned? To get the scroll back to Philäe without being killed? To serve my goddess? To discover what Khai's true feelings for me were? Or mine for him? I let none of those things show on my face.

'Thank you, child,' I said instead, all impassive priestess-princess. 'And the same to you. May Isis bless you and keep you.'

She smiled up at me, her face serene and innocent, a smile to make the heart feel glad, but there was sadness in it too, as if she knew something I did not.

The Pharaohs had not yet arrived, so I wandered about through the crowds, clutching my lotus pot, desperately trying to think how I could get hold of Khai, how I could get the map away from Alexandria before the Dark Feast of Serapis. Horrible pictures of what might have happened to Charm floated through my head, overlaid with the vision of those two dead bodies at my feet. Unfortunately I could imagine them in far too much detail.

I was so distracted that I hardly even noticed Captain Nail and the warriors keeping the more intrusive courtiers away from me. Cat Isle was full of noises – the chatter of gossiping voices, the soft rustle of sandals, the high, sweet sound of a mizmar, the twangling of a shaken sistrum and the low thump of drums. The scent of delicious foods wafted past my nose, and my mouth watered. I hadn't eaten since I woke, and I was hungry. Then the harsh blare of trumpets broke into my reverie, and I looked towards the sea. A great barge, covered in beaten gold approached. The oars were silver, and the sound of flutes kept the rowers in time. The deck was lined with torch-bearing Nubian Guards, perfectly matched in height, and at the prow stood two priests of Am-Heh, dressed all in black, swinging golden braziers which poured out a heavy, greenish smoke, whose cloying scent mingled with that of the food and killed my appetite completely.

Under a purple canopy in the centre were two raised thrones, on which my vile sisters sat, in full royal regalia, shimmering with jewels. Behind them were pretty, dimpled boys, chubbier than my Mamo, plying ostrich feather fans dyed in bright colours. I had eyes for none of them. All I could see – all I wanted to see – was Khai's dark head bowed at Tryphena's side, her ringed fingers resting in his hair. I wanted to rip them away from him.

I bowed not quite as low as the rest of them when the Pharaohs' procession passed me, and got up sooner. It made Tryphena notice me.

'Ah, sweet Cleopatra,' she said. 'Come, join us. I see you found some suitable cloth for your dress.' She sniffed. 'Not what I would have chosen, but still, I suppose it suits you well enough.'

I tried not to grind my teeth at her patronising tone.

'Thank you, dear sister,' I said. 'It does suit my Ptolemy colouring, I think, doesn't it?'

Berenice grimaced.

'What one can see of it under that truly dreadful hairstyle. What was your body slave thinking to have sent you out with hair like that? I should have her whipped if she were mine.'

'Ah yes,' said Tryphena. 'Your precious body slave. I do trust she is enjoying her time in the palace. Charmion, isn't it? The one who's been with you forever?' She smiled like a cat in the cream, and all the hairs stood up on the back of my neck and right down my spine.

'I'm surprised you remember,' I said, my voice cold as iced sherbet. 'She is well, thank you. And under the protection of Isis, as are all my people.' I knew what the wish of my heart was now. It was that anyone who'd hurt my best friend should die a horrible, painful death. If it involved covering them from head to toe with stings from Isis's giant scorpion, so much the better. I'd gladly pick the creature up in my own hands and point its stinger the right way.

'How delightfully fierce you are, Cleopatra. One would almost think you cared. Now, come. We must honour Nefertem, and make our little wishes. So quaint, this Lotus Ceremony, but one must humour the people, and be seen to do the right thing.'

After that we walked in silent procession to the other side of the isle, where the singing was reaching a crescendo. Khai slipped back into the crowd behind, and as he passed, I smelt his now-familiar scent and saw his lips move slightly. The word 'later' came to me on the ghost of a breath, so faint that I didn't know if I'd imagined it. I nodded slightly, just a tiny movement of my head. I knew he'd pick it up. Then I set my eyes forward again, trying not to let the squeezing thump in my belly overwhelm me.

Hail, you of the Lotus, hail!
Your names are known to Nefertem.
Rise like Him from the blue water lily,
Rise to the nostrils of Ra,
Rise with the dawn each day.
Rise, you of the Lotus, rise!

The choir sang in unison, and then the single voice I'd heard before rose again, clear notes tinkling against the starlight as the yellow edge of the full moon peeped over the horizon of the Great Green Sea.

Come forth, you of the Lotus, come forth.
Luck, luck be with you,
Each and every one.
Light now the flame of heart's desire!
Come forth, you of the Lotus, come forth.

Acolytes and priests of Nefertem were waiting for us with lit tapers, moving first to Tryphena and Berenice, then to me, and afterwards to everyone else who held a silver lotus pot. The small candles inside flared and then wavered as a puff of breeze whispered over the water. I cupped mine carefully. I knew the legend. Anyone whose pot floated on the waves without the candle blowing out would get their wish from Nefertem, along with a healthy dose of luck for the year. I needed both desperately. Fat purple cushions were set on the ground for the Pharaohs to kneel on – Isis forbid they should ever have to touch the sand with their precious royal knees – and they set their small pots adrift. Almost at once, another, harder, puff of wind made both their pots rock dangerously before tipping over and sinking, the flames extinguished. Berenice made a gesture of annoyance, quickly stifled, and then rose to her feet, beckoning one of Am-Heh's black-clad minions over to her.

'The pot-maker has clearly offended Blessed Nefertem with his shoddy work,' she said, her voice a savage hiss. 'Find him and take him to Am-Heh's mercy.'

The priest nodded and scurried away through the suddenly still crowd of courtiers. I could see the fearful indecision in their eyes. Should they place their own pots in the water and risk the wrath of the Pharaohs if they floated? Or should they simply blow the candles out themselves and throw the pots away, risking the possible wrath of the god? Present circumstance won. With one collective indrawn breath, the candles were blown out, and the lotus pots discreetly dropped. A cascade of small, muffled musical clangs rang out as silver hit sand, and the crowd turned as one to follow my sisters towards the waiting feast.

I did not blow out my candle. Ignored for the moment, I walked forward and knelt beside the cushions, feeling the damp sand soak through my dress. I closed my eyes and carefully set my own pot on the waves. The prayer bubbled up from deep inside me.

Please, Nefertem. Save her. Let her be safe. Let me have my Charm beside me again. And please, Nefertem, grant me your luck. I really do need it.

In the end, it seemed that revenge wasn't the most important thing after all. I opened my eyes, and saw my small candle still alight, sailing out along the path of the full moon's rays, and hovering above it, the figure of a young man with a shining blue lotus as a crown. He smiled at me before flashing out of sight.

'You are truly blessed by the god, chosen of Isis,' said a voice in my ear. A hand reached down to help me up, and I put my own in it, rising to see a priest of Nefertem beside me, dressed in blue-striped white. His eyes were distant and unfocused as he spoke, like someone in a trance. 'You must believe you are not to blame for what will happen now. Remember that your luck will come with the opening flowers of the blessed blue dawn. No sooner than that.' He bowed and withdrew quickly before I could ask him what he meant, but I knew his god had spoken to him directly.

Captain Nail stepped up beside me.

'Best we return to the feast before you are missed, Chosen,' he said quietly.

I nodded and turned to go, seeing little Mamo out of the corner of my eye. He looked pale as a ghost, and his mouth was pinched shut.

'Art thou well, boy child?' I asked.

His eyes widened with fear.

'Y-yes, Great Lady. I am well.' He began to ply his fan vigorously, as if to show his health, but I wasn't fooled. If he was frightened, it was because he'd just seen Berenice in action. Berenice would want a report from him, and soon. He wouldn't want to give it, because I'd been kind to him, but he wouldn't have a choice. He'd just been reminded that Am-Heh's crocodiles were waiting for any who displeased the Pharaohs, hadn't he? I sighed. Any hope of keeping what had just happened secret was now gone. I would have to be even more careful from now on when Mamo was around.

'Thou art the best waver of feathers in the palace,' I said, hoping it would make him feel a little better. I knew how it was to be powerless and afraid.

Am had his work cut out tasting for me at the picnic

feast. Servants and slaves darted round with baskets full of tiny morsels, traditional sweet pastries shaped like lotus flowers, bite-sized skewers of meat marinated in spicy sauces, small pies filled with a variety of delicious things, tiny lark's thighs rolled in honey and sesame seeds, quail's eggs with gold-leaf speckled salt to dip them into, and delicate glass goblets filled with wines and sweet sherbets. I ate only as much as I could manage – which wasn't a lot. My eyes darted round constantly, seeking for any sign of Khai. Where was he? He wasn't with the Evil Sows, who were sitting above us all on thrones woven from rushes, painted blue, and garlanded with more lotus flowers. I caught a glimpse of shiny black hair. There he was! I hoped he'd come to me, even as I knew it was too dangerous. My heart squeezed in my chest as he settled himself in his usual place at Tryphena's feet. What had he meant by 'later'? Should I try to get a message to him? I wanted to talk to him so badly it hurt – not just to make plans for stealing the map, but for myself. I wanted to tell him about Charm, to ask if he knew anything, had heard anything. I was sure that Tryphena had had something to do with her disappearance now – she'd as good as said so. What might Charm be suffering at that moment? Had she been fed to Am-Heh's crocodiles already? Abruptly my stomach roiled, and I knew I was going to be sick. I rose as quickly and discreetly as I could, blessing Captain Nail for falling in behind and not asking any questions, and hurried behind a nearby bush, where my stomach promptly turned itself inside out. Captain Nail handed me a square of linen to wipe my mouth with. He looked worried.

'Is it poison, Chosen?' he asked, his face anxious.

I shook my head. Am was standing a little distance away, looking healthy and clueless as ever.

'No. It's just…you know…' I whispered.

He put out a tentative hand, and then withdrew it, the first glint of sympathy I had ever seen in his eyes. He coughed, clearly embarrassed.

'I understand, Chosen. Would you like to go back to the palace now, if you are unwell?'

'I'd better not. It would be rude to leave before Their Splendiferousnesses.' I hesitated. Could I trust him? Yes. For all his stiffness, he was definitely on my side. I beckoned him closer.

'Do you see the boy with the Pharaoh Tryphena – the one with the dark hair?' I breathed into his ear. He nodded. 'He is a friend, marked by our goddess. Trust him as you would me. He may enter my chambers at any time of day or night, with no questions asked. But no one must know. No one, especially Mamo. Do you understand? It is vital no one sees him if he comes.'

He nodded again, and cleared his throat.

'I will see to it myself, Chosen,' he said. 'At once.' He waved his hand at Am. 'You, taster boy, fetch the chosen a tisane of peppermint leaves. Quickly now. And oversee the making of it yourself.'

Am set off towards the servants at a run.

'Thank you, Captain Nail,' I said formally. 'I couldn't wish for a better guard in time of need.'

He bowed, the corner of his mouth creaking up into what might have been a half smile.

'My duty and pleasure to serve you, Chosen, as always.'

Maybe he is human after all, I thought. It was a small comfort.

The full moon rose high in the sky. I could see Thoth and Nefertem dancing dreamily together in its creamy rays. The food was cleared away, and then the fire dancers came, twisting and turning, their blazing ribbons filling the night with streaks of flame and the smell of ash and smoke. I saw Khai rise and bow, saw Tryphena dismiss him with a flick of her hand, seemingly mesmerised by the patterns of light. Thinking quickly, I turned to Mamo, still fanning me like a small demon of air.

'Go thou, and find the small girl of the silver pots. I

wish to give her a gift. Bring her to me, and if thou art hungry and find thy way takes thee past the place of food, I shall not be angry.'

His eyes flicked quickly to Berenice, then back to me. Then he bowed.

'I hear thee and obey, O Great Lady,' he said, before slipping off into the darkness. As soon as he was out of sight, I stretched lazily, got up and coughed a little.

'I need some air,' I said to Captain Nail, giving him a pointed look and fanning my hand in front of my face. 'This smoke is choking me.' I hoped he had seen Khai leaving too.

He muttered some orders to the two warriors, and followed me alone into the darkness. I walked away from the lights, my footsteps lit only by the moon's glow behind me. My shadow wavered eerily, long and mysterious, seeking out the path before me, hoping I was going the right way. As I brushed past some bushes, the scent of crushed tamarisk rose around me, like a cloak of sweet liquorice. I had no idea where I was headed, but I prayed to Isis wordlessly as I walked, trusting her to guide my footsteps. We soon reached a tiny beach, where several small feluccas were pulled up onto the sand. Khai was sitting on the edge of one of them. I let out a breath I didn't know I'd been holding.

'I will stand guard, Chosen,' Captain Nail said. 'But hurry. These are the boats of the palace servants, I think, and they may come back at any moment.'

I hurried forward as Khai came towards me. Our hands met. His were warm and dry, mine cold and clammy with exertion and nerves.

'I have news,' he said, before I could speak. 'Your Charm is held below the palace, waiting on the Pharaoh's pleasure.'

I didn't ask how he had found out, just squeezed his hands. He was a spy, after all, as I was.

'Can you get her out?' I whispered. 'Or can I? Tell me where to go. I'll do anything to save her. Anything.'

'I know,' he said, squeezing back. 'But it'll be easier for me. Don't worry, Cleopatra. I'm used to this sort of thing.' He jerked his head towards the captain. 'He's to be trusted, then?'

I nodded.

'Yes. He has orders to let you into my rooms at any time of day or night. If you succeed, bring her by the slave passages. Charm knows the way. I…'

He stopped my lips with a quick, darting kiss. I had only just time to close my lips. Did I taste of sick? Oh, please not, dear Isis!

'I know what to do,' he said. 'Stop fussing.' He took

my hand, put it to his chest and knelt at my feet. I could feel his heart beating steadily under my palm. 'Give me Isis's blessing, though. Just in case.'

I squeezed my eyes shut.

Please, Isis. Keep him safe, I prayed. *Help him get Charm out.* Once again, I didn't know if she'd heard.

'Whatever blessing I can give is yours,' I said. I leaned forward, but just as my lips touched his forehead, Captain Nail cleared his throat loudly, and I heard rustling and chattering in the distance.

'Go!' I said, pulling back from him. 'You mustn't be caught with me. Not now.'

He smiled – just a quick flash of white teeth. 'I'd rather be caught with you than anyone else, my beautiful priestess.' Then he scrambled to his feet and slid away silently into the darkness. A few seconds later, a file of servants appeared through the bushes, bearing kitchen pots and pans. Captain Nail was now at my side, and they stopped dead on seeing us. They dropped their pots with a clatter, and prostrated themselves immediately.

'Get up,' I told them, trying to keep the irritation out of my voice. 'Go on with your work. I am just leaving.'

With sidelong glances, and reverent murmurs of, 'Yes, chosen of Isis,' they obeyed, and I walked away, my heart bounding like that of a dik-dik with a hyena after it.

The fire dancers were just finishing as I returned to the main party. Am had brought my tisane, and I drank it gratefully, the taste of mint washing away the last sourness of vomit. My eyes slid to where the Evil Sows were sitting. Khai was already back in his place, but I caught Berenice glancing at him, and then back at me, looking thoughtful. Maybe it was nothing, but there was a cloud of darkness around her again and one of the foul Am-Heh priests was whispering in her ear. Had we been careful enough? Or had we been seen? I shivered. If she suspected...! No! I wouldn't think that way. I would be strong, and confident. I had good people and my goddess on my side, and I was a royal princess. I was, whether I felt like it yet or not, a leader by birth and by blood. I would reclaim Isis's power for Her, drive Am-Heh's foul taint from the palace, and save Egypt – however long it took.

Straightening my back, I lifted my chin and looked back towards the two thrones. One was now empty. Berenice and her priest had disappeared, but Tryphena was still sitting there, head craned round, staring at something behind her. Her face was half-avid, half-disgusted as she watched whatever it was. Figures were moving in the shadows, but I couldn't make out who it was, or what they were doing.

A low, sickening buzz of chanting started, stopping abruptly as a flash of silver rose, fell. I heard a small gurgling scream, quickly cut off, a soft thud, then, after a pause, several sharp cracks and a high wail, which echoed into the night. I surged to my feet, frowning, peering forward, trying to see. Surely I recognised that young voice. My stomach clenched, sickness rising again. I took one step forward, two, then came to a sudden halt as I saw Berenice re-emerge from the darkness. Mamo was being dragged along behind her by the priest, a raised whip weal across both cheeks. I fought the urge to run towards him, fury rising within me. What had they done to him, poor child?

Berenice smiled at me out of the black cloud of Am-Heh which surrounded her. She reached behind her, snagging Mamo by one small ear, and pulled him forward, throwing him down at my feet, where he cowered, weeping silently.

'Ah, Cleopatra,' she said, her voice a cruel purr. 'You really should take better care of my gifts, you know. My priest found this one with a girl, no less, and at his age! I have punished him a little, as you see. I leave it to you to decide whether you return him to me, and I send him to the mercy of Am-Heh or not. He is yours, after all. I have already blessed the girl with His mercy, you will be glad to hear.'

As I saw her smile widen, and noticed the fresh red splotches staining her dress and hands, I felt even sicker.

Now I knew what the silver flash and that gurgling scream had meant. Now that pretty, innocent lotus child was dead because of me, all because I had sent Mamo on a useless errand to find her. I sent my fury and shame down to a distant part of myself. There was nothing I could do for the girl now, and Berenice knew it, but I vowed to Isis that I would have my revenge one day.

I made my voice colder than iced sherbet in summer.

'As you say, sister, he is mine to punish. After all, I do need a fan bearer in this heat. I shall see that this slave gets exactly what he deserves. Exactly.' I bared my teeth in a smile that promised terrible things. She wasn't to know that none of them involved Mamo.

'All this fuss over slaves,' Tryphena said, rising. 'I really don't know why we bother with them. Such a bore, training the stupid things up, but I suppose we must have them, and at least there are always plenty more if one should meet with a little…accident.' She smirked at me again, but I just raised a bored eyebrow at her. I wouldn't give her the satisfaction of responding to her taunts, and I made myself keep my eyes off Khai. I just prayed to Isis, Ra, Zeus and every other god of my ancestors that his rescue plan for Charm, whatever it was, would work.

After the Pharaohs had left in their golden barge, we waited for an age till ours arrived. I'm sure that greasy adviser had made it be late on purpose. The journey back across the bay seemed to take forever. I could not comfort Mamo in public, but I gave his shoulder a small squeeze as I passed him. He let out a stifled cry, and my fingers came away sticky. The iron tang of blood reached my nostrils, and I wiped them hurriedly on my dress.

'Hush thyself, boy child' I murmured softly in Amharic. 'Be thou brave and all will be well.' I could not stop thinking about the little lotus girl and the sadness I had seen on her face. What had her name been? Where was she from? The priest's words came back to me.

You must believe you are not to blame for what will happen.

How had he known? Had his god told him? Had her fate been laid out for her by Nefertem? I shook my head. Whatever the priest had said, I still felt guilty and sick. One day, when this was all over, I would make time to go to the temple of Nefertem and give an offering in her memory. It was the least I could do, and I would take Mamo with me. For now, all I could think about was Charm, and wonder if Khai was really going to get her back for me. I had wanted to go with him so much, but I knew it was impossible. I had to trust him, let him tread the paths he knew so well, let him be the rescuer as he had been so many times before. I couldn't contemplate Charm suffering the same fate as the little lotus girl. I wouldn't. But, of course, a treacherous little voice in my brain said: *What if you have to?*

I had no answer to that.

11

Death in the Morning

The blue lotus flowers were still firmly holding their petals closed as we passed the long pool in the palace gardens. I looked at them in the fading moonlight, willing them to open soon. Nefertem had promised me luck with the dawn, and I hoped he'd keep his word, because I really, truly needed him to – or rather, Khai and Charm did. The nearer we got to my apartments, the more my stomach began to flutter with hope. Would Charm be there? Had Khai managed to save her yet? He must have got back long before me. I began to worry about the two warrior guards we'd left behind. Would whoever was on guard by the slave passages even let him in?

Come on, Khai, I thought at him fiercely as I quickened my steps. *Be there!*

I wanted to call out Charm's name as soon as we entered, but I controlled myself, letting the warriors and Captain Nail do their job, fanning out slowly to make sure there were no intruders. I could see for myself that there was no sign of her in any of the main chambers. Captain Nail spoke to Sergeant Basa in a low voice, but he shook his head, sending me a sideways glance of sympathy. He was a kind man, and I was glad he and his huge muscles were on my side.

'No sign, sir, and none of the rest have come back, neither our boys, nor the eunuchs.'

I walked slowly around the room, hope sliding out of me, to be replaced by despair. Captain Nail went through into the bedchamber to talk to Warrior Rubi, who was guarding the slave passages, but there was no news from him either. The captain came back to stand beside me. I beckoned him in closer.

'Is there any way you can neutralise the eyes and ears in the walls?' I whispered.

He moved me slightly to one side, with a discreet push of his hand.

'Not here,' he said, his lips hardly moving, then, louder, 'I will escort you to your chamber, Chosen. You are tired and need sleep.'

I took the hint.

My bedchamber seemed empty and cold without Charm in it, and I choked back a sob, as the door shut behind us.

'We can do nothing about the outer chambers,' he said quietly. 'It would look too suspicious. Here, the men moved some furniture and hangings around before you arrived to, er, discourage, any unwanted eyes, and although we cannot completely prevent the ears, they will hear nothing that is spoken softly. The bathing chamber is also safe, we think, and the courtyard too. It was Charm's idea to do this. She acted the part very well, I'm told, as she gave orders for her mistress's comfort. It will just seem an unfortunate coincidence, we hope – and there's nothing they can do, short of moving the furniture back.'

'Oh, Charm,' I whispered. Always thinking of what was best for me. Always guarding my back, even when I wasn't around. 'Where are you? Why hasn't Khai brought you back?' I felt a fleeting spurt of anger at him, then a long shiver of fear shook me. What if neither of them came back? Oh, *why* hadn't I insisted on going to rescue Charm myself? Doing something, however dangerous, would have been far better than this awful waiting and inaction.

'I will have to tell my men about the young man,

Chosen,' Captain Nail said, very quietly. 'I cannot be on duty every minute of the day, so they must know in case I am not here. They are all sworn to Isis. None will betray you.' He looked worried. 'We are spread much too thin. I wish I'd brought more men to guard you.'

I nodded slowly. He was right – on both counts. But there was nothing we could do about the numbers of my warriors now.

'Tell them, then.' I looked at him. If he were to trust me too, I would have to be truthful as well. 'I already know at least one of your men can hold his tongue.' I took a breath and confessed to my night-time trip to the library to meet Khai. 'Don't blame Warrior Sah,' I finished. 'I threatened him with Isis's wrath.'

The tight lips were back for an instant, and then a miracle happened. The Captain actually smiled properly – a real grin that showed his white teeth.

'Did you really think he wouldn't report back to me, Chosen?' he asked. 'We who are Isis's warriors take your safety very seriously. Warrior Sah came to me the instant he was off duty.'

'Oh,' I said. My cheeks heated with embarrassment. I should have known, really. 'Well…well, why didn't you say something?' I burst out.

Captain Nail shrugged.

'There seemed little point,' he said. 'I gave orders that the next time it happened – as we all knew it would – you were to be discreetly followed and protected. We will not allow your own stubbornness to get you killed or harmed, Chosen. We would all rather die first.'

That was the moment everything that had happened caught up with me. I couldn't stop them – the held back tears overflowed and ran down my cheeks, and I flung myself at the captain's chest. He caught me, and held me awkwardly, patting my back with a hand that was clearly more used to handling a spear than a sobbing girl. He reeked of oil, sweat and metal, and I had a brief hysterical thought that the beautiful dress I was wearing would smell as if it had been on a battlefield, what with me having wiped Mamo's blood off on it too. Gradually, I stopped crying, and found that he was holding out another square of linen. It was getting to be a habit. Did the man have an endless supply of them? I scrubbed at my eyes and nose, noticing too late that the material was now streaked with black and red and green – the remains of my makeup. I must have looked like a camel's backside – a backside with an upset stomach, too – but I didn't care. I straightened my shoulders and cleared my throat.

'All we can do now is wait,' I said, trying to pretend my lapse of emotion hadn't happened, even though small hiccupping sobs kept welling up. 'But at least I can patch up poor little Mamo while we're doing it. Bring him to me, if you would, Captain. We both know where he came from, but I won't have another child hurting on my account, whatever the consequences. If he tells my wretched Am-Heh-loving sister I was kind – well, too bad.' I was fed up with pretending to be someone I wasn't – I'd told High Sister Merit I wasn't cut out to be a spy, and it seemed I truly wasn't, though I would still have to try.

'And in that you show your quality, Chosen,' he said. 'It proves that Isis does not make mistakes.'

I blushed a little. If he was not careful, Captain Nail would be in danger of becoming positively soft-hearted.

I had to soak the robe away from Mamo's back with water from the bathing chamber. It took a long time to soak the dried blood away, but he was very brave. He had been slashed over the shoulders with a sharp blade, as well as being hit in the face with a whip. I found some honey and herb of Achilles ointment in Charm's chest, and carefully smeared it over his wounds before binding a dressing of linen around him as best I could. I blessed the lessons in healing I'd been given as part of my acolyte training at Philäe. Those days seemed very far off right now, and I muttered curses as the material slipped and slid in my fingers.

'Go thou and sleep now, boy child with the lion's courage,' I said when I had finished. 'The dawn will bring better things to thee, I hope.'

'May the Thunder Father bless thee, Great Lady,' he said.

I lay down on the bed. Captain Nail was right, I did need to rest. But all I could see when I closed my eyes were endless pictures of Charm being tortured, fed to crocodiles, dead. Tossing and turning restlessly, I began to pray to Isis, saying the same thing over and over again, in case my goddess was still listening.

Please, dear Isis, keep Charm and Khai safe.
Please, dear Isis, keep Charm and Khai safe.
Please, dear Isis, keep Charm and Khai safe.

I must have finally fallen asleep with those words on my lips, because I found myself waking with a start, sitting up as a slight commotion came from the direction of the slave passages. I leapt off the bed, and ran towards the closet at full tilt, colliding with a dishevelled Charm as she limped into the room. She stank of rank sweat, blood and a musky, stale scent I didn't recognise, but it didn't matter to me how much she smelt – I cradled her in my arms as if she was a precious jewel, feeling the beat of her heart against mine, the rough rasp of her breath against my neck, and, finally, the hot wet of her tears soaking into my shoulder.

'Thank Isis, you're alive,' I whispered, never wanting to let her go. I felt a hand squeeze my shoulder.

'I brought her back to you, Cleo,' Khai said. 'I keep my promises.'

I moved my hand a fraction to clasp his tightly, to bring it to my mouth and kiss it. He'd earned the right to call me that now.

'I know you do,' I said, laughing and crying at the same time, not knowing how else to express my passionate gratitude. 'I know you do, Khai.'

Charm's was the second battered body I treated that night. She had bruises everywhere, like deep purple-black flowers on her brown skin. They blossomed on her back, her hips, her thighs, her legs – even her stomach hadn't escaped. There was blood in her hair from a deep cut on her scalp, and her wrists were sore and weeping where she had been tied and had struggled against the ropes. There was a look in her eyes I remembered from long ago, when she had first been sent to me. It was a look I'd hoped never to see again. It spoke of despair and helplessness and impotent fury. I bathed her gently, wiping off the crusts of dirt and smears of filth, pouring jugs of cool water over her. It was a measure of her pain and distress that she let me. The old Charm would have batted my hands away and scolded me for doing her job. She would have asked me if I thought I was the Sultana of Scrubbing. She would have made me laugh. This Charm sat silent and staring inwardly at the horrors in her head. She hadn't spoken a word since she arrived. I wrapped her in thick towels, and left her sitting on the side of the bath while I went out to the closet to fetch one of my softest robes.

Khai was talking to Captain Nail when I entered. His black hair was mussed and untidy, and I saw that his tunic was covered in cobwebs and dust. He turned as I entered.

'How is she?' he asked.

I shook my head.

'Not good,' I said. 'Will you tell me where you found her? How did you manage to get her away.'

'Your sisters,' he said, then stopped. Disgust made his mouth turn in on itself. He started again. 'The Pharaohs have a secret route down to Am-Heh's temple. Nobody is really allowed to use it except them, but some of the brotherhood use a short section of it to bring the bodies away into their own underground chambers. Or the bits of them that are left. It's usually not much.'

I winced.

'I'm not supposed to know about it, but I've been doing some sneaking around since I've been with *her*.' He made a face as if there was a vile taste in his mouth, as he had before when he mentioned Tryphena. 'I guess I was lucky. There are no guards down there, and the priests were...otherwise occupied. Charm was tied up in one of the outer chambers they use for their dirty laundry, so I just grabbed her and carried her out through the brotherhood tunnel and then through the slave passages.' He looked at me.

'She just said one word when she saw me. "Cleo". That's how I knew it was her. She...she was just lying there on a pile of filthy black robes, moaning. I think they hurt her badly. She only just managed to give me directions for how to get here.'

'They did hurt her badly,' I said, my hands knotting into fists. 'Isis curse them for ever. But it will never happen again. I'll make sure of it.' My best friend would have a warrior to guard her wherever she went from now on, whether she wanted one or not. She was too precious to lose again.

Charm was sitting in exactly the same position I'd left her in, staring blindly at the marble walls. I dressed her carefully, feeding her arms and head through the openings of the robe as if she were a child like Mamo. Then I sat down beside her and put my arm round her waist, pulling her gently against me.

'Do you want to tell me what happened, dear one?' I said softly.

She stirred a little, clearing her throat as if to make room for words to come out.

'Not really,' she said, and her voice sounded hoarse as a crow at dawn. 'Not now, anyway.'

I remembered the finger-shaped bruises on her inner thighs, and closed my eyes in pain for her. Talking could wait till later.

'All right, then. Come into my bed and lie down. I'll make up a sleeping draught for you.' I knew that sleep would be the best healer for her, even if it brought nightmares.

She followed me like a ghost, and I tucked her under the coverlet. She was shivering, despite the close, warm air, so I searched for a blanket. I sent Captain Nail for hot water, and brewed her an infusion of passionflower and valerian, which I made her drink. She took small, painful sips until it was all gone, then lay down on her side with her back to me, unmoving. I felt helpless, but knew there was nothing more I could do for now.

All this time, Khai had been pacing up and down like

a caged leopard. I asked the captain to wait outside, then went to him.

'Thank you,' I said huskily. It was so natural to lean against him and put my head against his shoulder. I felt his head turn, felt the roughness of his warm, slightly chapped lips against my temple. I turned my face up to him, and our mouths met, gently, tentatively at first, and then deeper. The reality was so much better than the years of dreams. Small, fizzing bolts of lightning flared all over my body, until I felt liquid as warm honey against him, and entirely breathless. Everything went away except our lips, our touch on each other's skin. It was blissful, and I was glad that Khai seemed as enthusiastic about the kissing as I was. I tried not to wonder how he'd got so good at it.

Eventually a small clicking sound brought me back to reality. I opened my eyes and saw a small brown head retreat round the door, which closed immediately. Mamo! He was meant to be sleeping. How much had he seen? A little nagging voice in my head told me that this wasn't what I was supposed to be doing, and that it was my own fault if I'd been caught. Would he tell Berenice, or – even worse – Tryphena?

My heart began to thump in quite the wrong way – with fear. Oh no! What had I done? I pulled away, reluctantly, wanting so much to stay lost in those new, exciting feelings. But Isis wouldn't thank me for wasting our precious time together with kisses, and it was a risk I couldn't take again – though I wanted to with every bit of me. If we were found out…if word got back to Tryphena. I didn't want to think what would happen then. Khai held onto me as if he never wanted to let go, murmuring my name, burying his nose in my hair. But I was determined.

'Khai… Khai! Let go of me! We have to talk.'

He laughed, a small, rueful sound, and moved away a little. I tried not to be distracted by his still-stroking fingers on my shoulder.

'Our beloved Isis is a demanding goddess, Chosen.'

'Yes,' I said firmly. 'But she chose us for a reason. We mustn't disappoint her. There are things I need to tell you, and I don't know how much time we have. And… and I don't want to be responsible for your death, Khai,' I blurted out without meaning to. He stilled, tensing, pulling away from me now.

'What do you mean, Cleo? How could you possibly be responsible for my death?' He had that dangerous look in his eyes again. 'What do you know? Tell me!'

I explained quickly about how he and Charm were involved in the new vision from Saïs, and then, at last, about the map and the urgency of the mission I'd been given by Isis. 'Do you have any idea where we might start looking?' I finished.

He took a step back and ran his hands over his face and up into his long, dark hair, finally clasping them at the back of his neck. Then he began to pace again.

'This is all a lot to take in,' he said. 'I thought you… I thought Isis – well, never mind what I thought, it doesn't matter now.' It was as if the kissing had never been. The eager lover was gone, and the spy was back in his place.

'Let me get this right. If we don't get that map out by the Dark Feast of Serapis, then she,' he gestured towards the sleeping figure in the bed with one hand, 'and I die?'

I nodded, as he sat down on the nearby couch with a dull thud.

'Then we've got till dusk of the fifth day from now. The feast won't end till sunrise of the third day after that, but we can't risk that the seer misinterpreted Isis's meaning. We must have the map before it begins.'

Set out starkly like that, it sounded as if we had terrifyingly little time. I sat down beside him.

'We'll have to sneak into the brotherhood's secret archives tonight then, Cleo.' He tapped a fingertip on his knee, thinking.

'I'll leave the how of getting us in to you,' I said. 'But we must get hold of that map and get it out of the palace. Then…'

Oh, by Ra's golden toenails. I hadn't really thought the 'then' or the 'afterwards' through. I needed a plan to get us all out of Alexandria and on the way back to Philäe.

'Then what?' he asked. 'Have you actually thought about what will happen next, Cleo?'

'Not…not as such,' I said, a little waspishly. 'There hasn't been a lot of time.'

He frowned. 'Always set up a foolproof escape plan. First law of spying.'

Now I was annoyed.

'My spying education is clearly lacking in the legal department then. Perhaps you can give me lessons.'

He sighed, wiping the back of his hand across his mouth. The part of me that wasn't cross with him hoped that he wasn't wiping away the memory of our kisses.

'I'm sorry, Cleo,' he said. 'I just want to get everyone out of here safely after we've got the map – especially you. It's hard to remember that you're new to this sneaking around thing sometimes.' The corner of his mouth lifted. 'You're the chosen of Isis after all, you should be infallible.'

'Well, I have news for you. I'm not,' I said. 'I may be chosen, but I can still make silly mistakes.'

His arm snaked around me, drawing me close again.

'Good,' he said. 'We can be fallible together, then. But we do need to set up something – you can't just run out of the palace into the night. You'll need transport, and a fast exit in case you're pursued.'

My heart sank a little. Was he going to stay behind, then? What if he was caught? I didn't think I could bear to be parted from him again – even if he was an annoyingly superior spy.

I ducked my head, suddenly shy. 'I'll talk to Captain Nail about it. And Cabar. But won't you come with me, Khai? Back to Philäe, I mean? It might be dangerous for you to stay here, and I couldn't stand it if…' My voice faltered to a stop.

He took my hand, pressing it against his chest as he had before. The steady, reassuring thud of his heart made my palm tremble.

'If Isis wills it,' he said. 'Then I will come.'

Isis had better will it, I thought. *Or else.*

Just then, Charm let out a long, low moan and began to thrash, half raising herself off the bed. I ran to her at once. Her closed eyes were flickering, with only a small crescent of white showing beneath the lids.

'Oh, don't, please don't, *please*,' she whimpered, in a high, scared voice I didn't recognise as hers. I scrambled onto the bed beside her, taking her in my arms, rocking her gently.

'It's all right, Charm. I'm here. You're safe,' I whispered.

She sank back down.

'Cleo,' she murmured, and then was still again. I looked over at Khai, not wanting to leave her.

'Where shall I meet you tonight?' I said.

He gnawed the corner of his lip for a second, thinking. 'The brotherhood usually make their prayers to Seth just before the middle hour of the night. Can you get to the library a little before that? It should be at its quietest then. Where we met before? There's a door hidden behind one of the scroll racks.'

'Yes. But I don't think the captain will allow me to come on my own this time.'

'That could be a good thing. If there are any nosy eyes or ears about, he can head them off. Say you're studying, or something.'

It was a perfect idea. Everyone knew how studious I'd been as a child. Perhaps it wouldn't seem so unlikely if I wanted privacy to look at some old scrolls in the middle of the night. I began to smile at him, but the smile turned into an enormous yawn, and I realised just how exhausted I was. Khai's eyes crinkled with laughter as he fought off a huge yawn of his own.

'I think we'd both better get some sleep,' he said.

I stretched out a hand to him, and he came to me and took it, pressing it to his forehead and then to his lips, kneeling beside the bed.

'Did I say thank you already?' I asked, a little breathless again.

'You did, my Cleo. But I would do what I did a thousand times over with no need of thanks.' His eyes met mine, direct and honest. 'Isis has blessed me with loving you, you see. You are the true path I have chosen for myself.'

Now I was totally breathless.

'Sh-she gave the same blessing to me,' I said, hardly able to get the words out. 'I-I mean, loving you, not me,' I stammered, wanting him to understand, then feeling foolish at having explained.

He grinned, the dimple at the corner of his mouth making me want to kiss him all over again.

'I know what you meant, and it makes my heart glad,' he said. 'Now, I really must go. I'll see you tonight, Cleo.' He walked back through the closet, and I heard him greet Warrior Rubi there. I fell asleep clutching his words to me like a cup full to the brim with warm sunshine, curled into Charm's back as if I was her armour against the world.

Several hours later, near dusk, Captain Nail woke me with terrible news. Charm was still asleep beside me – well, I had fed her enough valerian and passionflower to knock out a herd of camels. Her skin looked a little less grey, but the bruises were even more pronounced now, blackish-purple with blood.

'I'm sorry to tell you that we have found Dennu,' he said, low-voiced. 'He is dead.'

I shook my head stupidly, trying to clear it of the cobwebs of sleep that hung around it.

'Dead? How? Where?' I asked.

'He was outside the kitchens, lying beside a pile of rubbish. I'm afraid he…' The captain stopped, clearly unwilling to tell me the worst.

'He what?' I said. 'Tell me.'

'His lower legs were missing. Torn off as if by a wild beast. His face was so battered as to be almost unrecognisable, but Corporal Geta knew him by his blue amulet.'

My lips were stiff as I asked what had to be asked. 'When you say a wild beast, do you mean a crocodile?'

Captain Nail nodded. 'That's what it looks like, Chosen. I'm sorry.'

'It's not you who should be sorry,' I hissed. 'It's those Evil Sow bitches. I know it. If they hurt one more of my people, just one more, I swear I will ask Isis to blast them from the earth, Pharaohs or not. Let their precious Am-Heh protect them then.' I hurled myself out of bed, forgetting that I had thrown off my dress in the night, and was only clad in my breastband and loin cloth. The captain averted his eyes politely, as I found a robe.

'Is there any way we can get more warriors, Captain? Ones we can trust?' With Dennu gone, our little troop would be spread thinner on the ground than ever.

'Not unless we send to Philäe. And that will take moons, both for the message, and for the return. No, Chosen, we will have to manage with the men we have. One man sacrificed in battle doesn't lose a war. We are diminished, but not dead yet. Dhouti is a little upset, not being a soldier, but he will recover.' The Captain's eyes promised sharp words if he didn't.

'Where is Dennu's body?' I asked.

'With the Brotherhood of Embalmers, Chosen,' he said. 'I took the liberty of ordering in your name that he be taken to the Valley of Royal Servants when his

242

body is ready, with full rites of Osiris and Isis, and the proper grave goods for the afterlife.'

'I will ask our goddess to intercede with Osiris and make sure Dennu's afterlife is easy and pleasant,' I said. 'He has died in Her service, after all. He deserves that at the very least.'

I followed him into the outer chamber. Dhouti was slumped in a corner, his head in his hands. As I went over to him, he fell to his knees and prostrated himself.

'I am sorry, Chosen,' he said, his high voice ragged. 'I saw him taken and I hid. I am not worthy to serve you. I am a coward.' He began to weep and wail, and I squatted down beside him, as he writhed on the floor with shame. I saw a couple of the warriors' lips curl with distaste, and little Mamo staring wide-eyed, but I took no notice of them.

'Hush, Dhouti. You are not a coward, and you did the right thing. If you hadn't, you would have been taken yourself, and then I would have lost two good eunuchs instead of one. Get up now, and calm yourself. We must all be strong now, and I need you.'

He snuffled a bit, but picked himself up off the floor.

'How may I serve you, Chosen?' he said, wiping his eyes and standing up straight.

'That's better,' I said. 'Now, will you and Am go and

find us all something to eat? We must keep up our strength.'

I saw him wince slightly, whether at the thought of food, or at the idea of going out into the palace corridors again, I didn't know. I thought it was probably the latter. I beckoned Captain Nail over.

'Will you send one of the men with them, Captain? I believe none of us should go anywhere alone now, just in case.'

'Yes, Chosen,' he said, saluting. Then, in a lower voice, 'And that includes you.'

I could see I would have a fight on my hands, later.

12

The Hidden Door

While Dhouti was away, I took Captain Nail into the bedchamber to discuss tonight's meeting with Khai.

'It is a good time,' the captain said. 'The Pharaohs are away from the palace tonight and tomorrow. They have gone to bless the waters. The river is much too strong this year, and many granaries and houses have been flooded and destroyed upstream.'

I'd forgotten that the blessing of the waters came right after the feast of Nefertem. It was something of a relief that my sisters weren't around to summon me at an inconvenient moment – perhaps they'd do us all a favour and drown in the Nile flood. But what if Tryphena had summoned Khai to attend her on the royal barge? What if he wasn't there to meet me? I hoped he'd be able to make some excuse not to go with her – his duties for the brotherhood, perhaps? I would have to trust in Isis to get him to our meeting place on time.

I made very sure that we discussed our escape plans too. I wasn't going to let Khai rebuke me a second time.

'We need to be away from here as soon as my mission is complete, and at the latest right after the Dark Feast of Serapis begins,' I said. 'So everything will have to be in place.'

Captain Nail scratched his chin, the bristles rasping. He clearly hadn't had time to shave. That showed the measure of his worry. He was always very precise in his dress. I think he felt it set a good example or something.

'It is too risky to command a barge or a felucca to stand ready for all that time,' he said. 'Too many people would talk. We need fast camels or horses to take us to Canopus. We can hire a boat onwards from there. But the problem is buying the beasts. All our people will be watched, we must assume now.'

'Maybe Cabar can help. She was going to give me some doves. I could send her a message. She's used to helping people escape from Alexandria.'

'They arrived earlier, Chosen. My apologies. I meant to tell you. Perhaps that would be best. They may not be watching her.' I didn't tell Captain Nail that Cabar was a

Sister of the Living Knot and Khai's spymistress. He knew about my mission, but I didn't know how much he knew about all of that, and it wasn't my place to tell him. High Sister Merit's words of caution still rang in my ears after all these moons.

Tell nobody about the sisters, on pain of your own death.

That seemed fairly clear, although, of course, I'd told Charm. A cold snake of dismay wriggled down my spine. Had she told her torturers anything? I wouldn't believe she'd betrayed me till she told me with her own mouth, but pain does strange things to people. I knew that from my readings on the medicine of the mind. I shivered, dismissing the idea. Whether she had or not, I still had to carry on. If I had to answer to Isis for my loose tongue where my best friend was concerned, then so be it. She was another part of me. I couldn't not have told her.

'Chosen?'

Captain Nail's voice broke into my thoughts and I turned towards him.

'Make sure the men are packed and ready to leave at a moment's notice. Try not to let Mamo see.' I suddenly remembered the small head which had poked around the door when I was kissing Khai. Had I imagined it? I couldn't take the chance. 'Keep an eye on him, and don't let him run off anywhere. I'd like to trust him, but I think he's too frightened of his real mistress not to tell everything he knows at the first threat. We'll have to take him with us and drug him when we go. Otherwise he'll just raise the alarm. We can use the passionflower and valerian mix I gave Charm – he'll drink it if you say I told him to.'

The captain left to give the orders, and I was alone with the still-sleeping Charm. I moved carefully around the room, straightening things, picking up my ruined dress and hanging it in the closet, just to have something to do with my hands. I wasn't used to it, but I found it strangely soothing.

'What are you doing, Cleo?' came a sleepy voice from the bed.

'Tidying,' I said.

'But that's my job. Princess hands aren't made for housework.'

I ran over to her, leaping onto the bed. She winced.

'Oh, Charm, I'm sorry… I didn't mean to hurt you.'

'It wasn't you that hurt me,' she said, a bitter note in her voice. 'And no, I still don't want to talk about it.'

I suddenly didn't know what to say to this new, serious Charm – the one who'd had horrible experiences I could only imagine. I wanted so badly to comfort her, but I didn't know how. Instead, I asked her if she was hungry. Delicious smells were wafting under the door, and I knew Dhouti and Am must be back.

'Not really,' she said. 'My teeth hurt. But I suppose I'd better have something before I get back to work.'

I stared at her, shocked.

'You don't have to work, Charm,' I said. 'You must rest, get better, before you even think…'

'I want to,' she said fiercely, interrupting me. 'I need to be busy, Cleo. They're just bruises. They'll heal. If I work, I don't have to think.'

We walked in silence to the outer chamber. Am was busy tasting small morsels from several steaming pots. There were also plates of dates, soft curd cheese and flatbreads. When he had finished, I went to pick up a bowl, but Charm got there before me.

'I'll do it,' she said. 'What do you want, Chosen?'

The formality of it hit me in the chest like a blow, and I wanted to weep again. If only I hadn't brought her here. If only I'd left her safe in Philäe. But wishing wouldn't change things, however much I wanted it to.

'I'll have a bit of everything, please, Charm,' I said, keeping my voice cheerful. If she wanted to take refuge in the pretence of being my servant, I would let her.

Right now, I would pretty much let her do anything she wanted. She'd survived being torn from her family and her home all those years ago, so I knew she was tough. She'd survive this too, and I'd give her however long it took.

We ate together in the bedchamber. I made her share my food, but I could see it hurt her to eat the harder-to-chew things. The bruises on her jawbone rose and fell as she ate. It was painful to watch.

'Oh, do stop staring at me, Cleo,' she said irritably. 'I told you, I'll heal. I feel like a performing monkey with you watching me all the time.'

I bit my lip.

'I'm sorr—'

'And stop apologising. I told you that too. It wasn't your fault. I got stupid. I got caught. I wasn't watching hard enough.'

'But it *was* my fault,' I burst out. 'If I hadn't brought you here…'

'Huh!' She snorted. 'Do you really think I would have stayed behind to serve those stupid, whining acolytes at Philäe? I've been with you since I was six, remember. I don't know anything else but you, and I don't ever want to.'

'What have I done to deserve you?' I asked, genuinely

curious. I really didn't know.

She put down the date she was nibbling at, staring down at the floor.

'At first it was because you were kind to me,' she said slowly. 'I was lost and alone and afraid, and you treated me like a sister, not a slave. I could see that was unusual for a royal princess, even then. After that, well... I suppose I began to love you for being you. That's all, really.' She cleared her throat. 'When they took me, that's what I hung onto, what kept me going.' She turned to look at me at last.

'I didn't tell those horrible priests anything, you know, Cleo. I'd have died, rather than betray you.' She gave a small, choked laugh. 'They, er, they didn't like that very much, Ra and Osiris curse them. Hence my new decorations. I think I shall call myself the Princess of Pain from now on.'

I forced my lips into a smile. She was trying so hard to be normal. 'Pharaoh of Pain is more like it,' I said. 'I'm the princess round here, remember? And, yes, Ra and Osiris will curse them, and Isis too. I'll make sure of it.'

'That's the thing about having a best friend who's in with the gods,' she said. 'You can always call in a good curse when you need one.'

It was a very small step, but my old Charm was back with me. Sort of.

'My cursing powers are always at your disposal, O Beater of Bruises.'

'I think it might take me a little time to beat these, Cleo,' she said, inspecting the bits of herself that were visible, holding her arms out and turning them back and forth. 'But I will. Just…just let me do my job as usual, will you? No special treatment or anything. I don't think I could bear that.'

I knew then that I had to force myself to tell her what I'd discussed with Captain Nail – even if it made her angry.

'There is one thing,' I said. 'I've given orders that nobody is to go out alone from now on. If you have to do something, then you take a warrior with you. It's for your own safety.' I knew I shouldn't have let those last words out the moment they left my mouth.

'My safety?' Charm snarled. 'Do you really think one warrior can ensure my safety? Don't be ridiculous. Wasting one of our few warriors when I want to go to the wash-house, or to the middens, or the women's quarters? What about when I gather all the palace gossip and news for you? Do you think they'll tell me anything with a great tall man with a shield looming over my shoulder?

It just won't work, Cleo, and anyway, they should be guarding you, not me.'

Annoyance welled up in me at her stubbornness. Did she really believe she was that unimportant? I closed my lips on several sharp words that popped into my mouth. I would not shout at her. I would not. Why could she not see that I was doing this because I cared about her too much to let her risk herself again?

'It's not just you, Charm,' I began. 'The others…'

She rounded on me.

'I don't give a monkey's arse what the others do. If I have to have a guard, I can't do my job properly. So I won't have one.'

I promptly lost my temper.

'Yes you will – and that's an order,' I shouted. 'Or you won't leave these rooms.'

'Fine,' she snapped, 'one prison's as good as another to a slave.' She stalked into the bath chamber and slammed the heavy wooden door behind her with a final-sounding clunk.

Charm and I still hadn't made up by the time I was ready to leave for the library with Captain Nail and two of the warriors, and I suddenly realised we'd never had a real fight before in all the years we'd been together. I hated that she wouldn't talk to me, but I wasn't going to apologise for wanting to protect her. She'd come out of the bath chamber, carrying wet cloths and a determined expression, and had proceeded to get down on her hands and knees to wash the bedchamber floor from one side to the other. If cleaning helped her, that was fine by me. But when I saw her wince as her bruises came in contact with the hard marble, I couldn't keep quiet.

'I wish you'd stop,' I said, trying to keep my voice light. 'I'm sure I can live with a little dust.'

She just turned her back on me and carried on. After she'd finished the floor, she took every single thing I owned out of the closets, and began sorting and folding them. At that point I just gave up. She'd said she wanted to be busy, so I wasn't going to stop her. A determined Charm was nearly as much of a force of nature as High Sister Merit. I'd learned that early on in our relationship. The warriors we'd left behind were under strict orders to let her go nowhere unless one of them was accompanying her. She was almost as stubborn as me, so I thought that was about as likely as a flying pyramid. We also left Dhouti, Am and Mamo behind, although Mamo pleaded with Captain Nail to come.

'I must fan Great One. Is hot,' he said, in his broken Greek.

'It is cool in the place of many scrolls, boy child,' I told him. 'I do not need thee there. Stay here with the taster of food. He will teach thee to play the game of sticks.' I knew from our journey from Philäe that Am always carried a pouch of Senet pieces with him, and would take on all comers, given the chance. There'd been a permanent Senet board chalked out in a corner of one deck. Am nodded eagerly when I told him what I wanted.

'I'll show him, Chosen. He'll soon pick it up.'

Dhouti we left in the small inner courtyard, in charge of watching for messenger doves. I'd scribbled a note to Cabar, using the secret priestess cipher we'd agreed on, then rolled it small and attached it to one of the small bird's pink legs with the thread she'd provided. I went outside, cupping its fragile body in my two hands, and threw it into the dark air, sending a quick prayer Isis's way, asking her to guard it on its short journey to her temple. The grey wings flapped frantically for a moment, and then it was gone.

That done, we left. I had changed into priestess robes, and my most comfortable reed-soled sandals. Charm had whipped them out from the pile and held them out to me, when I'd asked for them, her face expressionless. She still wasn't talking to me. Warrior Sah was carrying my writing materials and a large papyrus scroll. Sergeant

Basa was carrying a badly-trimmed oil lamp, from which gouts of thick smoke guttered with every step, hanging in the still air like greasy blots of ink. Even at this hour of night, there was bustle in the passages. Once again, people bowed low when they saw me. I smiled and gave them the blessing of Isis. The more people who were reminded that my goddess was a power, the better.

There were only a few scholars studying late, their oil lamps casting pools of light over the scrolls they were poring over. I thought I recognised the back of one particular head, the white hair closely cropped against the scalp, and I stopped.

'Master Apollonius?' I said. The head swivelled round to reveal a wrinkled face, with pouchy bags under the eyes, and a snub nose.

'Yes?' he growled. 'And who might you be, young lady?'

Captain Nail made a move, but I put out my arm, smiling.

'Shame on you, sir. Don't you recognise your old pupil? The one you used to call Little Pest? How is your study of female philosophers coming along?'

He squinted up at me, then his face lit up.

'Heh! Young Cleopatra, is it? You had a good mind, as I remember. Always interested in my lady philosophers.

Then you disappeared.' He frowned, looking puzzled. 'They said you were dead, by Zeus. Are you alive, then?'

'I am, Master Apollonius. I'm a priestess of Isis now.'

'Ah well, even though death is not evil, as old Zeno tells us in his writings, I am glad to see you still on this earth, child. Mind you keep that mind of yours sharp, now. Follow where reason leads.' He turned back to his scroll, as we went on again, deeper into the library, and I realised I'd missed talking with the scholars. Even though most of them were grumpy old men like Master Apollonius, they'd always taken the time to talk to me and to answer my many questions.

There was a small desk in an alcove near the pillar of Seshat, and I sat down there, with my pens, ink and scroll, pretending to be studiously at work. The warriors and Captain Nail were stationed at every entry point, on the alert for intruders. Sergeant Basa was nearest me. I smiled at him, wanting some sort of human contact. His dark eyes crinkled at the corners and the corner of his lip twitched upwards for a second before he started scanning for danger once more. The sheer bulk of him made me feel safer, somehow, just by being there.

It felt strange, sitting in the library as if I were a student again. I found it oddly comforting. I was in the place where I belonged. I got up and picked out a scroll at random, rolling it out carefully. It was an account of the famous horse of my ancestor, the great Alexander. Bucephalus was his name, and I was soon lost in the description of his prowess in battle, and his loyalty to his master. Reading always calmed me, and the familiar story helped to take my mind off the worry about whether or not Khai would come.

I heard the scuffling sound of sandals turning fast, and looked up. A door-sized portion of the scroll racks swung out from the rest, creaking slightly. A smell of musty decay, and something else, both sharp and sickly at the same time, reached my nostrils. Within moments, Captain Nail and the two warriors had surrounded me, spears pointed outward and at the ready. I was tense, watching for betrayal, but then a dark head appeared, followed by the rest of Khai's body, and I relaxed for about half a candle flicker before my nerves kicked in. He had come, and our mission to steal the map could finally begin.

The fight with Captain Nail wasted long minutes, as I'd known it would – another stubborn person. I seemed to be surrounded by them. Not that I could talk.

'With the greatest respect, Chosen, you cannot…'

'I can,' I hissed, trying not to let my voice rise. 'And I will. This is my task, and mine alone. Armed men can't sneak, and that's what we have to do, don't we, Khai?' I turned to him in appeal, and he nodded.

'I'll guard her with the last drop of my life's blood, Captain, but our Chosen is right. The tunnels of the brotherhood are no place for a warrior. You'd put us at risk of being caught.'

'Exactly!' I butted in. 'See? He agrees with me.'

'And how will you defend her if things go wrong? You carry no weapon!' Captain Nail's face was dark with anger and frustration.

'I know every twist and turn of every passageway. I know where the traps are hidden. If things go wrong, I will get her out to safety. Can you say the same?'

The Captain's shoulders slumped. He knew defeat when he saw it.

'Very well. We shall remain here till you return, Chosen.'

'And if I don't return, you will make arrangements to get Charm and the others away.' I gave him a hard stare. 'Won't you?'

He sighed. 'If those are your orders, Chosen.'

'They are. If we're not back by dawn, then go back to my apartments and start packing.'

He came to attention, as did the other warriors.

'Good luck, Chosen. And please, be careful, both of

you.' He frowned at Khai menacingly.

'We will,' I said. And with that, Khai and I turned and slipped into the gap behind the scrolls. He put his hand to the wall and fumbled a little, before pulling on a small lever, just visible in the faint light of the oil lamp we'd left behind us. The scroll rack was closing again, with the same creaking sound as before. It clicked shut, and then we were totally in the dark.

'Come here and take my hand, Cleo,' Khai said.

I groped around, waving my fingers back and forward, trying to locate him. I hit something soft.

'Oof!' he said. 'That was my eye. Here.' I felt his hand grasp mine. It was warm and dry where mine was clammy and cold with nerves. 'It's only this first bit that's dark. Don't touch the walls if you can help it.'

I didn't ask why. I didn't really want to know.

I tried not to stumble as he led me along the close, womb-like passage. It was both like and unlike the realm of Isis – but this time I had Khai with me instead of the kite, and that made a big difference. I had a strange sensation in my head, as if a far-off voice was whispering to me. It was creepy, and I didn't like it. I shook my head, trying to dislodge it and nearly lost my balance.

'What's the matter?' Khai asked, stopping. His voice sounded slightly strained.

'I've got this weird sound inside my head,' I said.

He cursed.

'I'm a Ra-touched idiot. I should have warned you, Cleo. The brotherhood have some kind of Seth mind trickery going on down here. It's supposed to lead intruders astray. All of us who are meant to be down here have an amulet to protect us from it.' He let go of my hand for an instant, and his elbow dug into me as he fumbled inside the neck of his robe. The whispering voice instantly got louder.

Come! Come to me, loathsome thief. Come to me and die.

I could recognise the voice of a god when I heard one. Its flat, monotonous tone, full of evil intent, gave me the chills, but I found my feet yearning to go towards it. I couldn't help it. I took one step. Then another.

'Here,' Khai said, fumbling for my hand again, pulling me back. I felt a round metal disc pressing between his palm and mine. 'This will help.'

It did. The voice went away, my feet were released, and although I could still hear a very faint whisper, it was now bearable.

'What happens if we have to stop holding hands?'

'Then you take the amulet. Better that you are protected than me.'

Suddenly I knew just how Charm felt. I squeezed his fingers. 'Better that neither of us lets go,' I said firmly.

I felt him shake with silent laughter.

'Much better,' he said, squeezing back.

I wondered if it was the same kind of amulet that the filthy murderer had worn when he was escaping with the map. Then I wanted to hit myself in the head. I hadn't told Khai about the stuff I'd seen at the end of High Sister Merit's vision, had I? I tugged on his hand.

'Wait, Khai,' I said. 'There's something you need to know.' I conjured up the vision in my head again, trying to see every detail. 'There's a green statue with a donkey's head. And a...' I faltered a little, remembering. 'And a pile of skulls with red eyes. The map is near there, in an ebony box.'

'Are you sure about the skulls, Cleo?' he asked.

I nodded in the darkness, then realised he couldn't see me.

'Yes,' I said. 'Quite sure. Red-eyed skulls aren't something I'm going to forget in a hurry.'

He cursed again. 'I wish you'd told me before. That makes things a lot more dangerous,' he said, sounding annoyed. 'The skulls are right near the underground temple where all the brothers will be worshipping right about now. We'll just have to be quick and very quiet. I want you to promise me you'll do exactly as I say, otherwise I'm taking you straight back to the library.'

'I promise,' I said. 'You're the boss here, not me.'

He didn't answer, but walked on, picking up the pace a little. My heart was already thumping uncomfortably, and now it too sped up, till I felt as if I had a large rock banging about inside my chest. My hand became even clammier, and my palm made little sucking, clicking noises against Khai's as we walked. I would have felt embarrassed if I hadn't been so nervous. I was praying to Isis continuously in my head to protect us, but I didn't even know if she could hear me or act in this place given over to the power of Seth. Maybe Khai and I were completely on our own. It was a scary thought.

A little way on, Khai stopped again. There was a barely perceptible lightening of the darkness up ahead.

'No talking from now on, Cleo,' he said in a whisper. 'I mean it. Watch my hand, I'll point the way with that. And try to follow my footsteps exactly. There are traps all over the place, and I don't want you to step on one and set it off.'

'All right,' I said. 'I'll do my best.'

I could just see his face, dim and indistinct as he turned. With his free hand he reached behind me and pulled me forward, pressing a hard kiss on my lips, which I returned with interest.

'That's just in case I never get another chance,' he said. And with that cheerful thought he took me forward into the secret archives of the Brotherhood of Embalmers.

13

The Bray of the Donkey

The passages were lit by some kind of dim, green light. I couldn't see where it was coming from. It shone on our clasped hands with a numinous pallor, making our flesh look ghostly and insubstantial. The sweet, sickly smell was much stronger now, and I stuffed my spare hand into my mouth to keep from gagging. Then I saw Khai's head swivel frantically from side to side as, from behind us, the faint, papery shuffle of reed sandals came to my ears. His hand pointed right, to a door that stood ajar, and he pulled me through. I just had time to see a long stone trough with a legless body lying in it before he pulled me around and down behind it.

Khai's eyes were shut, and his lips were moving silently in what I assumed was prayer as the sound of sandals grew louder.

My eyes were open and I was trying not to be sick, breathing shallowly through my mouth.

I knew the person in the trough, despite his swollen face.

It was Dennu.

I could tell from the ragged stumps of his crocodile-chewed legs and his blue amulet.

Just to my left was a large earthenware bowl full of offal. Coiled grey-pink snakes of intestine lay on top of dark pink wings of lung, with the deep bloody purple of liver poking up from underneath. The whole thing was scattered with the dirty yellow crystals of salts of natron. A smaller bowl beside it held a greyish mush with a long, thin metal hook leaning up against it. I didn't even want to think about what that had been used for.

The shuffling sandals were right outside the door now, and I felt Khai's grip tighten on mine till it was almost painful.

Don't stop, don't stop, don't stop, I thought at them urgently, my heart banging so loudly I thought it would burst from my chest.

They didn't. *Shuffle shuffle shuffle* they went along the passage, till they were out of hearing. I breathed out, then sucked in a deep lungful of air, forgetting for an instant where I was, and stood up. Bad mistake. I doubled over, retching, my stomach finally rebelling against the truly revolting smell. Bitter fluid filled the back of my throat, but I choked it back down, trying desperately to keep the gagging noises quiet, to show some respect to my former eunuch. I fixed my eyes on four pretty canopic jars which were standing on a shelf, so I didn't have to look at Dennu's flabby, empty body lying just in front of me, also covered with a layer of salts and seeping fluids into a drain spout at one end with another basin set underneath it.

The figures of Falcon, Jackal, Baboon and Man looked back at me from the jars, their painted gaze fixed and staring, and somehow disdainful of my weakness, I felt. I had never known exactly what happened to a dead person during the embalmers' secret death rites. Now I did. It was information I would much rather have continued to do without. Khai tugged at me, pointing towards the door with a finger to his lips. I nodded, silently asking my goddess to send Her blessing Dennu's way. The sooner we were out of this place, the better.

As we crept onwards, I couldn't help thinking about my mother. Was this where the embalmers had brought her? Had they cut her earthly shell open and left her guts in a bowl too? *No!* wailed the long-ago child inside me, and I hurriedly thrust the horrible image away, feeling sick again. I'd spent so many years wondering what had happened to my mother's poor little broken body after I had escaped to Philäe, but with everything that had gone on since we'd been in the palace, I hadn't even thought to ask Khai about it. A big wave of guilt washed over me. I hadn't even found out where she was buried, or been to visit her tomb. What kind of awful daughter forgot to honour her own mother's grave like that? I made a vow to ask him as soon as we got out of here. One more to add to the long list of vows I seemed to be making lately.

We were in amongst stacks and stacks of crumbling scrolls now. Square stone pillars appeared between them at intervals, painted with Seth's sacred animals – snarling hyenas, a fierce boar piercing the moon with his tusks, roaring river-horses, braying donkeys with evil eyes, desert dust storms, black clouds spitting lightning, and altogether too many scenes of death and destruction. Khai's pointing hand turned this way and that, snaking left and right with a sureness that spoke of long familiarity. Then he held up his hand, and I stopped. He turned sideways, flattened his back against the scrolls, and began to edge around something in the floor. I followed, trying to match my footsteps exactly to his. Staring down at the tiles, I strained to see what we were avoiding, but in the faint green light I could see nothing unusual, except, perhaps, an almost invisible line in the stone.

Despite the protection of Khai's amulet, the feeling of malevolence was becoming almost unbearable now. I blocked out the chaotic pictures on the pillars and instead conjured up a vision of my goddess as I had last seen her, veiled, in that small room, painted with pictures of Her in all Her glory.

Isis is my shield and my protector, I whispered inwardly, believing it with all my heart. I wished I could hear her voice again, wished she would send me some sign that she was with me, but I knew that this was a test I would have to pass or fail on my own. The reek of foulness and hatred was almost tangible now, somewhere off to my right, and I broke into an icy sweat. Khai tugged on my hand urgently, leading me away from it, down a left-hand passageway, which was so narrow that the overhanging scrolls felt as if they would topple down onto my head at any moment. All I wanted was to get away as fast I could.

We stole along like thieves in the dark. Gradually I began to hear chanting. I couldn't make out any words, but the sound was dark and grim, rising and falling with monotonous regularity. It wasn't at all like the joyous songs of praise we had sung to Isis in the temple. The passage suddenly widened out, and we were in a small open space with a green donkey-headed statue right in the middle of it. I recognised it immediately. Then I saw a glint of red and white off to one side, and ran forward, forgetting that Khai was supposed to be leading. Bad mistake. My foot slipped sideways and into a small depression in the floor, where it hit something that made a loud click. Immediately there was a grinding rumble underneath me, and the donkey head let out a shattering bray that echoed and rang around us, drowning out the chanting. Khai jerked me sideways with all his strength and I fell on top of him as the floor opened at my feet. As we rolled, he pulled me upwards, all in one movement, and I could see his face go pale. The bottom of the hole was lined with sharp spikes, around which huge glowing cobras were writhing and hissing. I had been here before, except that now I had no way to dance across the pit. There was a moment of silence, in which I realised that the chanting had stopped, and then I heard yells and the pounding of feet on stone.

'Run!' said Khai in my ear, but I dug in my heels.

'The map!' I said. We were so close! I could see the skulls with their ruby eyes just up ahead, and the corner of a shelf just beyond. Surely the map box was just there, within my reach. I must get it! I must! Everything depended on it! I stretched out a hand towards it, but Khai was just as determined as me.

'No!' he said, hauling me away with a wrench that hurt my shoulder. 'No, Cleo! You promised. Come now, or we'll both die, and Isis's power will be gone forever!'

I heard a louder hiss from the hole, saw a shining, yellow-banded, brown body rear up, its hood extended. I ran, dodging round the still-howling statue, feeling a puff of air hit my heel as the cobra lunged and then a spatter of liquid. Had it bitten me? Oh, Isis, Isis! If it had, I would be dead in moments, the breath all stolen from my body. I ran anyway, leaping where Khai leaped, expecting my lungs to fail, to collapse at any second. With a deadly flat clunk, holes opened in the walls, and more glowing brown and yellow bodies slithered out, pouring down the scrolls and onto the ground behind us. Isis curse them – cobras were our royal sigil. How dare they come after me, a Ptolemy princess? A kind of reckless madness seized me. I skidded to a halt and turned to face them, holding up my free hand. I heard Khai moan behind me, felt his clutching fingers shake.

'Sisters! Brothers!' I said. 'I am of your blood, the blood of the Pharaohs. I serve the goddess Isis. Let me pass in peace.'

The snakes halted for one moment, swaying and

eyeing me with their dead gaze, then they surged forward again. I was still breathing, but I wouldn't be for much longer if they reached me.

'Run!' It was me shouting this time, and unlike me, Khai didn't hesitate. He took off like a long-legged desert hare, tugging me along with him, and I ran with him, back along the path we'd come until the snakes were left far behind. Pillars and scrolls flashed past, and then doors. Just as we ducked into the partially hidden entrance to the dark tunnel, we heard the *slap slap* of running feet. Khai's arm went round me and I buried my face in his shoulder, trying to muffle and control the heaving sounds coming out of my chest. We clung onto each other like burrs to a goat. More running feet! I envisaged a curtain of invisibility over the entrance.

Don't see! Don't see! Oh, Isis, please don't let them see!

Maybe my goddess was listening, maybe it was just luck, but eventually the sandals and shouts ran past, faded and were gone. I couldn't have let go of Khai even if I'd wanted to. The amulet between our hands was hot and pulsing and angry, and I felt it was welded to my palm. Hurrying as much as we could in the dark, listening for pursuit, we made our way up the tunnel, our rapid, panting breaths filling the close, dark air with a sound like an ironworker's bellows.

I had no idea how much time had passed since we left Captain Nail and his men, but I was now completely exhausted – in fact, I was stumbling and drooping so much that Khai had to hold me up. I'd had only a few hours sleep since Charm had reappeared, and my body was twitching with tiredness. I just wanted to lie down somewhere. I was too worn out for fear now. Instead, a dull disappointment filled my belly. We had failed. The map was still held by the brotherhood, and I saw no prospect of ever getting close to it again before the Dark Feast. The brotherhood would be more watchful, now, even though I didn't think they had seen us. They certainly wouldn't have known why we had been down there – and that was our only hope.

We came to an abrupt halt at the end of the tunnel. The library lay just ahead of us, behind the closed secret door.

'Cleo,' Khai said, then stopped, clearing his throat. He pressed his other hand against our two clasped ones, capturing mine in a double embrace, squeezing hard. 'Cleo, what were you thinking? You promised to obey me. You promised.' His voice was a low growl. 'When I saw you'd stepped on the trap, all I could think about was how to get you out of there...and then you argued.' I felt him shiver convulsively as he suddenly burst out, 'Bloody snakes! I hate those Isis-cursed things. How could you even imagine you could stop them?' His voice rose to a stifled shout, and his hands dropped mine, grasping my shoulders instead, shaking me back and forth for just one moment with a violence that made my teeth clash against each other. Then he stopped, hands falling to his side.

My body tensed, rage rising. How dare he treat me like that? I nearly struck him back. Then I heard his voice half catch on a soft sob.

'H-have you ever seen anyone die from a cobra bite, Cleo? I have, and it's horrible. His name was Embalmer Ibi – and he was my only friend down there. I... I couldn't do anything to save him. He swelled up and was gone in seconds. I can still see him choking, see the foam on his lips. If you'd been bitten back there, I couldn't have done anything to save you either...' His voice tailed away into silence, but the darkness finally gave me the ears to hear that the anger in it was because he'd been frightened for me.

My momentary rage drained away, and I leaned into him, putting up my freed hands to stroke his face, summoning up one last burst of energy. It hadn't been his fault I'd forgotten the rules he'd set.

'You saved me, Khai. If you hadn't pulled me away when you did, I would have died on those spikes. And you got us out, just like you promised you would. One of us will find a way back in. At least we know where the map is now. Maybe you can get it for me. Maybe it doesn't even have to be me.' Would it be against Isis's rules if he were the one to steal the map? Surely our goddess wouldn't mind who retrieved it as long as I carried it back to Philäe? Even as I thought it, a little niggling voice told me that she would mind, very much, but I chose to ignore it.

I felt a tremor go through Khai's body, then he straightened, as if bracing himself.

'I'll have to go back, Cleo. But if the Seth priests find out it was me down there with someone who's not a brother embalmer, I'm a dead man.' Then he laughed. It was not a funny laugh. 'I suppose I'm a dead man anyway if we don't get the map before the Dark Feast, aren't I?'

I closed my eyes, seeing again a vision of my bloodied hands and of his and Charm's bodies lying at my feet. I wouldn't let it happen. I wouldn't.

'They don't know, Khai. I'm sure no one saw us – unless you count that statue, and I would have seen if there'd been a god inhabiting it. If you go into the library now, and find a desk somewhere away from here, it will look as if you've been here all night.' I tried to think, though my brain felt as if it was made of thick, slow mud.

'Maybe I can bribe someone to say they saw you.' Would Apollonius do it for me? He was a cantankerous old man, but he did love me in his own way. Perhaps he would. I could try, anyway.

Khai shook his head again.

'No, Cleo. A bribe's too risky. Maybe you're right. If I sneak into my usual place in the library, they can't prove I wasn't there, working on my index. They may be suspicious, but they do trust me now. I've done good work sorting out all their scrolls into proper order. That's the reason they think I've been with them all these years, after all. They asked for a librarian, and they got one. They just didn't know I was Isis's spy first.' His right hand lifted to clasp mine again, and his left arm snaked around my waist, holding me tight.

'I'll have to go back to Tryphena later, you know. It'll look strange if I don't.'

I tensed once more. I couldn't help it. This time it wasn't rage rising, but an acid tide of jealousy that bubbled in my gut.

'If I see her stroking your hair just one more time, I'll bite her hand off,' I said savagely. 'Why can't she just leave you alone? Why can't she concentrate on seeing ambassadors and sorting out petitions like a proper Pharaoh? That's what my father used to do. Well, he did when he wasn't womanising and playing his flute.'

He laughed – a real one this time.

'Maybe I should shave all my hair off. Say it's a penance from Seth. She won't like me then.'

'Maybe you should,' I said, but my own fingers betrayed me by sinking themselves in its silken tangles. 'I'd like you just as well bald.'

'Little liar,' he said, his voice warm. And then he kissed me. It's surprising how much energy kissing gives you.

Some time later, I walked back to my rooms, trying not to yawn too openly. Captain Nail and the warriors surrounded me, their, long, brown, muscled (compared to mine, anyway) legs, covering the ground at a good clip. I had to concentrate hard to keep up without falling over. As soon as we were back in my rooms, I stumbled into the bedchamber and fell into my sheets. I barely had time to notice and return the tentative smile Charm gave me as she helped me out of my clothes and then climbed in beside me, hair crinkled and tousled-looking. I think I was asleep before my head hit the soft flax of the bolster on my head-rest.

I dreamed for the first time in days, floating above the gold and crystal of great Alexander's tomb, looking down on a pile of grubby rags that lay beside it.

Come to me, Beloved Daughter, said a voice I had never heard before. It was weak and old and far off, but it still sounded like the silent thunder of a waterfall in the distance. It was not Isis, I was sure of that, but it was definitely a goddess.

Who are you? I tried to call out, but I had no words in that place, and the dream soon faded into the darkness of deep sleep.

I woke to the smell of fresh hotcakes and honey, and the sound of a busy Charm. *Swish swish* went the familiar noise of a palm leaf brush.

'You can't still be cleaning,' I said sleepily, watching her through half-closed eyes. Her face was more swollen than ever, and the bruises had spread still further over her arms and legs. I knew if I said anything about resting I'd get my head snapped off faster than a feeding crocodile.

'Oh yes, I can. The stupid simoom was blowing early this morning, and there's dust got in everywhere. Can't you feel it?'

I ran a finger over my skin, sticky and clammy with sweat and sleep. The fine, sandy grit rasped under my touch, scraping me slightly.

'Ugh, yes. I see what you mean.' I inspected my arm. There were dirty smears all over it. I hadn't noticed them last night, but I must have got them from rolling around on the floor with Khai. Abruptly, I remembered. The map. I sat up in a rush, sleep falling away in an instant.

'We didn't get it, Charm,' I told her. 'Isis will be so angry with me. I'll have to try again. But we…we nearly got caught by the brotherhood.'

She tsked, palm brush whisking ever faster.

'You should let that boy of yours get it,' she said. 'No sense you putting yourself into danger again.'

I wanted to contradict her, but it was only what I'd suggested myself last night. Now that he knew where and what it was, Khai was the perfect person to steal the map. He could bring it to me, and then we could all leave together. I got out of bed, suddenly more cheerful, still wilfully ignoring the tiny voice that told me Isis would punish me if I didn't do the job she'd chosen me for specially, and get the map myself.

'I think I might need a bath, Charm,' I said, as I wiggled my toes and felt yet more grit under them. 'Would you be a dear and see to it, please?'

She turned, giving me a little bow.

'Would you prefer plain water, O Mighty Chosen, or warmed asses' milk with rose petals and gold sprinkles?' It was hard to tell with this new Charm whether the tone was her usual mocking of my orders or not. I chose to take it as if it was.

'The Mighty Chosen would just like to be clean, O Pearl Amongst Floor Sweepers. Plain water will be fine, and I'll do without the gold sprinkles, but if you felt like adding those rose petals you mentioned...' I looked at her with one eyebrow raised.

'Lucky I have some, then,' she said grumpily. 'Otherwise you'd make me go to the market with one of those Ra-bothered warriors, wouldn't you?'

Oh.

I clearly hadn't been completely forgiven, then.

'I'm afraid I would,' I said. 'Make you take a warrior, I mean. Sorry.'

Charm went to order the water with a distinctly annoyed swirl to her step, and when it came, she poured it for me with lips thin and pressed together, dumping in the petals before she left again. The silent treatment was back.

However, just as I was beginning to dry myself, picking small bits of dried red petal out from between my toes, there was a flurry of noise outside, and Charm rushed in, our tiff clearly forgotten.

'Oh, Cleo,' she said, her bruised face alight with emotion. 'Put this on and come quickly.' She threw me a robe, and I flung it round me and belted it, wondering what all the fuss was about. It couldn't be anything too horrible if Charm was smiling like a little girl who'd been given the moon. She took my hand and pulled me, still dripping a bit, into the outer chamber and then into the little courtyard with the mosaic fountain, which was crowded with my retinue. 'Look!' she whispered, pointing upwards in awe. I looked.

A flock of white and black ibises was circling, their wingtips outlined in gold against the shining orb of Ra. They were truly beautiful – a cloud of brightness against the blue sky – and a wonder to behold.

'Do you know what this means, Chosen?' Captain Nail said quietly, coming up to us.

I shook my head, my brain sifting through and discarding possibilities. Ibises were a common enough sight, weren't they? Obviously, they belonged to Isis, but I couldn't see that one flock meant anything special. They weren't in a shape, like the ones Isis had shown the river captain.

'Perhaps you hadn't heard that there have been no ibises seen in the palace grounds since your sisters came to power,' he said. 'Not one. For four long years.'

I hadn't heard. Now the sighting of the birds, and Charm's reaction to them, made sense. If the people of Alexandria saw the ibises returning, they would know that Isis was around the palace again. But what would that mean for me? I turned, pulling Charm closer. She'd know.

'Won't the people think that they're here for the Pharaohs?' I asked in a low voice.

She shook her head.

'Too many people have heard you're here by now, Cleo, and everyone knows what happened in the throne room when you arrived. Dhouti and Am told me that the cooks are already talking about you as if you're Isis returned to earth.' She snorted, quite in her old manner. 'If that's the way the kitchen gossip goes, you can be sure those rumours have already reached the streets.'

Captain Nail frowned, tapping a nail against one tooth.

'This will frighten the Pharaohs, I think, Chosen. If Isis, blessed be Her name, is showing her favour to you this openly, they will fear that power is shifting away from them and their vile god, and that may be dangerous for you. We must be even more careful than usual. One or both of our rulers may react badly to this.' He turned away, barking out new orders, and everyone scattered to their posts. I noticed he hadn't said how he thought Am-Heh would react. That was what was worrying me most. My sisters were only human – He was a god.

Charm raised one eyebrow at me.

'I'll just go back to sweeping the simoom away, shall I, Your High Holiness? Wouldn't want your newly immortal feet to be dirtied by mere dust, would we?'

I made a shocked face. 'Don't be disrespectful to my goddess, O Stupendous Sweeper of Floors. Or her representative on earth will smite you on the bottom.' I made a suggestive motion with the end of the cord that held my robe closed and chased her, smiling, into my chambers. Maybe things would be all right between us now.

Sure enough, a short while after the Pharaohs had returned from blessing the flood waters, I received a summons from Tryphena, commanding me to come to the Grove of Demeter at sunset. I knew the place. My father had often given parties there, dancing round the trees dressed as Dionysus and playing beautiful melodies on his flute. I remembered my mother laughing up at him, as he dropped the flute on a cushion and whirled her round in a mad maenad dance. Suddenly, I missed him unbearably, as I hadn't for years. Why was he still staying on in Rome, playing politics and sucking up to that devious Caesar person he owed so much money to? He had been a bad ruler – I knew that all too well by now

– but my sisters were worse by far. For all his drinking and merrymaking and flute playing, at least my father had taken his duty as a Pharaoh seriously – unlike the two of them. As far as I was concerned he still was the Pharaoh – and always would be. But my father wasn't here. I was, and I had a job to do. I spent the rest of the afternoon going over escape plans with Captain Nail and Charm, trying not to dread another long evening with my sisters. Cabar had sent a dove back, saying that fast camels would be waiting for us in the Jewish Quarter, near the Canopian Gate from tonight, stabled under the name of a Greek merchant called Alexander.

'How original,' I said. 'I'm sure my ancestor would approve. Perhaps I'll get really lucky and my camel will be called Bucephalus.'

Charm just looked at me, rolling her eyes.

'What?' I asked. 'I'm very grateful to Cabar, but honestly… Alexander? Couldn't she have been more creative?'

The afternoon progressed at the speed of a racing scarab beetle with a limp. Every time there was a knock at the door, my head went up, hoping for a message from Khai. But of course, there was nothing, only sycophantic notes and sumptuous gifts from courtiers who wished to curry favour with me after seeing the ibises. I tore the notes up and stamped on them, and had Charm pile the gifts in the closet. It wasn't the wisest thing I could have done, politically, but it made me feel better.

Even though I knew Khai couldn't try again for the map until tonight at the earliest, I still longed to hear that he was safe. Instead, my overactive imagination showed me pictures of him dancing attendance on Tryphena, flicking his beautiful black hair back and forth for her delectation. I closed my teeth on a snarl, my temper rising.

As sunset approached, I set off for the Grove of Demeter, dressed in deep blue robes, embroidered with peacock tail eyes, my mother's jewellery adorning my neck and arm. I appreciated old Nena's nod towards the goddess Hera, but tonight I felt less like the Queen of Heaven and more like a large frustrated hornet. I would have to keep a tight rein on my temper if I was to get through tonight without stinging somebody to death.

14

Petals and Plots

The shiny green leaves of the pomegranate trees were netted with tiny mirrors, which caught the light of the dying Eye of Ra, flashing jewel-like purples and reds over the assembled crowd of flower-garlanded courtiers lining the path on either side. The path itself was strewn ankle-deep with pink rose petals, and it led to a dais with a tall golden throne, on which Tryphena sat. For once I was truly thankful to see that Khai knelt in his usual place at her side – it meant he was safe, and hadn't been taken by the brotherhood.

Tryphena was dressed as the goddess Demeter, in a robe embroidered with overflowing cornucopias done in gold thread and precious stones of many colours. Flaring golden torches lit the scene about her. There were gilded sheaves of barley lying around her feet, and standing at her back was what looked like a whole chorus of nymphs and shepherds, dressed in filmy Grecian tunics and carrying lyres and pipes.

I stopped, taken by surprise at the carefully orchestrated scene. Behind me there was a series of muffled metallic clanks as Captain Nail and the warriors came to a hurried halt too. Mamo, just at my left shoulder with a large peacock feather fan, gave a small squeak as I stepped back onto his foot. What in the name of Hathor was going on?

Tryphena gave an imperious flick of her hand towards the choir, and the nymphs and shepherds started to sing:

Hail to the chosen of Isis,
Cleopatra, sister of Pharaohs!

Demeter-Nut, goddess of earth and sky,
Bids you approach, sister-daughter!
Praise! Praise to She who is mother of all Egypt,
Generous and wise!

I shook my head slightly to clear my ears. Had I heard right? What was all this 'sister-daughter' stuff they were singing about? Was Tryphena pretending to be Greek

Demeter now? Or Nut, mother of my own Isis? Or both? What a cheek! There was, of course, no sign of either goddess actually appearing, so it was all just an elaborate trick as far as I could see. What was my sister up to now? And where was Berenice?

I was very confused, but Tryphena was beckoning me forward, so I went, my sandalled feet sinking deep into the petals as an overwhelming and beautiful scent rose up around me, filling my nostrils with musky-sweet comfort. The courtiers on either side bowed low, though they didn't prostrate themselves, of course. In front of the Pharaoh, that would have been suicidally stupid, both politically and personally. There was a low susurration as I passed, like wind through corn.

Isissss. Isisssss.

My mind worked frantically as I approached the throne. Should I kneel before her as I had done before? Or should I go along with her charade, take on the mantle of Isis and stare my sister in the eye, goddess to goddess? I decided on the latter. Tryphena was clearly in a benevolent mood, even though the question of why Berenice was not present niggled away at me. I let my eyes scan the grove casually. No. Her Evilness definitely wasn't around, and that was very strange.

I reached the foot of the throne, and stood there,

waiting, as the choir trilled one last wavering note of praise. I kept my chin raised and my eyes up. I knew that if I saw Tryphena's hand on Khai, I would do as I'd promised and bite it off. He was not some pretty pet to be caressed. He was a person, and…and I loved him too much to put him in danger by showing my feelings for him in public.

I met Tryphena's gaze defiantly, wanting to rend and tear her to pieces for what she'd done to Charm, but she threw me completely by smiling. It was a tentative twitch of the lips at first, but then it blossomed into something that looked almost real. Now I was definitely more confused than ever. My sister hadn't smiled at me like that since I was very small. It was our father's smile, open, friendly, caring. I didn't trust it further than a cobra could spit venom.

'Chosen of Isis,' she said, her voice very clear, ringing out through the trees with the ease of one accustomed to being heard. 'Sister. We have been blessed. Sweet Isis has shown us a sign of her favour. Her sacred ibis have returned to their home today. All hail to Isis!'

'All hail to Isis!' roared the crowd.

'All hail to Isis!' bellowed Captain Nail and the warriors, clanging spears on shields.

'All hail to Isis,' I muttered, slightly stunned, as

Tryphena went on.

'We have summoned you, her chosen, here, to give you a gift, in celebration of this holy day.' She clicked her fingers once, and her fat adviser stepped forward with a small hammered silver chest, inlaid with ivory and studded with aquamarines and carnelians. His false oily smile was that of a vulture forced off a juicy carcass by a pack of hyenas.

'Your honoured mother, so sadly gone before us to the afterlife, left behind her certain jewels. We, in our incarnation as Demeter-Nut, would stand in her place, as we give you this gift.'

With that, the chamberlain flung open the lid to reveal a blinding array of many-jewelled necklets, earrings, bracelets, armbands, all set in buttery yellow gold. I recognised all my mother's old jewels with a small, wrenching grief.

I didn't know whether to laugh or cry. I couldn't believe her hypocrisy. She wanted to stand in my mother's place? Had she forgotten the scene at my mother's deathbed? Had she forgotten just why my mother was dead, and who had murdered her? And what was this sudden conversion to Isis's cause? Did she really think she could erase all the years of brutal sacrifices and Am-Heh worship with a few words and a smile? None of this showed on my face, of course. I had my impassive princess mask firmly welded in place again.

Inclining my head a fraction, I motioned for Warrior Haka to take the chest, searching for the right words to say. Those particular jewels of my mother's were tainted now. I didn't want them. I had the only jewels of hers I'd ever wear on my neck and arm already.

'Isis thanks the Pharaoh for her generous gift and her even more generous praise of one who was our Pharaoh father's truest love,' I said, ramming home my right to speak in the name of the only goddess who really mattered, and getting in a hearty dig on my mother's behalf at the same time. Then the perfect words flowed from me, as if Isis herself had put them in my mouth.

'My dearest mother would be honoured that you remember her so kindly. As a daughter I say to you that these jewels shall be used to adorn a golden statue of my mother as Holy Isis herself, to stand in the grounds of the Sema, where all true Ptolemy wives are buried.' It was the least I could do to make up for my horrible neglect of my mother's grave, and I knew Tryphena would get the unspoken message immediately.

She did. The smile cracked and faded.

'Very well,' she said, her voice several degrees colder. 'Let it be done.'

By uttering those words, the very ones used to sign off on every Pharaoh's written orders, she signalled that she would go along with me – for now. She was playing a dangerous game here, trying to play two sides of the obol at once, I realised. Am-Heh was the least forgiving of gods, and this sudden championing of Isis could be seen as a potential betrayal of the highest order.

As if the mere thought of Am-Heh brought him near, I shivered, sensing something bad close at hand. There was a movement among the trees, and Berenice walked out from among them, her usual retinue of Nubian guards, servants and black clad Am-Heh priests at her back. A cloud of darkness hung about her, and once again I caught a glimpse of long, cruel jaws, more like a crocodile's than a hound's. The god was here in person.

I could see that Tryphena somehow knew it too. Her face paled underneath its make-up, and swallowing as if her throat was suddenly dry, she bent down, whispering something in Khai's ear. He shuffled backwards, prostrating himself, then sprang up, shouldering his way through the choir. I tried not to let my eyes follow him, but I couldn't help it, just for one agonised moment. Where had she sent him? What was he doing? His absence made a tiny but perceptible gap just where my heart was.

'Naughty, naughty,' came Berenice's voice, harsh and overlaid with a cruel tone that sent shudders through me. 'Are you having a party without me? Did my invitation get lost? Dressed as a goddess, too! Do I smell a tiny hint of disloyalty to our lovely Am-Heh, sister mine?'

I wondered for a second which sister she was talking to.

'I didn't want to bother you with something so trivial, dear,' Tryphena said in a tone that cut like a blade. 'I know how much you hate fancy dress. This was just a little something to remind our dear Cleopatra how highly we regard her – a few jewels...a rustic party, nothing special.'

Berenice was stalking through the crowd of courtiers now, and wherever the shadow around her touched, people wept and trembled, their faces damp with cold sweat. The mirrors on the trees reflected only darkness and a faint glimmering of lamps now. Ra's Eye had fallen behind the horizon, and it was night.

There was a sudden scream as Berenice's arm shot out, grabbing a courtier by the throat, a young girl clad in a pretty sky blue dress, with a garland of sapphire-petalled flowers in her hair.

'You!' she spat. 'Daughter of a drunken donkey's

vomit. How dare you look at your Pharaoh with disrespect?'

'I… I didn't…' the girl choked out.

'Do you dare to contradict me, spawn of a syphilitic monkey?'

The girl tried to shake her head, but Berenice's grip was too strong. She thrust her at the priests. 'Take her to the blessed crocodiles. And make sure she receives Am-Heh's most special mercy. I want it to take a very long time.' Her tongue came out and licked her lips, caressing the words. 'A very, very long time.'

I wanted to step forward, to countermand the order, but it was as if my arms and legs were held in iron shackles, my tongue paralysed in my mouth.

Be still, my Chosen, said the familiar voice, full of the music of desert storms, smooth and sweet as honey dripping from the comb.

This is her fate, and it is not your place to act here. Her sacrifice is not unnoticed. I will escort her soul to the afterlife myself when the time comes. Remember that.

For the first time in ages I wanted to shout and scream at my goddess. I was too angry to moderate my tone.

Really? I thought at her. *You speak to me here? Now? Why couldn't you save that girl, or Dennu or Charm? Or that poor little Nefertem acolyte? Do you actually want*

Am-Heh to win? Since I couldn't move a muscle, I raged at her in my head.

She cut off my furious thought tirade like a dam in a stream, and her voice now rang in my ears like the roar of a thousand lions in the night.

Do not dare to judge me! Seek out my enemy's map, above all else, and do not be tempted by the easy path, or I cannot be answerable for what will happen. Your destiny will no longer be in my hands alone.

Just as suddenly as it had come, my goddess's presence left me. My limbs felt as limp as an unstrung puppet, and I staggered forward one step, before forcing myself upright again. It took all my determination to do so. Isis had never chastised me before, and my head hurt as if a blunt axe had battered the inside of it for the last ten days and nights.

The girl's piteous screams were fading into the darkness now, and I saw Berenice slump slightly, as the black shadow of Am-Heh left her and glided after the priests, presumably to oversee their grisly task.

'Dear me,' said Tryphena, her face still pale. 'Well, that was a little unfortunate.' She clapped her hands.

'Music!' she commanded. 'Song! Let us have something cheerful, for Ra's sake.' She shook her finger playfully at Berenice. 'Spoiling my little party like that, dear sister,' she scolded, as if dragging an innocent off to be sacrificed was no more than breaking a nail. As the music started up again, Khai reappeared beside her, holding a delicate glass goblet, rimmed with gold, and filled with a deep red liquid that looked uncannily like blood. He knelt, offering it to her with his head bowed, and his hands high above his head. I hated to see him in such a servile position.

'Ah, my pomegranate juice,' she said. 'Taste it for me, there's a dear.' She watched him like a cat does a mouse while he took a sip. I held my breath, praying that it wasn't poisoned, as four slaves struggled to fit a second golden throne onto the little dais. Barley sheaves fell like ranks of slashed down soldiers, and I saw one slave kick them surreptitiously out of the way. The time of Demeter-Nut was definitely at an end – even the crushed rose petals now smelled fetid and rank after Am-Heh's noxious touch.

Berenice stood there for a moment glaring out at everyone, ignoring her throne.

'Where are the dancers?' she asked petulantly. 'It's a party. Why aren't there dancers?' Immediately, the lyres and pipes struck up a rustic dance, and a troupe of performers appeared, as if by magic. Such was the power of the Pharaoh, whose every wish or command was anticipated. But Berenice grimaced with disgust.

'Oh, really, sister dear,' she said. 'Couldn't you have found better than these uncouth street rats to entertain you? I don't think I can be bothered to watch any more. There's better fun to be had elsewhere.' She directed a feral smile at both of us, and stalked off in the direction the priests had taken with the girl, followed by her guards. I felt almost ill with hatred of her. She was vile and contemptible and just like the most evil of my ancestors. She was the worst kind of Pharaoh possible. Why did Isis not strike her down?

When she was out of sight, Tryphena reached over Khai's head and patted the throne beside her. 'Come. Sit, Cleopatra,' she said. 'See how you like the feel of it. Who knows, some day soon one of these might even be yours.' She paused, giving me a very direct look. 'Life is so uncertain here in Alexandria. If you take my meaning.'

The music wasn't helping my pounding head, but even the stupidest brain could have worked that one out. My sister really was trying to play both sides of the game if she was offering me a chance to be Pharaoh at her side. Not that I wanted the job on her terms, but still . . . I sat down heavily on the cushioned golden seat, trying to ignore the warmth of Khai, kneeling between us, still as a statue. Small flickers of lightning flashed inside my eyeballs, and everything seemed bathed in a sickly green aura as I looked out over the courtiers, chattering brightly and artificially as the whirling dancers capered and leapt. I would not be sick this time, I told myself firmly, battling to keep the nausea down. I could not. My sister raised the glass to her lips and tipped back her head, draining the blood red liquid in one long gulp. Then she tapped Khai on the shoulder.

'Bring the chosen some pomegranate juice,' she said. 'In fact, I need more too, so bring us a pitcher. And something to eat. You know what I like, my own sweet Khai.'

My hands curled into fists. Her own sweet Khai? How dare she? I bit down hard on my tongue, drawing blood, to keep the hot words behind my teeth. It made me feel even sicker. Then Khai crawled away backwards, and was gone.

'Off you go too, Pothinus,' she said, flapping a hand at her oily adviser. 'Go and sort some of those boring papers you're always bringing me or something.'

He went, shooting me another nasty look. Pothinus. I'd have to remember that name.

We were alone and private – or as alone and private as a Pharaoh could ever be. Tryphena leaned in close, putting her lips to my ear. She smelled heavily of jasmine and patchouli, mixed with sour fear sweat. I pressed my lips together, feeling my stomach rise. I would not be sick. I could not.

'Tell me how to win the favour of Isis again,' she whispered. 'I can see I have made a terrible mistake. I wish to restore *ma'at*, bring back balance to the throne. I wish to return to the gods of our ancestors. I know you can help me. Please, Cleopatra. For the sake of our beloved Egypt.'

Ma'at is the feather which balances the scales of the soul. You could have knocked me backwards with it. A part of me wanted not to believe this, to see it as some sort of trap. But I could hear the fear and sincerity in her words. I thought she meant them – at least for as long as it suited her to. Maybe this was my chance to bring at least one of the Pharaohs back to Isis. But I had to be sure she was serious. I turned slightly towards her, putting my hand over my mouth to hide it.

'What brought this on?' I asked, my lips barely moving. 'And why now? Why should my goddess show you any mercy after what you've done?'

Her eyes rose to meet mine, but faltered at the last moment. She looked down at her hands, clasped in her lap, the knuckles white.

'I-I know I've done terrible things,' she said. 'Berenice

and I…we've always liked the darker side. We…well, you probably wouldn't understand.'

Too right, I thought.

'It was partly your slaves…'

I growled, low in my throat, and she flinched back a bit.

'So loyal to you and Isis. Apparently neither of them would say anything at all, whatever the priests did to them. It was so admirable. And then, this afternoon, the birds returning. That was what decided me. Isis is a strong goddess, and…and I don't want to burn in the Devourer's lake of fire.' She put one hand on mine. It was hot and dry and felt like it might go up in flames at any moment.

'I just want to make amends,' she said, squeezing my fingers hard enough to hurt. 'I want to go to the afterlife and face the gods with a clean conscience. A Pharaoh has few friends, and fewer who are loyal, I know, but I have none – only my sweet, sweet Khai. I really don't know what I'd do if I lost him.' She sighed in a way that made my teeth clench, and I cursed Cabar yet again. Her stupid desire for a spy at the Pharaoh's side had backfired badly. If Tryphena found out about me and Khai, she'd turn to Am-Heh again faster than a dog could snap a rat's back.

What was I to do here? However much I hated the

thought, this was a real opportunity to enter an alliance, to throw Berenice off the Double Throne, and take one side of it for myself. It was a chance to stamp on Am-Heh and his foul priests, throw them out of the palace and bring my own goddess back to her rightful place. It seemed like the perfect opportunity – except that I'd found that perfect opportunities were much like scorpions. They usually had a sting in the tail. My goddess had just ordered me to seek out the embalmer's map above all else. She'd also told me not to be tempted by the easy path. So I wouldn't be.

I'd play for time instead. I needed air, badly, and a few hours to think. My headache and sickness had receded, but still lurked, waiting.

'I will go and consult Isis,' I said, still keeping my voice down. 'We can't talk here, anyway.'

She nodded.

'I will do whatever it takes to get back into the goddess's favour,' she said. 'Berenice and I leave just after dawn for the Blessing of the River Ships. I will send for you on my return. Don't fail me, Cleopatra. You have much to gain from this.'

Yes, I thought. *Like spending the rest of my undoubtedly short life wondering when you're going to stab me in the back. I don't think so!*

I left her moodily tapping a foot to the music, with a crowd of sycophantic courtiers queuing up to flatter her and tell her how marvellous she was. Her eyes darted round restlessly, and I knew she was looking for Khai.

Some of the courtiers drifted towards me, looking hopeful, but Captain Nail fixed them with his most ferocious glare, and they veered away hurriedly. He knew me very well by now. I didn't want to play politics or indulge in vacuous conversation with people who only wanted to talk to me for their own advantage. I'd spent long enough in the world outside Alexandria to realise that the Greeks who made up the bulk of courtiers in the palace thought they were better than everyone else in the city, let alone in the rest of Egypt. I didn't like that. It simply wasn't true, anyway. Captain Nail was a hundred times better than any of them, and he was Egyptian to the last drop of his blood.

As we went back through the gardens, I caught a glimpse of Khai, carrying a large pitcher and a covered tray of something that let out small wisps of steam in the still air, trailing out behind him like tiny ghosts. Should I try to catch up to him? Was it worth the risk? I hesitated, then turned back on myself, and quickened my pace to cut him off.

'What are you doing, Chosen?' Captain Nail asked.

'I have to see Khai,' I said quickly. 'I'll just be a minute. Wait here.'

But of course, he didn't. He gave some swift orders to the rest of the warriors, and wheeled round to march beside me.

'This is not the wisest course of action, Chosen,' he said.

I knew it, but by now I could tell Khai had seen me. He stopped, put the pitcher and tray down, and bent as if to fasten a loose sandal. There was a secluded alcove just off the path, and I ducked into it, the delicate, butterfly wing petals of bougainvillea brushing my head.

'Chosen, no!' Captain Nail hissed.

I ignored him, and moments later, Khai had slipped in beside me, a small questioning frown wrinkling his forehead. I reached up and kissed him, hard.

'Think of that every time she puts her hands on you,' I said fiercely. I knew it was unfair. I knew it was dangerous and stupid, but I just needed to have him near me, to erase the memory of her touch on him, even if it was only for an instant.

'Is that it?' he asked, his face incredulous and his tone withering. 'You just wanted to kiss me? Was marking me as your property really worth putting everything at risk for? If one of her spying toadies sees me with you, we're

303

probably both dead. I thought it was something really urgent, or I'd never have come.'

I felt as if he'd kicked me in the belly, and then the realisation crashed over me. He was right. In that one selfish moment I'd used him just as much as Tryphena ever had. I was no better than my sister.

'I-I'm so sorry, Khai,' I stammered. 'I-I didn't…'

He cut me off, his hands gripping my shoulders, shaking me.

'There's no time for any of that now, Cleo. I'll get the map as soon as I can tonight and bring it to you. Stay in your rooms till I come, and by Isis, you'd better be ready.' His eyes were like black stones, and they met mine sternly. 'Please tell me there's an escape plan in place?'

I nodded mutely.

'Good. At least you listened to me on that.' He peered round, looking for danger, wary as a leopard at bay, then turned back to me. 'I have to go to her now. She'll be wondering where I am, and she doesn't like cold food.' His eyes might look hard as stones, but he cupped my chin with one hand, running a gentle thumb over my lips, telling me without words that I was forgiven. 'Stay here – and pray to Isis we haven't been seen.' Then he was gone, swift and sure, walking away as if nothing had happened at all. I watched through the screen of thorny striped stems and green leaves as he picked up his burdens again and went off quickly down the long marble-tiled path, not looking back even once.

Oh Isis, how I wished this were all over. If only Khai succeeded in getting that wretched map out, we could all leave at dawn, be away from this poisonous sink of intrigue and death. But Isis's voice beat on my brain insistently.

Seek out my enemy's map, above all else, and do not be tempted by the easy path, or I cannot be answerable for what will happen.

I was just about to leave the bower when those words became a horrible reality. In the distance, four kilted Nubian guards stepped out in front of Khai. They seized him by the arms, so that the pitcher and tray fell to the ground with a clatter. Pomegranate juice spilled over the white marble like a flood of dark blood. Khai let out just one muffled cry, before they dragged him away. I bit back a horrified scream and started after him, but Captain Nail snatched me back.

'No, Chosen,' he growled as I fought against him, tearing my arms and hands on the bougainvillea thorns, petals falling around me like tears. 'I will not let you be taken too. There is nothing you can do for him now.'

I struggled even more, cursing at him, feeling my

heart tear in two. It was all my fault. Khai had been right to be angry with me – and so had my goddess. How could I have been so selfish? My own possessive desire had ruined everything. One of the Evil Sows had the boy I loved, and I needed to find out which, and fast, before they killed him. Was this really Isis's punishment for not going after the map myself? Surely she couldn't be so cruel? But I knew she could and would. It wasn't as if she hadn't tried her best to give me advance warning.

'We must rescue him! We must!' I said, beating my bloody hands on Captain Nail's chest. But the sad look in his eye told me that my chances were not good.

Not good at all.

15

Blackmail and Betrayal

All the way back to my chambers, my mind had been turning over plans and rejecting them.

We would storm the dungeons!

No.

Not enough men.

I would enlist Cabar.

No.

She would probably just kill me for exposing her.

Isis would strike Khai's captors dead.

Definitely no.

She hadn't saved Charm and Dennu, had she? And she was angry with me already.

Frustrated and frantic to find a way through this, I pushed past Captain Nail and slammed open the doors to my chambers with a bang.

The scene that met my eyes stole every last breath from my lungs.

Dhouti, Am and the warriors we'd left behind stood helpless in one corner of the room, each with a Nubian guard's silver spear tip at his throat. Charm was lying face up on the floor, her sore wrists bound to her ankles. She was making small whimpering sounds. Berenice, lounging on a low couch, had her foot on my best friend's throat. The black Am-Heh cloud hovered at her back. It was giggling – if a hound could giggle like a madman.

I should have been afraid. Instead, I was instantly so enraged that I felt as if a small furnace had ignited inside my brain.

Now I knew exactly which Evil Sow had taken Khai.

'Get. Your. Foot. Off. Charm,' I said, biting off each word as if it was a piece of her smooth, scented flesh. She smiled. This was definitely not our father's smile. It was evil and calculating and cruel.

'I hardly think you're in a position to make demands, dear sister,' she said, her voice lazy and smug. 'But I suppose she doesn't really make a very comfortable footstool.' She withdrew her foot and kicked Charm in the ribs. 'Move, you worthless rat dung.'

Charm rolled aside, groaning. I went to her, as a clash

of spears broke out at my back. Captain Nail and the warriors who had been with me were attacking. I bent hurriedly to undo the bonds tying her.

'Are you all right?' I whispered.

'Been better,' she croaked.

I felt a small prick at my throat.

'Stop! Or your mistress dies!' Berenice had raised her voice only slightly, but it was enough that the crash and clang of fighting men stilled immediately. 'Throw down your spears and shields.'

I looked up, disregarding the long scratch the sharp knife tip left down my neck. Was it poisoned? In my fury, I didn't care.

Captain Nail's whole face was frozen in an impotent snarl of rage.

'Do it!' I said to him, putting all the force of command I could behind the words. I thought for one moment that he would disobey. But then his expression smoothed itself out into an impassive mask, almost as good as mine, and he nodded once. There was a clatter of dropped weapons and shields, and soon he and the other warriors had joined the men already held. Only my little Mamo stood free, shaking with fear, his peacock fan drooping and limp at his side. Charm lay on the floor, still bound, her eyes glaring black murder at Berenice. I knew she felt the same way I did, but I was as helpless as she was just now. I sent her a pleading look.

Don't do anything stupid. Don't get yourself killed.

Her eyes met mine, sending the exact same message back to me.

Berenice took the knife away and patted the couch beside her.

'Come. Sit. I think we should have a little chat.'

'What do you want?' I asked, keeping my voice as steady as I could. I wanted to gouge her eyes out with my nails, but if I did, my people would die. So I locked it all down deep inside me.

'Here's the thing,' she said. 'I have something I think you want very much. And I think you could help me get something I want very much. We could make a lovely bargain – a life for a life, if you see what I mean.'

'I don't,' I said, though I feared I did. 'Why don't you explain?'

Berenice tittered.

'Oh dear. You're going to be difficult. What fun!' she said. 'Very well, then. A little bird tells me you're very fond of our Tryphena's library boy.'

I tensed, I couldn't help it. We were sitting so close together that Berenice felt it at once. 'Now don't deny it, dear. You can pretend all you want, but my little bird says you've been doing all sorts of naughty things together. You know,' she leant in close, shaking her head in mock outrage. 'Cleo and library boy in a palm tree, k-i-s-s-i-n-g.'

I saw Mamo drop to his knees suddenly.

'Mamo is so sorry, great lady,' he whispered in Amharic. 'He had to tell or…or the Magnificence would have killed his brother.'

So that was it. No wonder he'd told Berenice everything he'd seen. I cursed myself again for not being more careful.

'Even the greatest warrior has a weakness, my boy child,' I said. 'Do not be ashamed. I forgive thee.'

Berenice pouted. 'I'd forgotten you spoke worm boy's language,' she said. 'Such a waste of brain space, all those foreign words, but then you always were a scholar, hiding out in that stupid library.' She made the words 'scholar' and 'library' sound unclean. 'Now, what about our little bargain?'

I took a deep breath. What should I say here? What bargain did Berenice want to make in return for Khai's life? Should I pretend to be as ruthless as her, make out that I didn't care about him? No – she'd already felt my reaction. She'd see straight through it.

Isis! I prayed. *Dear Isis! I'll do anything, but please help me. Please tell me what to do here.*

But there was no answer. I was on my own, just like I had been when my mother died. Very well, then. I would have to do the best I could with no divine help. I decided to risk it.

'What little bargain?' I asked, ice in my tone. 'I don't remember agreeing to any bargain.'

'Let's see if we can change that, shall we?' she said, smiling that evil, calculating smile again. 'Bring her.' Getting up, she snapped her fingers, and two Nubian guards fell into place beside her. Two others came towards me, their hands out.

'Do NOT touch me,' I said. 'I will walk on my own.'

Berenice sighed.

'If she tries to run, do feel free to skewer her with those lovely sharp spears of yours, boys,' she said. 'Actually, do it if she even wriggles a finger in the wrong direction. I'd like to see if Isis chooses to save her chosen, or if it's all just a big fat fib. Like her pretending not to care about library boy.' Without another word, she walked out of the room. The black cloud of Am-Heh rushed past me as she left. It did not touch me, and I was truly thankful for that. I didn't think I could have borne its hateful miasma on my skin. I saw Captain Nail's agonised glance as I passed. I did not turn my head for a last look at Charm. I didn't dare, for fear of the threatened skewering. I just hoped that they would still all be alive when I got back.

If I got back.

I followed Berenice to her rooms, the guards exactly one pace behind me, hemming me in. This close I could see the grubby stains on their white kilts, and smell their sweaty, unwashed male bodies and the stale iron tang of old blood. I breathed in through my mouth so as not to have their scent in my nostrils.

I knew where we were going as soon as she pressed the carved acanthus leaf and a section of wall slid back to reveal a door. This was the Pharaohs' secret route to the dungeons, the one Khai had told me about. As we walked down the shallow stone steps, I tried to steel myself for what I would find there. The air was still and damp, filled with the smell of burning oil and a faint fishy odour that became stronger with every step. There were closed and bolted doors on either side. Storage rooms? Priests' quarters? Torture chambers? I couldn't tell. Soon I began to hear the sound of water.

'Blessed of Am-Heh,' said a harsh voice up ahead of me – a priest, I thought. 'We were not expecting you. Do you wish to visit the sacrifices?'

Sacrifices? Oh no! My heart began to pound. Khai could not have been sacrificed already, could he? Berenice would not have offered to trade me his life otherwise. Doubt crept into my mind like grey fog. Surely – oh, *surely* – she wouldn't have killed him if she wanted me to cooperate? But who else could they have down here? Then it came to me.

The girl in the blue dress – of course, it must be her. I shivered. She was still alive, then – but the cowardly part inside me shrank from seeing what had been done to her. I thrust it away. She deserved better from me than that. I probably couldn't rescue her, but she deserved that her suffering should be witnessed by someone who would remember her and send up prayers for her. Isis's words came back to me.

I will escort her soul to the afterlife myself. Remember that.

It was a terrible thought, but if Isis took the girl's soul, then she had to be present at her death when it came – and come it would, I was horribly aware of that. Maybe my goddess would hear my prayers if she was actually in the same room as me. It was all I had to pin my hopes on now – what hopes I had left, anyway.

The guards pushed me out into a wide circular space with several arched openings leading off it. Berenice went through the nearest, following the priest. It led past a series of barred niches in the walls, just deep enough for a man to stand up in and no more, and then out again into a larger room with a deep pool at its back, barricaded off with a spiked metal gate with thick chains to raise it up and down, and further chains running to it over the floor. Evil slitted green eyes and snouted nostrils floated in the still water, just visible in the dim light. The smell of old, rotten fish and damp stone was overwhelming.

Khai was shackled by the feet to one of the chains, the girl in the blue dress to the other. Both seemed unconscious, but Khai, to my relief, looked unharmed, apart from a trickle of crusted blood over his left eyebrow. The poor girl in the blue dress was another matter. Like Charm, she was covered in bruises, and her clothing was ripped to shreds. Sapphire petals from her lovely garland lay crushed and bloodied about her. I wanted to run to her, to comfort her, but I could see the faint shining of her *ka* beginning to emerge around her lips. I could see that she hung on to life only by a thread.

The priest went over to the gate, and started to crank it open with the larger of two wheels. The high, rusty creak it made screamed through my brain, reviving memories of the headache Isis had caused earlier. Soon the gate was half open, and the water surged and rippled slightly, lapping out onto the floor, as the crocodile eyes and nostrils swam forward and began to crawl out, their claws making a slight clicking sound on the stone. They were giants, there was no other word for it. They had iron collars round their necks, attached to more chains running back into the darkness behind them.

Berenice moved to stand beside me, as the priest chanted a monotonous litany of praise to Am-Heh. I tried not to listen to the evil, ugly words.

'Time for that demonstration. We'll see how much it takes to make this little bargain of ours, sister mine,' she said. My two guards came one step closer, pressing their spear tips against my neck, so that I couldn't move without a vein being slit. I didn't say a word. If I'd opened my mouth just then, I would have screamed obscenities at her, and that would have helped no one. So I fixed my eyes on Am-Heh, who was now crouched astride his two crocodiles, long jaws slavering with red drool, glaring my hatred at him. I knew nobody else was aware that he was actually there in the flesh – except maybe Berenice. If I hadn't seen gods around me all my life, I would have been even more terrified inside than I already was. But I wouldn't give that Evil Sow or her foul patron the satisfaction of seeing me quiver and shake.

Turning to the chanting priest, she motioned with one hand. 'I believe the Devourer is hungry for his sacrifice,' she said, confirming my guess. 'Shall we give the chosen here a nice look at what will happen to her precious library boy if she doesn't cooperate?'

The priest was tall and muscular and strong. It didn't take much effort for him to turn the smaller wheel. The chains holding the girl in the blue dress tightened, and her body began to slide across the floor, feet first. I knew what was going to happen, and for a second time, I could do absolutely nothing to prevent it. I began to pray to Isis.

Please, I begged. *Please keep your promise. Please come and get her soul. She's done nothing wrong. Don't let the Devourer take her. Don't let her go to the fire.*

As the girl – oh, how I wished I knew her name – slid closer and closer to the water, foul Am-Heh began to caper and giggle with glee. The chained crocodiles thrashed and snapped their jaws. Suddenly, the girl opened her eyes. A tiny despairing bleat came from her mouth as she saw them. I don't think she had the energy for anything more. And then, so quickly that I let out a horrified gasp, they were on her, jaws ripping and tussling as they tore her apart. I both heard and felt the mist of warm red droplets spatter on my feet.

Am-Heh leered obscenely, reaching out a curved claw to smear heart blood on his long, hound muzzle, licking it with his fiery tongue.

I couldn't, wouldn't look away. I'd promised to be her witness. I owed her that at the very least. I would not be sick. I *would* not.

The crocodiles quickly pulled her remains under the water and swam away with them. I saw a small sparkle as the girl's *ka* body rose from the spreading ripples, hovering above them like silver mist. She had a confused expression on her face, as if she didn't quite know what was happening. Am-Heh reached for her, his jaws gaping wide. Invisible fire was about him now, setting the water ablaze with a red-gold light. If he took her now, she was lost forever.

ISIS! I cried out wordlessly. *ISIS!* Then my goddess was there, reaching out a hand to the girl's spirit, opening a door in the air and handing her through to the jackal-headed god on the other side. I saw her *ka* form step into Anubis's reed boat, and then she was gone. Safe.

Isis came to me then as she never had before. I felt her slide within me, filling me with power. Even weakened as she was, her presence within me was almost more than I could bear and I turned to my sister, ignoring the spear points digging into me. I knew they could not hurt me now.

Am-Heh had slithered over to Berenice, surrounding her with a black shroud, and his hound muzzle overlaid her features like a strange mask.

'You dare!' she snarled, her voice hissing and strange, full of the sound of flame on wet grass. 'You dare to rob me of my sacrifice! This is MY place.'

I laughed.

It was not my laugh, but the laugh of a goddess, and it tore at my throat with honey-coated claws.

'You forget yourself, hound,' I said. 'You may not devour an innocent soul. She must submit to the judgement of Osiris and Thoth. There will be a reckoning from the Ennead if you break the rules again.'

They were not my words, but the words of a goddess, and my chest echoed with the sound of a thousand angry bees.

'Beware the path you tread, O Pharaoh,' Isis said with my mouth. 'Beware the company you keep. The Devourer will not rule in MY palace forever. Think what you do, for the reckoning of the nine gods awaits you also.'

Then, quite suddenly, she was gone, out of my body. I saw her catch Am-Heh by the scruff of his hound's neck, drag him out of my sister and fling him into the far depths of the pool, where he disappeared.

Both Berenice and I fell to our knees, gasping for breath. The priest was prostrate and writhing on the floor, muttering prayers to his foul master, and the guards had retreated back into the doorway, their eyes wary and a little wild. They were brave men, but they had just heard the gods speak, and that was hard for any mortal, as I knew very well.

I was the first to scramble to my feet. Khai was stirring, and as he opened his eyes, he saw me.

'Cleo,' he murmured. 'Cleo, what…?'

I put my finger to my lips.

Berenice wiped her own lips with the back of her hand, as if to scrub away a vile taste. Then she stumbled across to the priest and kicked him.

'Get up, fool,' she said. 'Close the gate.'

But he just clutched at her feet, still muttering prayers and praise to Am-Heh. She shook him off and turned to her guards.

'Why have you left your posts? I shall have you whipped.'

The two Nubians who had been guarding me slunk towards me, fear on their faces, the spears in their hands shaking visibly.

'Really, Berenice,' I said irritably, flipping a dismissive hand at her guards. 'Where do you think I'm going to run off to? Now, release Khai, and we can all be on our way.'

She had seen the power my goddess wielded, even weakened as she was, in Am-Heh's stronghold. She couldn't possibly refuse me.

But she did. She shook her head.

'I think you've forgotten the matter of that little bargain I mentioned, Cleopatra.'

I wanted to slap her so badly it hurt.

'We have no bargain,' I said. 'Your god has been banished by my goddess. End of story. Now, let us go.'

Again she shook her head.

'I don't feel any gods here now,' she said. 'So I believe I still hold the power, don't I? I can kill your precious library boy in an instant.' Her hand went to the thin-bladed knife at her waist. 'I will only let him go if you do exactly as I want.'

If I'd still had the power of Isis just then, I would have blasted her to ash. She held all the Senet pieces here, though, and I would have to go along with her, for the moment.

'What do you want, then?' I asked. It was an effort not to let my shoulders slump.

'Didn't I tell you already? Silly me! I want the throne, of course,' she said bluntly, finished with playing games. 'For myself. I want to be the only Pharaoh in Egypt. So you're going to help me get rid of darling Tryphena.'

I felt my jaw begin to drop, and clamped it shut before it could. The only Pharaoh in Egypt? It was against all the laws of *ma'at*. The lack of a second Pharaoh queen at his side after Tryphena and Berenice's mother died was what had finally turned the people against my father and tipped him off his own throne. Egypt must be balanced between two rulers – it was the law of all the gods. Everyone knew it.

Berenice must be mad.

It was only at that moment that I realised she actually *was* mad – god-touched in entirely the wrong way.

'And how do you suggest I do that?'

'Let me give you an incentive,' she said. 'For every hour that passes from now, the priest will give your precious library boy one quarter turn of the wheel. I'd say you have until about dawn tomorrow to save him from my god's lovely crocodiles. They'll want a fresh meal by then.'

I saw Khai give a convulsive jerk at her words, but he didn't let out a sound. The chains holding him clanked dully at the movement.

Berenice smiled. 'I don't think he likes that idea very much,' she said.

I didn't like it either. If I helped her, I would be no

better than any of the other sister-murderers in my family. If I didn't help her, Khai would die horribly. Not much of a choice. I would have to play along with her and convince her that I had a plan which would work.

'Poison,' I said, thinking out loud.

Berenice snorted wetly, much like the sow I was always calling her. 'Don't be stupid. She has tasters. We all do.'

'No,' I said slowly, remembering something Cabar had told me. 'Not in the food. I know someone who specialises in undetectable poisons. She might have something which would work in another way. Perhaps something like the cloak Deianeira gave Heracles.' I knew she'd know the tale of how Heracles died. Stories like that were part of our Greek heritage. We'd all taken them in with our mothers' milk.

She nodded.

'That could work. And then I can flay the cloth merchant who provided the material. Go and talk to this someone, then. And don't fail, or your boy here dies.' She prodded the priest with one foot. He was kneeling now. 'You hear that, imbecile? One quarter turn of the chain for every hour that passes.'

'Yes, Blessed of Am-Heh,' he said, his harsh voice cracked and afraid. 'I understand.'

Behind her back, Khai's eyes caught mine. I looked at him pleadingly, hoping he'd understand that this talk of poison was all a ruse to save him, hoping that he'd know I wasn't really a murderess.

'Don't worry about me, I'll be fine, Chosen,' he said, heartbreakingly formal. It was too late to pretend I didn't care.

'I know you will,' I said, putting all my love for him into those four words. I couldn't just leave him to Am-Heh, could I? I felt like I was being torn in two. The Dark Feast of Serapis started at dawn tomorrow, and my angry goddess was waiting for her map. The fate of Isis and all Egypt was in the balance – and Berenice had just upped the stakes to include the Double Throne. Right now I didn't feel I had a choice, though. I would rather be blasted from the earth and have it crumble under me than live in a world without Khai or Charm.

'Much as I hate to break up this touching scene, I should remind you that time is wasting,' said Berenice with a meaningful glance at the priest and the wheel. 'Come with me, Cleopatra.' Turning, she walked out of the door, with her guards trailing at her heels. I followed, leaving my heart behind me.

It was fully light before I finally got away from her revolting presence. She made me walk beside her litter as she left to meet Tryphena for the Blessing of the Ships, just for the pleasure of taunting me with threats and sly references to tightened chains. Finally, I lost my temper.

'Do you want me to do this or not? If you want me to find the poisoner, I have to leave right now,' I hissed, as we passed the Sema, where all my ancestors lay in their tombs. She smirked evilly, making a ripping apart motion with her hands.

'Go then! You're no fun anyway. But come to me as soon as you get back to the palace. Dawn tomorrow, remember!'

I felt soiled and disgusted with the lies I'd had to tell, and the bargains I'd had to make. I might hate Tryphena, but I didn't want to murder her – especially not after our conversation in the Grove of Demeter. It was Berenice I really wished ill towards – but unfortunately she had me exactly where she wanted me. I'd eventually managed to make her agree to let Charm and the rest of them go, by promising that she could leave her Nubians on guard outside the door to my chambers. If they were left alone, I was sure they could escape via the slave passages – if Captain Nail didn't go all noble and refuse to leave. I sighed. I could just see him doing it, too. Even Charm wouldn't be able to bully him.

I was so tired, and so torn between duty and love that I couldn't think which way to go. Every hour that passed would bring Khai closer and closer to the crocodiles' jaws. Pictures of him, of a bound Charm, of a helpless Captain Nail flashed through my brain over and over, making the fear in my belly rise until it nearly choked me. I tried to block out the other pictures – the ones where Khai and Charm lay dead at my feet. That was just not going to happen. I wouldn't let it.

Come on, Cleo, I said to myself. *There's only you now. You can do this. You HAVE to.*

The early morning streets were bustling now, and I was dressed in garments and jewels that marked me out as a highborn courtier at the very least. I would have to get rid of them somehow – people were already giving me strange glances. They'd recognise me soon. I looked around me. The gates of the Sema lay open, and behind the endless walls surrounding it, I could see the roof of Alexander's mausoleum rising high against the blue sky. Alexander's tomb…what was it I should remember about great Alexander's tomb? Suddenly, I had a very strong feeling that if I visited my ancestor, I would find help.

I ducked through the gates, and stepped out into the graveyard of the Ptolemy Pharaohs. Tall statues rose on every side, covered with hieroglyphs of praise, and garlanded with many flowers. Over in one corner, his back to me, was a sweeper with a palm brush, lazily flicking at the dust on a plinth. I made my way over to great Alexander. I hadn't visited him since I was a child, but his glass and marble tomb was as magnificent as I remembered. There he lay in deep shadow, locked in a golden cage, hands crossed on his breast, his proud gaze staring up at the sky. The whole tomb smelt of roses – petals were strewn all about it, offerings from the people to one who they saw as a god. The only jarring note was a pile of dirty old rags which lay in a dark corner nearby. Could I put them on over my dress? Wait! Those rags… I'd seen them before! My dream rushed into my head again. Yes! I'd been hovering above the tomb. I'd seen those rags and I'd heard…what had I heard? Trying hard to remember, I moved towards them, not seeing until too late the wrinkled brown hand which stuck out from underneath them. It was beckoning to me with a dirty fingernail which glowed yellow.

Come closer, Beloved Daughter, whispered the weak, cracked old voice from my dream. It filled my head with a soft thunder. I have a gift for you.

As she spoke, I felt a blow from nowhere hit the back of my knees, and I knelt abruptly, compelled to do so by a force I didn't understand. I reached out, trembling, to touch the wizened fingers. As I did so, a blue flash struck me, and everything went black.

16

The Poisoned Temple

I woke to find myself sprawled on my back, words in a language I didn't understand spilling out from my mind like sand through a glass. What had just happened to me? Had I been struck by lightning? No. The sky was still blue and cloudless above me. The shadows had barely moved – I hadn't been out for long. I rolled over onto my front, and crawled onto hands and knees. A set of ragged brownish robes lay beside me, folded neatly. Where had they come from? I shook myself, and squinted around me. There was something, something I needed to remember, something…what was it? I strained and strained my brain, but it was no good. My memory of the last few moments was as empty as a beggar's bowl. I did feel different inside, though. There was a space in my head that was bigger, or wider, filled with something that remained tantalisingly out of reach. I shook my head again, trying to pry it loose, but I couldn't make sense of it at all. All I knew was that I had to get out of what I was wearing, and make my way to find Cabar as fast as possible. Worry about what was happening to Khai and Charm and the others flooded back into me, driving out all other thought. If only I could go back to my chambers, check that Charm was alive and all right, rescue them all. But I couldn't – not if I wanted Khai to live. Every minute brought him closer to those foul beasts and a death I could now imagine only too well.

Reaching forward slightly guiltily, as if someone close by might be watching, I picked the heap of clothing up, sniffed them. They smelt clean and dry, of lye soap and a hint of dust, no more. I was somehow convinced they should have smelt much worse, but it was hard to tell with the perfume of roses all around. My brain was so scrambled that I didn't stop to question whether this was stealing or not, or who had put them there so conveniently. I needed a change of clothes badly, and here they were.

Apart from being unsuitable for street wear, my peacock robes were also splashed with dirt and blood. Nipping behind a shaded statue of Cleopatra II (my namesake and wife of yet another murderous Ptolemy ancestor who'd had his own son cut up and sent to her as a birthday present), I quickly stripped off, swapping rich fabric for ragged. The rough, hooded robe was too long, and slightly tight around the bust, but if I hunched over it wasn't too bad. At least there weren't holes in too many embarrassing places. I tucked it up and around me as best I could, and, taking my mother's precious jewellery off, I laid it as far inside the cage of Alexander's tomb as I could reach, piling rose petals over the gold to hide it from prying eyes. It was the best I could do. A ragged beggar could not be seen to be carrying a queen's ransom. I would have to send someone to retrieve it later – if I could.

'Please, great Alexander, guard my mother's jewels,' I whispered quietly, hoping his spirit could hear me from wherever it was in the afterlife. And then, pulling the hood over my head to cover my distinctive Ptolemy hair, I walked out of the Sema and into the streets of Alexandria.

After the relative peace of the palace, I'd forgotten how manic the city was – and how beautiful. Apart from the night Charm and I had escaped, which now seemed like a dark and far-off nightmare, I'd never walked or been carried through its wide, regular streets as anything other than a princess or a priestess with a whole retinue to keep off the more fragrant citizens. Now I had the appearance of a beggar girl, and things were a little different. I was jostled and bumped at every turn. I was shouted at for getting in the way as I dodged donkey carts and flocks of skinny sheep, who had a nasty habit of leaving drifts of round black raisin droppings behind them. Before I learnt to navigate around them (and believe me, I learnt fast), my sandals were squelchy with liquid dung. I tried to rinse my feet off in a fountain, but that just got me shouted at by angry washerwomen.

I knew roughly where I was going – the Pharos was visible from almost everywhere in the city – but it was still an unfamiliar route. It took me too long to find and cross the Canopic Way, with its immense statues of winged sphinxes and yet more of my ancestors, along with Pharaohs from previous times. They loomed over me, enormous, at least ten times as large as in life. I could imagine exactly what they would have thought of one of their own, scurrying and leaping through the common citizenry like a spindle-legged jerboa – their haughty gazes told me I was a disgrace to the name of Ptolemy. I stuck my own Ptolemy nose in the air and narrowed my eyes at them. What did they know?

The main market was in full swing by the time I reached it, its wide open space filled with the shrill cries of vendors and bargaining customers. I stopped in the shade for a moment, wiping my hand over my dry mouth, tasting sweat and dirt on the back of my hand. Doves and chickens cooed and clucked in wooden cages, tethered goats mehed plaintively, and a litter of spotty piglets cried and squeaked in a small pen. All was normal on the surface, but when I looked closer, some were clearly ailing, thin and sad-eyed in the growing heat, and on some I could see signs of small suppurating sores. Piles of floppy-leaved cabbages and papery onions, beans, garlic and small sacks of grain lay piled on bright blankets alongside great jars of oil and brass bowls of many-coloured spice. Again, there was abundance here, but hidden under the healthy fecundity on offer I spotted the brown ooze of rot. I could smell it too, lurking quietly under the cumin and fenugreek and cinnamon as well as the sweeter scents of honey and quince and apricot from the fruit stalls. Small charcoal braziers held everything from savoury skewers of meat to char-striped, spiced flatbreads filled with sweet almond paste. Despite the underlying reek of decay, my mouth started to water. I hadn't had anything to eat since yesterday. I had no money, though, not so much as a bronze obol, so I walked on, ignoring my rumbling stomach and my worries about these further signs of Isis's receding power, until I came to the Heptastadion – the long, wide, raised causeway that led across the harbour to the island of the Pharos.

At this time of day, there wasn't much traffic going over it. The hairs on my arms stood up in goosebumps as I felt eyes on me from the small guard fort which stood at its left-hand side. Would the soldiers stop and search me? They had no reason to detain a poor beggar girl, other than boredom – but I'd heard Captain Nail and the warriors talking often enough. I knew the soldiers who guarded the city could be unpredictable where girls were concerned. Luckily for me, there was a donkey cart going across at the same time as I was, filled with supplies for the Pharos, I supposed – or perhaps for the temple. A kindly-looking woman was leading the animal, and I followed her, as close as I could. The sea was slapping gently at the stone below us, and a few seagulls fought halfheartedly over the small crabs which clung to the green, slimy weed at the tide's edge. The woman turned and saw me.

'Going to the temple for the midday meal, are you?' she asked, stopping.

I nodded. My Egyptian was impeccable now, but I'd never entirely lost my Greek accent, and I didn't want to say anything if I didn't have to.

'Hop up on the cart, then,' she said. 'You look tired

enough that you'll fall asleep where you're standing.'

I clambered into the back of the cart obediently, and sat by a load of large amphorae which smelt, quite pungently, of fermented grain.

'I'm taking my best barley beer to the priests and priestesses there. Bless Isis, but they do get through a lot of it, holy as they are.' She laughed comfortably as she chattered on, seeming to want no input from me, till we reached the gates. The noon-shortened shadow of the Pharos fell upon us, still darkening the world with its immensity, nearly blocking out the Eye of Ra. I shivered, hoping it wasn't a bad omen.

'There you are, girlie,' she said, pointing. 'Straight through there will take you where you need to go. I'm off round the back to the kitchens.'

I scrambled down and stood there for a moment, hesitating.

'Get on with you,' she said tugging at the donkey's halter to get it started again. 'They won't bite, you know.' And then she was gone.

The gate was huge, made of wood, painted all over in bright colours with images of Isis. The smooth marble walls were decorated too, but on the seaward side the paint was faded a little from the salt. This was the place of my goddess, but I was wary. High Sister

Merit's words came back to me.

I grew up there, among the vileness, hearing the name of my goddess taken in vain but helpless to stop it, learning things no child should have to, seeing sights…

What sights had she seen? I shrugged the thought off. It didn't matter. I had probably seen as bad, or worse this morning. The important thing was to get to Cabar without being unmasked. I lowered my head, and walked in warily, keeping my eyes down, darting small glances around me. There was a crowd of beggars milling about in one corner, but nothing else untoward that I noticed. A priestess in dirty white robes was coming my way. I walked towards her.

'Please, Your Holiness,' I said, making my voice whiny and shrill like the ragged Egyptian girls I'd just heard in the streets. 'I have a message for the Priestess Cabar. Can you tell me where she is?'

The priestess curled her lip. 'Cabar,' she said. 'Always finding drabs and drudges to play bountiful Mother Isis to. I suppose you're her latest project. Very well then, follow me.'

I followed, biting back sharp words. A priestess of Isis was supposed to help the poor and the sick. Didn't she know that? And also, didn't she know where the laundry soap was?

You should teach her a lesson, Isis, I thought. *Send her out into the streets to dress sores on beggars.* But even here, in what was supposed to be one of her homes, my goddess didn't reply. There were no studious acolytes here, no fat eunuchs lazing under the Eye of Ra, watching the dance classes. Instead there was an empty stillness and a silence which felt ominous to me. Temples of Isis were meant to be places of joy, where our goddess was worshipped and glorified. This place just felt dead and cold and deserted. Isis wasn't here now. I didn't think she had been for a very long time. It was a sobering reminder of her weakening power.

Eventually, we came to a small door. The priestess gestured.

'In there,' she said, and turned on her heel without another word. I knocked, and heard a muffled command to enter.

Cabar was sitting at a wooden table, writing, a dove in a cage at her side. She looked up, squinting slightly through the bar of bright sunlight which fell through the high window and across the floor.

'Who are...' she started, but then I stood up straight, threw off my hood and looked her in the eye. 'Chosen!' she gasped. 'What are you doing here?' She got up swiftly and came to me, taking my hands in hers. It felt so good to have someone on my side at last that I felt a lump jump suddenly into my throat. Hot tears pricked at my eyes, but I blinked them back.

'What has happened? Have you got the map?' she asked.

I shook my head, sitting down with a bump in the chair she offered.

'No, I haven't got it yet,' I said. I told her as quickly as I could what had happened over the last days, and why I was there.

'So I need something that will make Tryphena look as if she's on the way to death – but she won't be really. That will distract Berenice and everyone in the palace long enough for me to get the map, I think,' I ended. My heart thudded uncomfortably – would she be able to help?

Cabar looked thoughtful. 'For how long do you need the false death effect to last?'

'For at least a day,' I said. 'And it can't be something that's taken in food, otherwise it will affect the taster first.'

'Then I shall make you a strong tincture of mandragoras root and poppy sap, mixed with half a grain of dried four-tooth liver,' she said. 'If dripped into the ear while asleep, it will cause the heart to slow to almost

338

nothing, and the breath to still to a thread. The victim will appear to be nearly dead to all intents and purposes. Will that serve?'

'I think so,' I said, though I had only the faintest idea what a four-tooth was – some kind of blowfish, I thought. 'But...but she will wake up eventually, won't she? You have to promise me that.' I really, really didn't want to be responsible for murdering my own sister, however horrible she was.

Cabar nodded.

'If the dose is correctly applied,' she said. 'Three drops only. Any more will be almost certainly be fatal.'

I would have to apply it myself, then. I definitely couldn't trust Berenice not to double the dosage, just to make sure. More worries crowded into my mind. How would I get to Tryphena while she was sleeping? She would be guarded. And if she died just after I'd visited... Perhaps that was Berenice's plan – to blame me for our sister's death. It made sense.

'Could you give me a very small amount,' I said, thinking quickly. 'But diluted, so that if someone had, say, ten drops, it would come out the same way?' So that Berenice could apply the whole amount and it wouldn't matter, was what I left unspoken.

'I see,' she said, and I hoped she did. 'Yes, I can do

that. Wait here. I will have to go to the herb room to make it up. It will take a little time.'

'Please hurry,' I said, feeling the passing tick of every second in the rush and slide of each drop of blood through my body.

There was a bed at the back of the room. I got up and went to it. I desperately needed rest before I went on or I would collapse. Even a few minutes sleep would be better than nothing. I lay down and closed my eyes. The strange new space in my brain stirred into life. I felt it stretch and uncoil.

Use the gift well, Beloved Daughter, said a familiar weak, cracked voice in a language I didn't know and yet now understood completely. Knowledge poured back into me. The dream. The pile of rags. The old, wizened hand. The glowing nail. Suddenly, without any warning, I was hovering over my own body, looking down at my sleeping form. I stretched out a misty, insubstantial hand towards the silver cord that rose from my belly button, tethering me to myself. Was I a ghost? Or a spirit? I should have felt frightened, but I didn't. This gift, whatever it was, whoever it was from, damped my emotions down to a murmur.

Where do you wish to go, Beloved Daughter? asked the voice.

'Who are you?' I tried to say. But no words came out of my incorporeal mouth.

There was a breath of earthy laughter.

All in good time, Beloved Daughter, all in good time! Now, use the power of your mind to take yourself where you need to be.

It was gone. I knew that as surely as I knew my own name. Use the power of my mind to take me where I wished to go? I thought of Khai in his fetid, fish-smelling prison, and, as quick as the thought appeared I was there, floating over his chained body. He was a terrifying amount closer to the crocodile pool, lying in a patch of damp blood. Normally I would have shuddered, but shuddering was impossible in this new form.

'Khai!' I tried to say. No, that was no good. *Khai!* I thought at him.

He opened his eyes immediately, looking around him in a confused way. There was no one else in the room – evidently the priest had gone off to do other things between turns of the wheel.

'Cleo?' he said, out loud. 'Where are you?'

It's a bit hard to explain. I'm sort of here and not here. Are you all right?

I knew it was a stupid question as soon as I'd asked it. He gestured with one chained hand.

'I'm still alive, I suppose. For now.' His voice was low and strained, and I could tell he was in pain. There was a sudden flurry of movement. The priest was back.

'Who are you talking to, library scum?' he said, kicking Khai in the ribs. Khai groaned and curled in on himself, hugging the pain into his own body. A tiny spike of fury reached into me, spurring me to action.

Touch him again and you will regret ever being born, lackey of Am-Heh, I shouted, right into his head. Somehow, I knew I could. He whirled – looking about him in fear.

'W-wh…who is that?' he whispered.

Fear me, I said. *I am the wrath of Isis. I will be watching. And if you turn that wheel even one quarter of a small span, I shall know, and the death Am-Heh promises will be as nothing to the eternal punishment I will wreak on your wretched body. Now go.*

He fled.

Khai struggled to sit up.

'Cleo?' he said again. 'Was that you? Did you make him run away?'

Yes. He won't touch you again. I hope. I'll be back as soon as I can – properly, I mean. But I have to go now. I-I love you, Khai.

Somehow I knew that Cabar was on her way. I didn't

want to leave him, but I had little time if I was to get to Charm.

I heard him say, 'Don't go, Cleo,' but I couldn't stay. I focused my mind on my chambers, and then with that strange disconnection of time and space, I was there. There were no Nubian guards present, so Berenice – surprisingly – had kept her promise. Charm was arguing in whispers with Captain Nail.

'I don't know where Cleo is, and neither do you. If she comes back to anywhere, it'll be to here. I'm not leaving, and that's flat.' She folded her arms in a determined way I knew all too well.

Charm, I thought at her. *Charm. Don't go crazy…*

Too late. She let out a little screech and clapped her hands to her ears, looking round the room with wild eyes.

'What is it?' Captain Nail asked. 'What have you seen?' His whole body was stiffened and on alert. I noticed that he had no weapons – the Nubians must have confiscated them and the shields.

'It's Cl… I mean, the chosen,' she whispered. 'In my head. B-but I don't know how…'

I broke in.

I'm alive. I'm fine. I… I've got a new gift. Please…just listen. Tell Captain Nail I'm going to speak to him.

She nodded – eyes wider than those of one of Bastet's temple kittens.

'C-C-Captain. She says she's going to talk to you now.'

He swung round.

'Where is she, then?' he said. 'What nonsense are you spouting, girl?'

Not nonsense. It's me, Captain.

He jerked visibly, slapping at the air.

'Begone, fiend!' he said.

Oh, really! He thought I was a fiend? A thing to frighten naughty children with?

Stop being so stupid, I said. *I am Cleopatra, chosen of Isis, and you are the captain of my warrior guard. I have simply been…er…blessed with the power to speak to you at a distance.*

Now his eyes were bulging. If I could have sighed in my present form, I would have.

I will return when I can. Be prepared before dawn. We may need to leave very quickly as we agreed before. I…

But there was no more time. The silver cord was tugging at me, then I was back in my body with Cabar shaking me by the shoulder. She looked pale and worried.

'I let you rest for a bit, but then I couldn't wake you,' she said. 'You were so deeply asleep, it was almost as if…' She stopped.

'What?' I said.

'It was almost as if you yourself had taken the drug,' she said quietly. 'You could have been dead, apart from the small rise and fall of your chest.'

Should I tell her what had happened? No. It was still too new. I mostly trusted her now, but I wanted to find out more about who the strange voice had belonged to before I told anyone else. It wasn't Isis, I was sure of that – but who else would address me as Beloved Daughter? I felt as if I still had a block in my brain somewhere, preventing me from knowing. I shook my head, banishing the mystery for now. It would have to wait.

I sat up, feeling remarkably refreshed, but then I noticed the longer shadows on the floor. Oh no! How long had she let me sleep for?

I had to get back to the palace and give Berenice the potion soon, to give it time to work.

'Is that it?' I asked urgently, seeing the tiny green glass vial in her hand.

'It is,' she said. 'There is exactly enough in here to put a person into a false death sleep for just under a day at most. I'm sorry, Chosen – I couldn't calculate the dose any more finely that that or it would have been fatal. The four-tooth liver is most unstable in a higher dosage – its strength varies from fish to fish and season to season.'

Under a day. It was not ideal. I had counted on a lot more. I knew that Berenice would call the Pharaoh's deathwatch as soon as someone noticed that Tryphena wasn't breathing much. If she woke up in the middle of it, surrounded by the whole court – well, at least I would then be on my way to Philäe with the map. If all went well. It was a big if, but I just couldn't allow myself to think about failure.

Cabar held out the vial to me – along with something else in a small, soft leather bag on a long thong.

'What's that?' I asked.

'It is an infallible amulet against venomous snakes,' she said. 'I should have thought to give it to you before. Khai informed us about the cobra traps in the archives long ago. I am so very sorry, Chosen. I will ask our goddess to punish me for my stupidity.'

I took it and hung it round my neck, tucking it into the robes so that nobody could see it. It was hard not to wonder if I might have succeeded in getting that Seth-cursed map if I'd had it before, but I tried not to blame Cabar too much. Anyone could make a stupid mistake – including me – and what was done was done.

Cabar hurried me out of the temple, and walked back with me across the Heptastadion. She had given me a clean set of her own white priestess robes, and water to wash my dung-stained feet, so at least I looked a little more respectable. The Eye of Ra was lowering its gaze towards the west, and the towering shadow of the Pharos now lay across the waves. It was afternoon, and I didn't have much time left.

'I am glad to be away,' she said as we went out of the gates. 'I do my duty as I must, but our goddess...' She cleared her throat. 'I do not think our goddess is pleased with some of the things that go on during the rites. The needless wantonness between priestess and priest, the shameless lewdness during the sacred dances...' She stopped. 'Anyway, there have been signs, but our high priestess is old and sick now, and I think she just lets it go.'

'What signs?' I asked.

'A mysterious sickness that strikes those who have taken part, with no warning. A flock of ibis leaving stinking piles of dung in the temple. Two acolytes slipping during the dance rites and breaking their ankles at exactly the same time.'

'Can't you do something?'

'I have asked Isis over and over for more sisters,' she said. 'But as I said, our goddess does not love this temple, and she doesn't send them often. I was born here, and I was given no choice but to stay.'

Like High Sister Merit, I thought. Except that scary Merit had got out, probably by the force of her own will. Cabar was not cut from such stern cloth, but she was here and I was grateful for that.

'When I have the map, I will ask Isis to help you,' I said. 'To make this temple what it should be again.' I didn't say that if I failed, Isis would probably be unable to help any temple, because she would have no power left and Egypt would truly be on its knees.

'Thank you, Chosen,' she said humbly.

We parted at one of the gates to the palace. Cabar was going to check that the camels were all in readiness, and to buy supplies for our journey.

'Won't you come with us to Philäe?' I asked, as I kissed her goodbye. She shook her head.

'My place is here, Chosen,' she said. 'I must be ready to serve holy Isis where she has placed me.' Her voice was tranquil, accepting. She was a good person, and a worthy servant of Isis.

All at once, I forgave her manipulation of Khai. She had only been trying to do her best.

'I won't forget what you have done, sister – and neither will our goddess,' I said. 'I promise you.'

* * *

Walking briskly through the gardens, I enquired of a servant whether the Pharaohs had returned from the Blessing of the Ships ceremony.

'Not yet, Magnificence,' she said, bowing so low that her head touched the floor. 'They were delayed by the crowds begging them to do something about the flooded granaries. There will be famine soon.' Her voice sounded worried, and I sighed as I thanked her and walked on. More evidence that Isis's power to protect Egypt was unravelling.

I pressed down the unwelcome knowledge, stifling it, and looked up at the sky. It was still blue. There was no sign yet of the first faint purple streaks of sunset. When would Berenice be back? I had no way of knowing, but I couldn't risk missing her. I felt naked without the comfort of Captain Nail and the warriors behind me as I made my way to the Pharaohs' quarters, but the few courtiers I met did not approach me. Either they didn't recognise me in my plain priestess robes, or Captain Nail had done a good job of making my feelings about being pestered clear.

I kicked my heels in Berenice's rooms for a good two turns of her fancy water clock, becoming more and more impatient. I had made the servants let me in by putting on my most imperious princess voice and threatening them with dire punishment if they didn't. I looked at the acanthus leaf button with longing eyes. Khai was just down there. Could I get him out now? I glanced regretfully at the bustle of activity around me. No. There wasn't a chance. I would be stopped immediately.

By the time Berenice returned, the skin beside my thumbnails was gnawed and bleeding. It was a nervous habit I thought I'd broken in childhood. I knew she was coming from the shouting between her and Tryphena.

Damn! I'd forgotten they'd be together. What would Tryphena do if she saw me here? She had said she would summon me – but she wouldn't expect me to be in Berenice's rooms. I fingered the tiny green vial guiltily. She'd also said she wanted to turn to Isis. Was I denying her the chance by doing what Berenice wanted? She'd survive, I reminded myself. I'd made sure of it. That was as much mercy as she could be granted unless she changed her ways considerably. I didn't think Isis would mind very much if she was drugged, and I had other priorities now. I moved discreetly into the background, though. There was no sense in putting myself in her way if I didn't have to.

Tryphena came in raging.

'You have no heart, Berenice. Standing under the heat of Ra's Eye all day has made one of my bad headaches come on – and then listening to those wretches roar at us about the granaries. I simply cannot sign all those letters now. I must lie down and try to sleep. You'll have to do it.'

Although I was well hidden, I knew immediately that Berenice had spotted me lurking, because she put her arm around Tryphena and steered her in the opposite direction.

'There, there, dear,' she said. 'Perhaps you are right. Go and lie down, and I'll send one of my slaves with a cold compress soaked in lavender.'

Tryphena shook her off.

'I have my own slaves to do that,' she snapped. 'And I need more than lavender. I'll see you at the audience with the Syrian ambassadors tomorrow. If I'm well enough.'

As soon as she was gone, Berenice beckoned to me.

'Come, Cleopatra. Attend me while I bathe,' she said. 'We can have a nice sisterly chat before I do all that boring signing.'

I saw the row of men holding piles of documents slump visibly. Berenice was not known for taking short baths. They were in for a long evening. She leant close to me as processions of slaves came in and out, bearing buckets of warm water and large pitchers of asses' milk mixed with precious attar of roses.

'It's near moonrise,' she said, her eyes malicious. 'Dawn is coming. Nearly time for dinner.' She smacked her lips meaningfully, looking towards the secret door.

'I've got what you wanted,' I said very quietly, handing her the little vial so that no one saw, the lie ready in my mouth. 'Two drops in the ear, no more. It will send Tryphena into an unbreakable sleep, which will lead to guaranteed death within a day.'

Berenice pouted.

'I'm disappointed in you, Cleopatra. You promised me a poisoned cloak, and all you give me is this? That's no fun at all. I wanted her to die in agony.'

'Well, I'm so sorry,' I said sarcastically. 'I'm told poisoned cloaks are in short supply in Alexandria today. This will do just as well, and it's much more effective. Now, I've done my part, so keep your promise. Let. Him. Go.'

She shook her head, the mad look back in her eyes.

'I want to see if it works first, or if you've tricked me,' she said. 'Library boy has a few hours yet before he's crocodile meat. We'll wait and see.' She held out her arms for a slave to undress her. 'You can scrub my back for me, little sister.'

'I wouldn't scrub your back if you were filthier than a pig,' I snarled. But I made it quiet. She gave a loud shriek of amusement.

'So rude to your Pharaoh,' she said. 'I should have you whipped for insolence.' But she didn't. Instead she sent for her chief steward.

'Bring me the woman called Thea,' she commanded. 'The one who is chief attendant to my sister's bedchamber – you know the one I mean. And be discreet about it.'

I wanted to pace. I wanted to scream. Instead, I sat on my nail-bitten fingers and ground my teeth while slaves scrubbed and pampered every inch of her well-fed naked body. It didn't help much, but it kept me occupied.

As soon as the woman appeared, she prostrated herself, right in the milky, sweet-smelling water that Berenice had slopped out of her bath.

'Great Pharaoh,' she said, sounding scared. 'How may I serve?'

'My sister has one of her headaches,' Berenice said. 'Is she asleep yet?'

'Yes, great Pharaoh. The physicians have given her the usual draught. She is asleep and resting, praise be to Ra.'

'Good,' said Berenice. 'I'm so happy for her.' Then she reached out for Thea's hair, and pulled her face up, hard, making the woman look at her.

'Now, you remember that favour I did your husband?' she murmured.

At this, Thea began to shake visibly.

'Y-yes, great Pharaoh.'

'It's time to repay it.' She handed over the vial and gave the woman swift instructions. As I'd anticipated, she told Thea to use the whole contents. I said nothing, not wanting to signal my own involvement.

'Just to make quite sure,' she said, when the woman had left, white and trembling. 'And now we wait some more.' She shot me an unpleasant look. 'If it doesn't work...' She left the threat unspoken.

'It will,' I said.

Oh, Isis, please let it work, I prayed as the clock dripped towards the time when the Dark Feast of Serapis would begin.

17

Forbidden Territory

It was the oily adviser, Pothinus who came, puffing and pale with the dread of bearing bad news. A gaggle of courtiers and servants rushed in behind him.

'The Pharaoh Tryphena,' he panted, falling to his knees. 'The Pharaoh, Your Magnificence...'

Berenice stretched like one of Bastet's temple cats in a patch of sunlight. She set down her quill, dabbing daintily at the ink on her fingers with a small square of linen that appeared immediately by her right hand.

'What about the Pharaoh Tryphena?' she asked lazily. 'Has she decided to recover from her wretched headache and help me with this endless Ra-cursed signing of letters?'

'N-no, Your Greatness,' he said, now flat on his face.

'I-I believe her Blessed Radiance, the Pharaoh Tryphena, is near death. I beg you to come at once, Your Magnificence!'

There was a weeping and a wailing from the massed ranks who had now crowded into the room. Berenice put a solemn expression on her face, though I could see it was an effort.

'Then, Pothinus, I suggest you summon the physicians. Surely she can't be dying from just a little headache. Such a fuss over nothing…'

Pothinus dared to interrupt her.

'B-but they have been summoned, Most Gracious One. She cannot be woken. Her breath is nearly stilled, and her heart can barely be heard. Oh, Ra!' he wailed. 'Woe! Woe is Egypt.'

'Woe! Woe is Egypt!' the crowd echoed, beating their breasts and tearing at their hair and clothes. I supposed they thought it was the prudent thing to do. I edged backwards. I must not be caught up in this. I had to get away before they called the deathwatch.

Berenice swept out of the room without a backward glance, trailing the scent of rotting roses behind her. Am-Heh was not with her, but she wore his foul taint around her like a shroud. Now was to be her moment of triumph. She didn't need me any more – I had got her what she wanted, or so she thought right now.

The little green vial had worked. But I didn't feel good about it at all. Had Cabar really got the dosage right? What if Tryphena actually was dying? I would have given the throne into Berenice's hands. I would have offended against *ma'at*, ruined the balance of the Double Throne, just as my father had. Egypt would be in even more danger than it was already.

Even if I succeeded in getting the map and restoring Isis's power – what about the other gods? What about great Ra, and Horus and Osiris, Hathor and Bastet, Shu, Nut and Geb? What about Seth, whose realm I was going to try and invade later tonight? Would any of them forgive me? Or would they throw me from the face of the earth, down into the jaws of faithful Ammit, the underworld goddess who ate those who'd sinned against *ma'at*? I pressed myself behind a pillar, as if I was hiding from their condemning eyes, though I knew they could see me wherever I was if they chose to. Isis would not be able to protect me from all of them, and unless I somehow brought my father back to sit on the throne with me or Berenice, I could never make amends.

Please, I prayed silently, as the wailing, moaning crowd trailed out of the room behind Berenice. *Please let me not have done the wrong thing, O great gods of Egypt.*

I hid behind my pillar till everyone had gone, then I rushed over to the acanthus leaf carving, pressing it hard. Nothing happened. I pressed it again, then twisted it. Still nothing. Oh, Isis! Had I got the wrong one? Were the gods punishing me already? I pressed every acanthus leaf I could find, trying not to look too hard at the paintings on the walls. They were worse than the ones in Tryphena's rooms. Not one leaf press opened the hidden door. I began to sob with despair, tearing at them all over and over with my bitten nails – if I couldn't save Khai right now, everything I had done was for nothing.

I gave the original leaf one more desperate try, twisting it left, then right. There was a small click, and the door began to slide open. I sagged a little with relief, then rushed in as soon as the gap was wide enough, brushing against a lever inside the passage as I went. With a rumble, the door started to close again. I didn't care. I was on my way to rescue the boy I loved.

I moved cautiously down the damp stone passage, again passing door after bolted door on either side. I had no weapon – how Charm would scold me for that if she was here – and I didn't know whether any priests would be waiting. Just as I was getting close to the circular room, I heard a regular muffled *boom boom boom* and then the

harsh braying of a great horn, once, twice, three times –
muted by the stone. I stopped, heart climbing out of my
chest. Was it? It came again.

Boom boom boom! Taraaa-taraaa-taraaa!

It was! Unmistakably, I was hearing the deathwatch
called for a Pharaoh. I knew Tryphena wasn't dead – she
couldn't be – and I'd expected Berenice to set it in
motion, but it still gave me a horrible fright. As the last
bray of the trumpet died away I heard the sound of
running feet, and cries of alarm. I had to hide, but where?
I tried the nearest door, fumbled with the bolt. It was too
stiff, rusty with damp. I rushed to another, then another,
panting with panic.

'Open, curse you, open!' I muttered, shoving
frantically at the next as the footsteps and cries grew
louder. The bolt snapped back and the door opened,
surprising me, and I fell into a tiny room filled with reed
baskets of dirty robes and loincloths. I pulled the door
closed, and ducked behind them. The laundry stank of
stale sweat, old blood and rank crocodile fishiness. I
wrinkled my nose with disgust. Was this where they'd
kept poor Charm?

Voices were calling to each other just outside now.

'Come! Quickly!'

'Is it the blessed of Am-Heh?'

'Is it the favoured one? Who have they called the watch for?'

'I don't know. Come on, Sati. We can go through the Pharaoh's apartments. It's the quickest way out.'

I thought I recognised the harsh tones of Khai's jailer, and held my breath. I didn't think I could scare him twice.

'But what about the prisoner?' There was a small pause.

'Oh, never mind the prisoner,' said Khai's jailer hurriedly. 'He's not going anywhere except into the Devourer's mouth, may His name be feared forever. Leave him.'

I let my breath out thankfully, as the running feet passed through the circular room and away past me, up the stone steps to the Pharaoh's apartment, fading fast. I listened hard for long moments, trying to hear whether anyone had stayed behind, but there was no sound, just the occasional *pat pat* of water dripping from the ceiling, and the rustle of a rat or a hunting snake. I tiptoed out from the laundry room, poking my head carefully round the door. Nothing. Nobody.

I walked quickly down the passage to the round room, keeping my ears open. Still nobody. My eyes darted from arched opening to arched opening. Which entrance was the one that led to where Khai was held? I sniffed. There! That one! I knew it by the smell of old fish and rot. I went past the barred niches at a run, and burst into his prison, skidding to a stop as I saw him. His black hair was dull and matted with mud and blood where he'd been dragged along, and his robes were unutterably filthy, but his eyes were open, and he had not moved a single span closer to that awful pool. The priest had obeyed me!

I went down on my knees beside him and nearly cried with relief, cradling him in my arms, the heavy chains clanking against me.

'I knew you'd come,' he said against my shoulder. 'I knew you'd save me, Cleo.'

I half laughed, wiping a smear of wet off my cheek.

'I haven't saved you yet. I have to get those chains off you first.' I looked around. Were there keys? He jerked his head towards the wheel.

'Over there. The priest took a lot of pleasure in rattling them in front of my nose, showing me I couldn't get to them. Bastard son of a hyena's turd.'

I let him go, and went to unhook a set of heavy iron keys from where they hung on the dripping stone wall, and then I unlocked his shackles. He winced and grimaced as I took them off, and I saw the red, raw weals where he must have struggled against them, trying to get them off.

'Cleo,' he said, and then hesitated.

'What?'

'Was that really you earlier . . . in my head? Or am I going mad?'

'It was really me,' I said, helping him up. 'I don't know how it happened...there was this voice and then...' I stopped. 'It's very hard to explain. I think a goddess did something to me, but I just can't seem to work out which one – or why they should give me such a great gift.'

'It doesn't matter now,' he said, his voice gruff. 'We have to get out of here and back to your rooms before they find us."

'Khai, wait!' I hated to take him into further danger, but I had a job to do now he was free. 'We have to steal that map for Isis – right now.'

He grimaced again, then straightened, audibly gritting his teeth at the pain. He didn't look at me.

'All right, Cleo. We'll go through the embalmers' tunnel, then. Unfortunately I know the way very well by now.' He took my hand without another word and limped forward stiffly. He didn't mention the deathwatch drums and horn. Maybe he hadn't heard them. I didn't tell him what I'd done to cause them to sound. I couldn't bear to.

The tunnel was just wide enough for a body on a bier. We couldn't go fast – Khai was still limping a little – and we had to be quiet. As before, he ordered me to follow him exactly.

'And this time you'll obey me, Cleo. Won't you?' Our last encounter lay between us like an unlanced boil.

'Yes, Khai,' I said out loud, but I vowed silently that I'd never let him be hurt on my account again.

He fumbled his amulet out of his robes, and pressed it between our hands.

'Thank Isis, they didn't take it from me,' he whispered as we went in. 'I think I got off lightly. The priests kicked me a bit when I first arrived, but then they just chained and left me till you arrived with the Bitch Queen.' He swallowed painfully. 'They made me watch what they did to that poor girl, though,' he said. 'I kept shouting at them to stop, but they only laughed.'

He squeezed my hand tight.

'Cleo – that could have been you. I don't think I could have stood it if they'd done…'

I squeezed back.

'They didn't, though. And they never will. You saw how Isis protected me.' I hesitated. 'I-I just wish she could have protected you too. And that poor girl.'

He put one finger to my lips.

'Hush.'

Seth's strange mind magic battered at me, stronger this time, but I ignored it, holding the round disc of protection tightly between our clasped hands as Khai twisted and turned through the stacks of scrolls. We were coming a different way this time, and as we crept along, I pulled the snake amulet out from where it hung around my neck and clutched it with my other hand. I did trust Cabar's word that it was infallible, but it was hard not to flinch every time I heard a strange noise. How long did we have? I didn't know. It must be late in the evening – but had we passed over into the day when the Dark Feast of Serapis dawned?

I urged Khai to hurry with my mind – but my new gift refused to ignite again while I was awake. A clammy sweat broke out under my arms and on my palms. Had I left everything too late? There was no sound of human movement anywhere near. Had the embalmers all left to attend Tryphena's deathwatch?

Please, let there be nobody here, I thought over and over again. Then as we were tiptoeing down yet another passageway, I saw the red-eyed skulls right up ahead. I didn't rush off this time. I just tugged on Khai's hand a little. He nodded, creeping forward even more slowly. I could almost feel the map now, coming closer to it with every step. We were so nearly there!

I knew the map box as soon as I saw it. It was made of plain black ebony, and it called to me. Literally. The feeling was so strong that I had no choice. Letting go of the snake amulet, I wrenched my other hand out of Khai's, reached out, and opened it with trembling fingers. The malevolence of Seth shook my whole body as I first touched it, like a great simoom wind. My hair rose around my head, streaming out behind me, but I didn't care, because I felt Isis rise within me then, Her protection bathing me in desert heat. I lifted the map out, raising it in triumph above my head as it began to glow, turning from sick green to a pure white light which illuminated me and Khai like beacons. I had the key to restoring Isis's power in my hands!

My Chosen! The familiar voice of my goddess rang through my head, and then another joined it.

Beloved Daughter! said the other voice, the one which had come to me in the temple earlier today. We await you. Bring what you hold in your hands to us before the month of Mechir ends. You must hurry!

What? I nearly dropped the thing. *Who was that?* I nearly asked it out loud.

I-I don't understand, I said silently to the second voice. *Who are you?*

She laughed as she had before.

You hold all the answers in your hand already, Beloved Daughter, she said.

I did? I looked down at the glowing thing I held, stained with ash and old blood. The map to the place of the Old One. The grandmother of the gods. As the obol dropped, the block in my brain lifted, and I realised who was speaking to me, I fell to my knees and prostrated myself. I couldn't help it. The awe was too great.

I will not fail you, great goddesses, I vowed.

We know, they said together, and my head nearly flew apart with the wondrous ringing chime of both their voices entwined. We have great plans for you, Cleopatra Chosen! Have courage.

Then the voices were gone, and I was left with my nose pressed so hard into the stone that it was numb, the map clutched tight in my left hand.

I felt a tug on my shoulder. Khai was bending over me, his eyes wide with fear. He pointed, low to the ground, and it was then that I saw it

A red leather slipper, only the tip of it, far away at the end of the passage, but just visible. Someone was standing there. I could hear both our breathing catch and still at the same moment. I made a rapid decision, stuffing the precious map down into my robes, between the folds of my breastband, where it would be safe.

Go! I mouthed at Khai. *Go! Hide!*

He shook his head impatiently. I glared at him, then pointed with my other hand. Why was he hesitating? I still felt the protection of Isis within me, shielding me from Seth's wrath, but he only had his amulet. If he was caught now... *GO!* I mouthed again, widening my eyes and screwing my whole face up in the effort to command him. *Quick!*

NO, Cleo! I could almost hear the angry roar in his silent words. Isis give me patience, but he was stubborn.

Quite silently, a man stepped into view, and then it was too late. He was dressed in the red embalmer robes of a priest of Seth, and in his hands he held a silver double-headed axe, which he raised menacingly.

'Stop!' he shouted as we turned and fled. 'In the name of Seth, stop!'

But we didn't. Snakes poured out of the walls again, but I held up my amulet, and they recoiled violently from us, rearing back and away. Only one set of footsteps followed us this time.

Bite him, snakes, I thought. But of course they didn't. He was probably protected by his wretched god, just like the murderer Tebu had been.

'Library!' Khai gasped, turning sharply right and into the hidden entrance. We didn't stop this time, though. We carried straight on, through the darkness, bumping into walls as we went. This time our luck didn't hold. The priest followed us in, but he was slowed down, not knowing the way as Khai did. He cursed loudly as his axe clanged and clattered against the stone. Looking hurriedly back over my shoulder, I saw it strike small blue sparks off the walls, sparks that flickered and died like fireflies.

I could hear Khai's limp getting worse. The regular sound of his running footsteps had a curious hitch to them now.

Isis… I prayed. *Isis!* But the feeling of protection was draining away from me – weakening fast, then gone. How could she leave me now, just when I'd succeeded in doing what she wanted? Was her power totally sapped now? I didn't dare pray to the Old One, either.

With a pained grunt, Khai ran full pelt into the door at the end. I heard him wrenching at the lever, cursing.

'Jam the opening shut when we're out,' I panted, as a crack of light grew. The sound of pursuit was far too close, and I knew we only had moments. Squeezing ourselves through, we tumbled into the Great Library.

'Quick!' I said, pointing, but Khai was there before me, burrowing behind the scrolls. The door had closed to a crack and he was wrenching at the lever on this side, pushing at it with all he'd got, when I saw a hand reach through, trying to force the door open with brute strength. I needed a weapon! What could I use? Then I saw the chair by my old desk. I picked it up and smashed it down on the marble floor, hard. It shattered with a satisfying crash, and I snatched up one broken leg, battering and stabbing at the hand in a frenzy. There was a yell of pain from the other side, as a sharp splinter penetrated the skin, and the hand withdrew. Finally the door creaked closed, and Khai stood there, the lever broken off in his hand. I could hear thumps and more yells coming from the other side, but the door remained firmly shut.

We looked at each other, swaying on our feet. The cut above Khai's eyebrow had opened up again, and blood trickled slowly down beside his eye.

Then the horn sounded, mooing long and low like one of Hathor's cows in agony, on and on and on in one long, unbroken note.

Its grave, mournful tone gave the news I'd been half-dreading since I gave Berenice the small green vial of potion.

'Oh, no…' I whispered, sinking to my knees. 'No, no, no, no, no.'

But I knew it was true.

Tryphena was dead, and I had given Berenice her heart's desire.

She was now the sole Pharaoh on the Double Throne of Egypt.

Ma'at was broken again. I could feel it in the ominous heaviness of the air, in the stifling closeness that wrapped around me like a thick cloak. I rocked back and forth, clutching my head, moaning. What had I done? How had the plan I'd hatched with Cabar gone so wrong? Tryphena was never meant to die. Had Berenice put something else in the mixture? Or had Cabar just misjudged the dose?

Khai shook me urgently, his fingers digging into my shoulders till it hurt. The banging and cursing from behind the hidden door was becoming louder, audible even over the mooing horn.

'Cleo,' he said. 'Cleo, come on. We need to get away from here right now.' I felt an answering jolt in the middle of my chest, once, twice – like a second heartbeat. The map! It was tugging at me insistently, as if it was attached to a string with someone pulling on the other end.

I forced myself to my feet, thrusting the sound of the

death-horn and what it meant away from me.

'The passages,' I said hoarsely, through a throat which felt as if it had been screaming for a week. 'Where are the passages?'

'Follow me,' Khai said. Then he hissed with sudden pain, tearing at his neck.

I heard a clink as he threw something to the floor. It was his Seth amulet, smoking and glowing red. He grimaced at the broken chain, kicking it away.

'Guess that's a pretty clear sign,' he said, grabbing my hand and beginning to run, pulling me along behind him. 'Looks like I'm coming with you to Philäe to deliver that map to Isis.'

I had succeeded in getting the map. Khai was going to join us. I was on my way back to Charm. Those three things alone should have made me deliriously happy, but my mind was numb. It was all I could do to put one foot in front of the other as we sped through the dim, earth-tinged light, down the nearly-familiar route to my rooms. It felt as if an ants' nest had been stirred with a stick down there. Slaves and servants were rushing about aimlessly, their faces inward-looking and slack with shock and fear as they passed us, bumping shoulders, banging arms, brushing against us without recognition. The sound of Tryphena's death-horn echoed on and on, creeping into every part of the palace. They knew it meant that Berenice and her foul god were all-powerful now. It was that thought which eventually snapped me out of my stupor. Only my goddess could stop Am-Heh's reign of terror – and she would need her full powers back to do it. I had to get the map to her and the Old One, had to get us all out of Alexandria.

There was no guard at the uneven steps up to my rooms, and that made us both wary. I wanted to go first, but Khai motioned me back. He was getting as protective of me as Captain Nail. I saw his body stiffen as he looked into the bed-chamber beyond the closet. It looked as if it had been ransacked by destructive thieves, but it was empty of people.

'There's no one here!' he whispered.

My heart dropped like a stone. Had they left already? Had we come here for nothing? I cursed softly, just as Khai held up a hand.

'Shhh! Listen!'

I strained my ears. The death-horn was still sounding, but above it I could hear shouts, grunts and bangs from the outer chamber. The map gave me a great tug towards it, and I rushed past Khai, throwing open the doors without caution. He followed swiftly, instinctively ready to shield me from danger with his body.

It was chaos in there. Captain Nail and the three burliest warriors had their shoulders braced against the outer doors, which were shaking with blows from the outside. Warriors Rubi and Sah were bringing over furniture and piling it up in a haphazard barrier, helped by Dhouti, Am and Charm. Mamo was lying in a corner, apparently asleep.

'Open! Open in the name of the Pharaoh Berenice!' cried the guards outside in their harsh Nubian voices, over and over. But nobody inside took any notice. Khai streaked across the room to shake Captain Nail's shoulder, nearly getting himself punched in the process. Luckily, the captain had quick reactions. He took in my presence at a glance, just as Charm saw me too. Her face was grim, and her bruises more noticeable than ever, but as soon as our eyes met, her shoulders slumped with relief, and she ran to hug me. Her warm, familiar smell surrounded me, as I hugged her back, burying my face in her shoulder for an instant. Wherever she was seemed like home, even if home was, right now, in a place of extreme danger.

'Fall back,' I croaked, letting her go reluctantly. 'We must get to the camels.'

Captain Nail obeyed at once, giving low-voiced orders even as he helped Warrior Sah lift one last heavy piece up to lean against the rest.

'Chosen,' he said, saluting, his dark eyes as impassive as ever. 'That should hold them for a while.'

Khai slung the sleeping Mamo over one shoulder, as the others picked up the bundles which were piled neatly in a corner of my bedchamber. He did not wake. Captain Nail must have drugged him with the passionflower and valerian mix, as I'd instructed earlier.

The closet felt very full as we all crowded through and ducked down the steps and into the narrow passage beyond. Burly Sergeant Basa remained in the doorway, four long bits of smashed bed frame by his side. Their ends were sharp – but not as sharp as a spear. He had no other weapons, no shield, no silver Knot of Isis to give him protection against our enemies. I looked into his eyes and knew at once why he was standing there, as if Isis had whispered it in my ear. Someone had to stay to try and fend off the Nubians when they broke through – someone who had only fists and broken furniture to defend him, someone who loved Isis and me more than his own life.

'Farewell, Chosen,' he said, raising his palm to his heart and bowing. 'It has been an honour to serve you.'

The sergeant's dignity and courage in the face of his own inevitable death humbled me. I bowed back, as deep as I would have to my father.

'The blessing of Isis will be with you, now and forever,' I said, my voice choked up even more than before. 'I will never forget your sacrifice. Never.'

I turned away from him with an effort. I had to. Whatever pain and sorrow I felt at leaving my favourite warrior behind, there was more at stake here than one man's life – but I vowed his last gift to us all would not be wasted.

'Will you guide us to the gate, Charm?' I asked her.

'I will,' she said.

And then we began to run.

Who is Who, Where is Where and What is What in CLEO

The Main Players:

Cleopatra Ptolemy (Cleo): Princess of Egypt, marked and chosen of Isis

Tryphena Ptolemy: Evil Sow Sister One and stealer of the Pharaoh's Throne along with...

Berenice Ptolemy: Evil Sow Sister Two. Both are worshippers of Am-Heh, the foul Devourer of Souls (see below)

Charmion (Charm): best friend, body servant and the person Cleo thinks of as her real sister

Khai: Scribe, Librarian, Spy, all-round hot guy

The Minor Players:

Am: Cleo's food taster

Brotherhood of Embalmers: red-robed, Seth-loving cutters-up of dead bodies

Cabar: Sister of the Living Knot, priestess at Temple of the Pharos

Captain Nail: Warrior of Isis, and head of Cleo's guards

Corporal Geta: Warrior of Isis

Dennu: one of Cleo's eunuchs

Dhouti: one of Cleo's eunuchs

Ibi: Khai's only friend in the Brotherhood of Embalmers. Now dead

Halima: Priestess and Cleo's teacher of precedence and hierarchy at Philäe

Hesi: one of Cleo's childhood nurses. Now dead of a scorpion bite

Holy Salama: Sister of the Living Knot and seer-prophetess

Hu: slave and masseur at Philäe

Jamila: High Priestess of Philäe temple, political schemer

Kemsit: annoying girl at Philäe

Mamo: slave boy from Ethiopia, gift to Cleo from Berenice

Master Apollonius: Cleo's old tutor

Merit: High Sister of the Sisters of the Living Knot

Nena: royal dressmaker, brilliant with a needle, but with foul breath

Pothinus: oily adviser to Tryphena and Berenice

Ptolemy Auletes: Pharaoh, father and flute player. Ran off to Rome, deserting his family, his people and the Throne

Sati: Priest of Am-Heh

Sera: Sister of the Living Knot and traitor to Isis

Sergeant Basa: Warrior of Isis

Shu: an arrogant priest-acolyte at Philäe

Taia: High Priestess of Saïs Temple

Tebu: Embalmer and priest of Seth, lover of Sera

Thea: Chief Bedroom Attendant to Tryphena

Warrior Haka: Warrior of Isis

Warrior Sah: Warrior of Isis

Warrior Rubi: Warrior of Isis

Zeno: ancient Greek philosopher, long dead

The Gods and Goddesses:

Am-Heh: also known as 'The Devourer of Souls' – hound-headed, crocodile-clawed, river-horse-reared god of all things evil. Lives in a lake of fire

Ammit: judgemental underworld goddess

Anubis: jackal-headed Lord of the Underworld, who ushers souls into death

Apep: evil serpent god

Atum: first Egyptian god

Bastet: cat-headed goddess of protection, music and dance

The Ennead: group of nine powerful gods and goddesses

Geb: god of the earth, brother of Nut

Horus: falcon-headed god of the sky, son of Isis and Osiris

Isis: goddess of motherhood and thrones, protector of all Egypt

Nekhbet: hook-nosed vulture goddess

Nefertem: god of the blue lotus flower

Nut: goddess of the sky

Osiris: god of the afterlife, husband of Isis

Ra: god of the sun

Serapis: bull-headed god

Seshat: goddess of wisdom and writing

Seth: god of storms, chaos and the desert, murderer of Osiris, enemy of Isis

Shu: god of the air

Tauret: river-horse-headed goddess of childbirth

Tefen: captain of Isis's seven scorpion guards

The Old One: mysterious grandmother of the gods

Thoth: god of the moon

Other Ancient Egyptian terms:

Papyrus: paper made out of a reed-like plant

Hieroglyphs: Ancient Egyptian symbols

Ka: the spirit form of a person, the soul's life-spark

Ma'at: balance of the Universe, life and the Double Throne, must not be broken

River-horse: what the Ancient Egyptians called a hippopotamus

The Great Green Sea: what the Ancient Egyptians called the Mediterranean

Felucca: a sailing boat, usually with a high stern

Sihor: the star of Isis, which rose in late June or early July to herald the Nile flood

Senet: an Ancient Egyptian board game

Quanun: a stringed musical instrument

Amharic: language spoken in Ethiopia

Mizmar: a wind instrument

Sistrum: a percussion instrument

Simoom: a hot desert wind, also known as 'poison wind'

Obol: a small bronze coin

Four-tooth: a type of puffer fish with a poisonous liver

Places:

Abydos of the Tombs: ancient city on the Nile

Alexandria: capital city of the Ptolemy pharaohs

The Antirhodos: breakwater island near the Royal Harbour, Alexandria

The Canopic Way: main thoroughfare of Alexandria, lined with statues

Cat Isle: island within the harbour of Alexandria

Drakon Island: island within the harbour of Alexandria

Harbour of the River: southern harbour of Alexandria, bordering Lake Mareotis

Heliopolis, city of Atum: city on the Nile, sacred to Ra

Lake Mareotis: large lake to the south of Alexandria

Memphis of the White Walls: city on the Nile, sacred to Ptah, god of craftsmen

Pharos of Alexandria: one of the Seven Wonders of the World – a huge lighthouse in Alexandria

Philäe: island in the southern Nile, with a temple to Isis on it

Saïs: city on the Nile with a temple to Isis

The Sema: burial ground of the Ptolemy pharaohs and their families

Thebes the Great: city on the Nile, dedicated to Amun, god of the invisible

Author's note:

Nobody knows much about Cleopatra's path to the Pharaoh's throne, beyond the bare minimum of speculative dates, and even those are disputed. Who her mother was, when exactly she was born, what she really looked like are all mysteries. Her early life is a big fat hole in history, which I have jumped into with both feet and tried to fill. Where possible, I have done my best to make the known facts about life in Ancient Egypt at that time historically accurate, but this is a work of fiction, so any small twistings and turnings to suit my story will, I hope, be forgiven.

Acknowledgements:

I can't thank you enough for reading this book. You, my Lovely Readers, are the people for whom I spend hours/days/years, locked in a small room, making stories up in my head. Every person who steps into Cleo's world makes all that effort worthwhile, and I value you all immensely.

I may be the one who wrote *Cleo*, but no book comes

to publication without the help of a legion of wonderful people. Writing acknowlegements feels to me a little like an Oscars speech (I wish!). I'll therefore try and keep this as short as I can, so you don't nod off.

Further Massive Thanks go to:

- Marvellous Michelle Lovric, who lent me so much support (and gave me the gift of quiet space with no distractions to write in), read the book in many drafts, and provided amazing and detailed feedback. This book would be much less without her.
- My incredible daughter, Tabbi, who was happy to talk about the ins and outs of Cleo's, Charm's and Khai's life, discuss plot points endlessly, and without whose passionate encouragement and belief in this book I would not have survived till The End.
- My fabulous agent, Sophie Hicks of The Sophie Hicks Agency, who lifts me out of occasional morasses of writerly unconfidence, makes me laugh and who was the spark which lit the tinder for the original idea. She is unquestionably The Most Kickass Agent in the Universe.
- The efficient and super-friendly Orchard team, including my eagle-eyed editors, Rosalind McIntosh and Emily Sharratt, Laure Pernette and the enthusiastic

publicity and marketing team at Books with Bite – and of course, the very talented Thy Bui for designing The Best Ever Cover.

- My faithful beta readers, young and old – Kath Langrish, Gillian Philip, Venetia and Crispin Jolly and Olivia Maiden, all of whom challenged me to change things I might not otherwise have noticed.

- Nicola Morgan, Mary Hoffman, Liz Kessler and all my other Scattered Authors Society and SCBWI friends for encouragement in times of crisis, as well as the very supportive writing, librarian, blogging and bookselling community on Facebook and Twitter.

- The very brilliant Susan Rose of Susan Rose China (www.susanrose.co.uk) for designing the fabulous Cleo 'Mug Full of History' for me.

- And last, but very much not least, my remaining family, Richard, Archie and my mother, Prue (and the patient deskdogs, Sika, Hero and Teasel), for putting up with extreme grumpiness, growling and muttering, as well as quite a lot of pizza and missed walks.

Lucy Coats,
Northamptonshire, May 2015